DANGEROUS WITNESS

REDEMPTION HARBOR SERIES

Katie Reus

Cover art: Jaycee of Sweet 'N Spicy Designs
Editors: Kelli Collins and Julia Ganis
Author website: http://www.katiereus.com

Publisher's Note: This is a work of fiction. Names, characters, places, and incidents are either the products of the author's imagination or used fictitiously, and any resemblance to actual persons, living or dead, or business establishments, organizations or locales is completely coincidental.

Dangerous Witness/Katie Reus. -- 1st ed.
KR Press, LLC

ISBN-13: 9781635560312
ISBN-10: 1635560314

eISBN: 9781635560305

For Kari. Thank you for everything!

Praise for the novels of Katie Reus

"...a wild hot ride for readers. The story grabs you and doesn't let go."
—*New York Times* bestselling author, Cynthia Eden

"Has all the right ingredients: a hot couple, evil villains, and a killer action-filled plot. . . . [The] Moon Shifter series is what I call Grade-A entertainment!" —Joyfully Reviewed

"I could not put this book down. . . . Let me be clear that I am not saying that this was a good book *for* a paranormal genre; it was an excellent romance read, *period*." —All About Romance

"Reus strikes just the right balance of steamy sexual tension and nail-biting action. . . .This romantic thriller reliably hits every note that fans of the genre will expect." —*Publishers Weekly*

"Prepare yourself for the start of a great new series! . . . I'm excited about reading more about this great group of characters."
—Fresh Fiction

"Wow! This powerful, passionate hero sizzles with sheer deliciousness. I loved every sexy twist of this fun & exhilarating tale. Katie Reus delivers!" —Carolyn Crane, RITA award winning author

"A sexy, well-crafted paranormal romance that succeeds with smart characters and creative world building." —Kirkus Reviews

"*Mating Instinct*'s romance is taut and passionate . . . Katie Reus's newest installment in her Moon Shifter series will leave readers breathless!"
—Stephanie Tyler, *New York Times* bestselling author

Seven months ago

Darcy paused when her security system let out a little *beep-beep*, letting her know someone had opened the front door. Her boyfriend, Brooks, had been the one who insisted she get a security system in the first place. Other than her sister, he was the only person who had a key, but he wasn't supposed to be here for a couple more hours.

Not that she was complaining. More time with Brooks was always welcome. She was just getting her wedding planning business off the ground and he ran a huge ranch so sometimes it was a struggle to make time for each other. They always did, however. And even if she wouldn't say the words out loud to anyone, she was pretty certain they were heading toward marriage.

Which was something she hadn't even been sure would happen for her. She absolutely loved planning weddings—and the *idea* of finding a happily ever after with someone you loved and trusted. But actual marriage for herself? She hadn't contemplated it until Brooks. Her own family had been so dysfunctional, her father abandoning her mom, and her and her sister when something better came along. But Brooks had her questioning everything. He wasn't perfect; no one was.

But he was perfect for her.

Setting her laptop down, she hurried to the mirror over her dresser in her bedroom and ran her fingers through her hair. Not that it would matter or that he would even care what she looked like. He liked her any way he could get her—and she felt the same about him.

Casual in jeans, a T-shirt and bare feet, she felt free to be herself around him. When she was in work mode, she was a totally different person. Polished, put together, usually in heels and always wearing makeup. But with Brooks, for the first time in a relationship, she was simply Darcy, and he loved her anyway. That was why she'd fallen so hard and fast for him. He'd given her no choice. He'd just barreled into her life and she'd realized something was missing. Him.

As she reached the bottom of the stairs, she found Brooks standing in the foyer, hands shoved into his jeans pockets. Sans his cowboy hat, he had on dusty boots and his standard flannel shirt. She smiled automatically, but her lips froze as she took in his dark expression.

He looked...angry. Truly and utterly angry. She'd never seen him like this. She took another step toward him. "What's wrong? Did something happen at the ranch?" Oh God, what if one of his friends had been hurt? She knew how much he cared about the people he worked with.

He tightened his jaw once but didn't move from his spot by the front door. "I just had an interesting conversation with my father."

Ah. She'd been planning to tell Brooks tonight about the ridiculous offer his father had made her. He'd offered her two million dollars to walk away from Brooks. At first she thought he'd been joking. When she realized he'd been dead serious, she'd been shocked—and offended. As politely as possible, she'd told him to shove it. After all, he was Brooks's father, so she hadn't wanted to be completely obnoxious to him. Even if he deserved it.

Brooks stood there staring at her, his jaw taut.

Darcy wanted to tell him not to be too angry at his father. Even if the man had done a complete jerk move. She was pretty certain that deep down his father truly cared about Brooks and was just looking out for him. She thought the older man had just wanted to make sure she was serious about his son, and not someone after his wealth. Before she could speak, Brooks pulled out a small box from his jeans pocket and opened it.

Her eyes widened when she realized what it was. A huge, sparkly engagement ring. This seemed like a very strange time to be proposing, especially given his furious expression, if he even was. Because it seemed like he was angry at *her*. But that didn't make sense. What was going on?

His eyes were cold, colder than his expression. "I shouldn't be surprised, but I truly am. You really had me fooled. If you'd held out a little longer you'd have gotten more than a couple million." The disgust in his voice made her stomach clench.

She gasped at his words, and the rage accompanying them, as she registered what he was implying. This was a side of Brooks she'd never seen before. The anger rolling off him was palpable and he was looking at her as if she was a stranger, as if he *hated* her.

Stricken, reeling, she wrapped her arms around herself, unable to believe what he was saying. He thought she'd taken the money? "*Excuse* me?"

"You heard me. I'd planned to propose this weekend. But it turns out my father made you a better offer. Or maybe a more apt description is that he's already taken care of your *bill*," he snapped out, venom in his voice.

She jerked back as if he'd struck her. Without thinking, she crossed the distance to him and slapped his face. The sharp sound reverberated in the taut silence as her palm stung. But not as badly as the backs of her eyes did.

She could barely breathe, as though he'd just shoved a dagger into her chest. Her throat was too tight to even respond to his words. He'd just called her a whore without saying the actual word. Her bill? Oh God, she felt sick. He'd assumed she'd taken money from his father to—what, walk away from him? That she was a liar and a fake and had been acting this whole time? That she'd never loved him? When in reality he was the only man she'd ever loved.

"You think I took two million to walk away from you?" Her voice was incredulous.

"Don't bother to deny it!"

She wanted to rage at him, to tell him how wrong he was. But if he actually believed she'd taken that money, he'd never known her at all. No way in hell was she going to defend herself. Because she had nothing to defend herself from. She'd done nothing wrong. And he should have known better. Should have known her. She couldn't even look at him right now. "Get out. Now." Her voice was raw, strained.

If she stayed in his presence another moment longer, she was afraid she would slap him again. And the thought of turning to physical violence made her sick. She hated that she'd already lost control once.

Turning on her heel, she strode up the stairs on wobbly legs, her entire body shaking. It was her house and she should have shoved him out the door, but she was about to start crying and she refused to let him see her like that. He already thought she was a gold-digging whore. She didn't need him to think she was weak as well.

When she reached her room, she slammed the door shut and sank down against it as tears tracked down her cheeks, sick inside. She couldn't believe what had just happened, couldn't believe Brooks could ever think this of her.

He knew her background, knew everything about her family, and he still thought that about her? A sob rose in her throat and she heard the *beep-beep* of the door opening downstairs.

He was gone. Had tossed those horrible accusations in her face like a grenade and walked away.

Now that she knew she was alone, she let the emotions rip free as sobs racked her body.

This morning she'd been excited about seeing her boyfriend, and beginning to hope that maybe there was a happily ever after in store for her with him. Now...everything was shattered. Her heart, and her future.

She wondered if she should have told him how wrong he was about her, raged the truth at him—but it wouldn't have made any difference. Now she knew exactly what he thought of her. She didn't care if he apologized, they were through. She couldn't be with somebody who thought so little of her, thought she was actually capable of taking money in place of him.

He'd never known her at all.

CHAPTER ONE

—One stupid mistake can change everything.—

New Year's Eve

Brooks tapped the top of his beer bottle to Savage's champagne glass. It was strange to see Savage drinking something bubbly—or anything not beer—but the man had just gotten engaged. "Congrats, brother," he said. They might not be blood brothers, but Savage was the closest Brooks had ever come to having an actual brother.

And Savage certainly deserved this happiness. He'd fallen hard for single mother Olivia and her daughter Valencia.

His best friend grinned and looked over to where Olivia was showing off her ring to Skye, Mary Grace, and Martina. Though the women had already seen the ring, Olivia obviously didn't realize that. Brooks had seen it too. Savage hadn't been able to keep it a secret from any of them. He'd been a wreck the last month as he figured out how to ask her. Brooks hadn't thought anything could get the former Marine/CIA contractor spooked but Olivia had him wrapped around her finger. And so did her daughter. Savage would do anything for the two of them.

"Thanks," Savage said. "Now we've got to plan a wedding and find a place to live. It's going to be a busy few months."

"Months?" Brooks might not have any experience in the marriage department, but his father had been married enough times that he knew planning a wedding could take a while.

"Yep. We're not doing a long engagement."

"You know who you're going to use as a planner?" Okay, that wasn't subtle. And he already knew what Savage was going to say before he said it.

His friend lifted an eyebrow. "You volunteering for the job? What do you know about planning weddings?" Savage snorted out a laugh before taking a sip of the champagne. He grimaced then put it down on the nearest table. "I need a beer."

Brooks fell in step with him as they headed toward the open bar set up by the Olympic-sized pool on the lanai. Everyone had decided to have a New Year's Eve party at his family's estate since it had the most room—and privacy. South Carolina was cold this time of year and this winter had been a brutal one. His breath was visible in front of him, curling up like little wisps of smoke. Winter was his favorite time of year but lately he was anything but settled. And it wasn't a mystery why. "I know a wedding planner. Her company is new, but she's very talented and driven." He was also in love with her. But he left that part out.

Savage gave him a strange look as they reached the small wet bar. "How the hell do you know a wedding planner?"

It was a fair question. Brooks ran his family ranch—though lately he was doing more and more for Redemption Harbor Consulting and letting his foreman take over at the ranch. He also didn't have many female friends because of his job.

Savage knew everything about him. Almost.

Brooks didn't answer, just set his own half-finished beer down as his friend got one. Looking out at everyone having a good time, a pang of loneliness hit him square in the chest. He was happy for the friends of his who'd settled down. Even his dad seemed to have finally gotten his head on straight. He'd moved back to South Carolina from Florida and seemed almost content. The eccentric billionaire, who'd never been much of a father, had been married so many times before. He'd finally left wife number...four, maybe? He didn't always marry them, so technically he might have only been married three times. Brooks didn't know. And he didn't really care. It wasn't as if any of the marriages had produced other children, so he didn't have any half-siblings. And Brooks had never cared to get to know any of his father's significant others. Because they'd all been gold diggers who hadn't lasted long. And the previous one had actually hit on him the last time he'd visited Florida.

"So?" Savage asked.

"It's Darcy." Savage had never actually met Darcy. None of his friends had. Brooks had been ready to introduce her to everyone when his father had dropped a bomb on him. Douglas had offered Darcy a couple million to walk away from him. And like a dumbass, Brooks had assumed she'd taken it. When he'd accused her, she hadn't denied it. Instead she'd slapped him and walked out. Only very recently had he learned from his father that she hadn't. God, he'd been such a fool. He should have known she'd have never taken that money.

"Who's Darcy... Wait, that bi—"

"Don't finish that sentence," Brooks growled out. The sharpest sense of possessiveness swelled inside him.

Savage looked around the pool area, confused. "Valencia's asleep." And Savage didn't curse around his soon-to-be-adopted daughter. That was pretty much the only time the man didn't curse.

Brooks looked away from his friend. No one was paying attention to them. Everyone was in little clusters, scattered around the pool, talking, laughing, and drinking. Even though his father didn't actually live in the main house on the ranch, but in another smaller house on the estate, he'd still paid to have the event decorated and catered. There were glittery lights everywhere, tons of food and the highest quality alcohol. It was overkill since there were fewer than fifteen people there tonight, but Brooks guessed his father had simply been trying to do a nice thing. Trying to make up for a lot of lost years. Which was why he hadn't told his father that the big gesture wasn't necessary.

Right about now he wished Darcy was with him. He just wasn't sure how to make things right. "She didn't take the money," he finally said.

"*What?*"

"Darcy didn't take the money my dad offered her," he said, finally turning back to Savage.

His friend frowned, his normally harsh expression even harder. "What are you talking about? You said—"

"I was wrong. My dad only told me a few weeks ago, right after the end of the Miami job, that she didn't take the money. He thought I'd *known*." But Brooks hadn't. He'd gone to see Darcy right after his father told him about the offered money and he'd basically called her a gold digger. Not in those exact words. But he'd been harsh enough—harsher. And she hadn't corrected him. She'd just slapped him across the face and walked away with tears in her eyes.

Savage's expression was thoughtful. "Let me get this straight. You only *thought* she took that money? You never actually confirmed it with her?"

"She never denied it." Looking back, he understood why she hadn't. Because he should have known better. He should've known and *trusted* her. And he hadn't. Instead he'd betrayed her trust.

"She shouldn't have had to, dumbass." A short pause. "What exactly *did* you say to her?"

Brooks tightened his jaw. He didn't want to repeat what he'd said. Not even to his best friend. Because he was ashamed.

"That bad, huh?"

Brooks just lifted a shoulder.

"So I guess you're the bitch." Not a question.

"Pretty much."

"So?"

"So what?"

"Don't be a dumbass. Have you apologized? Have you gone to see her? Oh my God, you're such a pussy!" Savage said, guessing the truth.

"Hey!" Skye shouted at them across the pool, clearly having heard the word. The badass redhead who carried around C4 in her purse like some women carried lipstick hated it when anyone used the word pussy in a derogatory manner. Savage had learned that the hard way. And probably still had the bruise to prove it.

"Sorry." Savage threw his hands up in apology.

Olivia just rolled her eyes at her fiancé and Savage apologized again—this time more sincerely.

Brooks snorted. "No, I haven't gone to see her. I only just found out the truth right at Thanksgiving. We had so much shit going on, then I was on that job and—"

"Sounds like a whole lot of excuses, my man."

"I need to do it in person." That was at least the truth.

He didn't even want to be having this conversation with his friend. Guys didn't talk about this kind of stuff. At least he didn't. And...he'd sent her a few things. In hindsight, it had been stupid to send her anything before apologizing in person. No, not just stupid, but cowardly. His head was all screwed up where she was concerned and he had no one to blame but himself.

"Then apologize. Tell her you're a dumbass, that you're sorry. In person. Simple as that."

But it wasn't simple. Not with Darcy's history. No, Brooks had screwed up. Instead of responding, he lifted a shoulder. "I think I'm going to get out of here for a while."

"It's after midnight and it's New Year's. Where are you going?"

"None of your damn business."

"When I said apologize to her, I didn't mean *now*."

Brooks simply headed inside and grabbed his coat, shrugging it on over his flannel button-down. He figured almost everyone would end up staying the night. At least the ones who had been drinking. The ranch was certainly big enough to hold everyone. And it wouldn't be the first time his friends had stayed over. It was probably rude that he was leaving, but he couldn't find it in himself to care. Right now, he wanted to check on Darcy.

Yes, he was aware that it made him a pseudo-stalker, but he also didn't care. If he had to guess, she was probably working late. Her business was in a safe enough part of Redemption Harbor, but she was still a single woman who worked a lot of late hours. And he didn't like it. Of course, she wouldn't care what he did or didn't like at this point.

Forty minutes later, he cruised down the street where her shop was located and sure enough, there were enough lights on that he knew she was there. It was close to two in the morning and she was working. He loved how driven she was to be successful, and understood why she was the way she was, but hated that she often burned the candle at both ends.

He needed to man up and talk to her. Now wasn't the time, but when would be the time? After the Miami job, he'd taken on two smaller ones, and convinced himself to wait to see her, to wait until he could apologize in person. Which was just plain stupid.

Waiting only kept them apart longer. Because he could have asked someone else to take one of his jobs, could have stayed and fought for her. But the truth was he was pretty sure that even with an apology, it wouldn't make a difference. He'd betrayed her trust. He'd doubted who she was at her core, and insulted her.

Basically, he'd screwed up beyond redemption.

And some things couldn't be undone. Which was the real reason he hadn't gone to see her in person. Because once she told him to fuck off, that she didn't care about his apology, it would be final.

In the front two windows stood mannequins dressed in wedding dresses made by a local boutique. Darcy had once worked for Faith Olsen—owner of a bridal shop—and her former boss had encouraged Darcy to start her own wedding planning business. Faith had been sad to see her go, but had been a supportive friend. And now they worked together, both sending each other business. It was a smart collaboration. And Darcy was smart. She'd utilized many of her contacts when she'd worked with Faith and had never gone behind her friend's back. Everything about her was honest, and loyal.

Something he'd remembered too late.

As he sat there, the conversation between him and his father from a little over a month ago replayed in his head. It had been right around Thanksgiving and the conversation had changed everything.

"So...most of the house is headed to town to see a movie," his dad said, leaning against the doorframe of Brooks's office. *"I'm going with Martina. Skye wanted me to ask you guys if you wanted to go."*

Brooks straightened the slightest bit as annoyance crept through him. He wasn't sure he bought this whole "changed man" act by his father. His father had left his ex-wife and moved back to Redemption Harbor. And now he was cooking breakfast, being friendly to everyone, trying to be a father to Brooks. And Brooks wasn't sure how to deal with it. "Martina's not like the women you've been with in the past." He couldn't keep the edge out of his voice when he talked about Martina. She truly was a sweet woman and had already lost a hell of a lot in her life.

Surprising him, his dad snorted. "Yeah, no kidding. It's why I like her. Really like her."

Brooks let out a snort of his own. He was so out of here. He didn't need to stand around and make small talk in his own office with his father. Especially not when Gage was in here, clearly wishing he was anywhere else. It was too damn awkward.

But his father continued, "So when are you going to pull your head out of your ass and go after Darcy? It's time you started on a family and I'd like some grandchildren."

Brooks started practically vibrating with anger at the mere mention of the woman who'd broken his heart. "Are you kidding me? Go after the woman you offered a few million if she'd leave me? This is why we can't ever have a normal relationship! You can never just leave well enough alone! And I don't buy this whole changed man attitude." Not one bit.

His father shoved up from the door, put his hands on his hips. "I did it to make sure she loved you and wasn't after your fortune."

"Yeah and how'd that work out?" Bitterness laced his voice, but he couldn't even bother to keep it out. "Looks like you and I have something in common after all. Shitty taste in women."

His father gave him a strange look. "She didn't take the money."

"What?" Brooks rasped out as lead filled his stomach. No. No. He couldn't have heard that right.

Frowning, his dad nodded. "How do you not know that? She told me to fuck off—though more politely than that. I always wondered why you let that one go. She was a real class act," he murmured, respect in his voice. "And I know she could have used the money too."

No. Brooks shook his head, but couldn't find his voice.

"Son, I'm sorry, I thought you knew that—"

Brooks didn't respond, just strode out of his office because he couldn't be in the same room as his father right now.

What the hell had he done?

CHAPTER TWO

—Every time I see her, I stop breathing.
For just a second.—

Feeling like a psycho for showing up at two in the morning without calling, Brooks decided to get the hell out of there and vowed to call Darcy tomorrow. The worst she could do was hang up on him. Which she probably would do. But he would still call and apologize. She deserved an in-person apology. Of course, she deserved a better man than him. But he would at least start with a phone call. And if he could convince her to meet in person, he would.

As he pulled into the front strip of parking directly in front of her shop, ready to turn around and leave, a movement from the shadows caught his eye. Looking to the right, it appeared as if someone had ducked around the side of the shops. He'd been inside before, many months ago, and her place, as well as the other five connected to it on this block, all had back doors that exited into an alley. And it wasn't well lit.

He was probably being paranoid, but he'd been a scout sniper in the Marine Corps and he always trusted his instinct. He wasn't going to leave without checking out whatever he'd just seen. After turning off the ignition, he slid from his vehicle.

The street was lit well enough but as he stepped around the corner of the building, he wasn't surprised that it was dark. It took a few moments to adjust to the dimness and as he did, he reached into his jacket and patted his holstered SIG.

Not that he planned to use it. But it was always his "just in case" because some habits died hard. He'd seen enough of the world and how shitty people could truly be that he was always prepared to protect himself, and more importantly, the people he considered family.

At a scuffling sound, he picked up his pace, jogging along the side of the brick wall. When he heard a startled, female cry, a jag of adrenaline punched through him as he sprinted to the end of the building.

Though he wanted to barge around the side, he stopped and eased his head around the corner, wanting to assess the situation.

It was dark, but there were a couple lights out back, and when he saw Darcy with her hands up facing a man in a hoodie with a knife, crimson bled into his gaze for a moment. The unknown assailant was next to a dumpster with the top open and it looked as if Darcy had just stepped out of the back door. She parked back here so as not to take up space in the front.

She'd clearly surprised the suspect. The man could be homeless and just looking for food, but he'd pulled a knife on Darcy. That meant Brooks would deal with him.

Sticking to the shadows, Brooks eased around the corner and slowly moved down the wall, grateful for the lack of lights back here. If either of them looked in his direction, they would see him, but Darcy likely had tunnel vision as she stared at the man with the knife, and the man had his hoodie pulled over his face far enough that Brooks couldn't even see what color his skin was.

"How much cash you got on you?" the man demanded, his voice raspy, as if he was a lifelong smoker.

Only ten feet stood between Darcy and her would-be attacker. She was closer to her shop's back door than she was to the man but she appeared almost frozen in place. Her dark hair was pulled into a loose braid falling halfway down her back. She didn't even have her coat on, which told him she'd likely stepped outside to throw something away.

He catalogued all of these unimportant details even as he silently continued moving, using the shadows to cover him. *Closer. Closer.* Now he was only a few feet away from the man. Brooks was vaguely aware of Darcy telling the man how much money she had, but all his focus was on the threat.

He didn't bother pulling out his SIG because he wouldn't need it. *Only a few more steps...* Darcy turned in his direction, clearly seeing him in her periphery.

And that was it. He'd lost the element of surprise. Which he'd known was coming soon enough. Adrenaline surging through him, he raced at the man, using all his years of training to neutralize this threat.

The man let out a grunt of surprise as he turned in Brooks's direction. But it was already too late for him. Striking out, Brooks grabbed the wrist holding the knife, and twisted in a sharp, practiced move.

"Ahhhhh!" The man's scream filled the air as his arm snapped.

Brooks felt no pity as he slammed the man to the ground, face-first. There was no telling what could have happened if he hadn't been here. Maybe Darcy would have made it back inside. But maybe this man would have attacked her, stabbed her, and she could have bled out... Nope, he couldn't even let his mind go there as he secured the man's wrist behind his back.

Pulling out flex ties—because he always had at least two pairs, since he'd started Redemption Harbor Consulting with his friends—he tugged the cuffs into place.

He stood to find Darcy staring at him, her pale green eyes wide with shock and fear. Her mouth opened once, then snapped shut when he stepped toward her.

"Are you okay?" he asked.

She nodded, still staring.

"I've got to call the police," he said even as he pulled his cell phone out of his jacket pocket. Instead of calling the main dispatch line, he called Miguel Hernandez, a detective he knew from high school. Of all people, he'd never expected Hernandez to go into law enforcement, but after he got out of the Navy, Hernandez had joined the local department.

The call took less than five minutes, with Brooks promising not to go anywhere and to make sure Darcy remained safe. He'd nearly snorted at that. Like him leaving was even a possibility. By the time he'd ended the call, Darcy seem to have gotten her voice back.

"Brooks, what are you doing here?" She'd wrapped her arms tightly around her middle, shivering, probably from the cold and the shock running through her system. In black skinny jeans and a thin-looking tunic-style top, she must be freezing by now.

He wanted to pull her into his arms, comfort her. Keep her warm. Instead of answering, he said, "Why don't you go grab a coat?" He would have tried to tell her to simply stay inside until the police arrived, but he knew her better than that.

It appeared as if she wanted to argue, but she nodded and hurried back inside. Less than a minute later, she cautiously stepped back outside, bundled up in a knee-length peacoat, a white sparkly cap and a multicolored scarf. She spared a glance at the man on the ground, but he was passed out cold. Probably from the pain or from however much alcohol he'd ingested. Because the man stank of booze.

Not that Brooks cared if the guy was in pain or not. And he didn't care what that said about him. The threat to Darcy had been neutralized. And he hadn't been forced to pull a weapon, which was a very good thing. There would be a hell of a lot less paperwork with the cops. And considering what he and his crew did with their consulting company, the less involvement with cops, the better.

"Why are you still parking out back? It's safer in front." Brooks immediately winced at his tone. He hadn't meant to lead with that. Or to say anything at all. At least not right now.

She stiffened, her spine going straight. "I think the more important question is what are you doing here in the middle of the night?" Each word came out whiplash sharp.

"I had a hunch you'd be working late and wanted to stop by and talk to you." Mostly the truth. He'd gone out and decided not to talk to her at the last minute.

"It's almost two in the morning on New Year's. You just assumed I didn't have plans?"

"No. I just know you." She was getting her business off the ground and was driven in a way he only saw with the truly successful. If she wanted to take over the damn world, he had no doubt she could do it. Of course, she could have been out with another guy. But that wasn't something he was going to think about.

She snorted, the sound full of derision. "You never knew me at all."

Oh, how he deserved that. "Darcy, I'm sorry. I screwed up. There's no excuse for what I said to you. What I accused you of doing." That being an understatement. He didn't want to have this conversation here, out in the cold, next to a dumpster that smelled of old Chinese food, and an unconscious mugger at his feet.

"Do you remember *exactly* what you said to me? Because I do." A mixture of pain and anger sparked in her green eyes as she took a step toward him.

He remembered, but he didn't respond. Just watched her. She was petite and adorable, but she was all fire and rage right now.

"If you can't remember, I'll remind you. You showed me an engagement ring..." She swallowed hard and blinked rapidly for a moment as if fighting back tears, before she continued. "You said you'd planned to give me that ring but that you'd heard your father had already taken care of my 'bill.' You called me a whore without actually saying the word. You just assumed I took two million dollars to walk away from you. You didn't bother coming to me first. No, you made an assumption and treated me like garbage." She stepped back now, putting a couple feet between them at the sound of sirens in the distance.

"I'm sorry," Brooks whispered, because it was all he could force out. He remembered that night all too clearly and he hated himself for it.

He'd been in a rage, hadn't been able to think straight. He'd been ready to propose to her, ready to lock her down for life. Then when his dad had told him what he'd done, he'd lost it. It had been like Maya all over again. Brooks had been in love before Darcy—scratch that, he *thought* he had been. When he'd gotten out of the Marines, he'd been young and horny and had fallen hard and fast for the first pretty face to come along. It had been so stupid. Looking back, he knew that hadn't been love. Not even close. But he'd been looking for a way to deal with everything he'd been through. Luckily, his father had been smarter than him. Not that Brooks would ever tell him that he'd done him a favor. That experience had colored his reaction and he'd jumped to conclusions with

Darcy that had cost him everything. Hindsight was such a bitch.

Darcy looked down at the man who was now stirring on the ground. "Thank you for what you did," she said quietly.

She never had to thank him for anything. Shoving his hands in his pockets, Brooks tried not to stare at her as they waited for the police. The sirens were close now, right on Main Street if he had to guess by the noise.

Which meant their conversation was tabled for now. Hell, who was he kidding—their conversation was over. But he wasn't done, not by a long shot. He might have screwed up, but he didn't want to believe that things were over between him and Darcy. It was unfathomable to accept that he'd had the perfect woman and let her go because of his own stupidity. He had to figure out a way to convince her to give him another chance.

CHAPTER THREE

—Today is the kind of day where I wish vodka came
out of my shower.—

Sitting on the back of the ambulance, Darcy tried to stop
her covert looks at Brooks. Because nothing about her ac-
tions were covert. She would have made a terrible spy.
Or...any job that involved lying.

Every time she looked at him, he was looking at her. And
he had this sad puppy dog expression on his face. Which made
her want to punch him. Right in said adorable, handsome,
stupidly sexy face. *Gah!*

She was still reeling from what had happened tonight. Or
technically this morning, since it was now two thirty. And the
really sad thing was, she was embarrassed that Brooks knew
she'd been working on New Year's Eve. Not out dancing with
friends, having a good time. Though the thought of going to
a crowded bar for New Year's Eve wasn't actually her idea of
fun, but still, it wasn't the point. She didn't want him to know
anything about her life. Especially how pathetic her social life
was lately. Aaaannnd, she realized the EMT had said something to her.

"I'm sorry, what?" she asked.

The man half-smiled. "I just said we're about to get out of
here. I'm glad you're okay. You're lucky your friend was here
tonight. Things could've been a lot worse." The tone in his
voice said that he'd seen worse.

Nodding, she slid off the back of the truck. He was the second person to tell her that in the last half hour, and she knew it to be true. Even if she was angry at Brooks, she was still glad he'd been there tonight. She thanked the EMTs as they left, surprised they'd even come down here. One ambulance had left with her would-be attacker. The police had told her that he would be taken to a hospital for treatment then booked.

The second ambulance had stayed. Apparently the entire police department was working tonight and the hospitals were fully staffed. They'd been at a nearby call that turned out to be nothing and instead of heading back to the hospital and PD, had all come here. It felt like overkill, and she wondered if the reason so many people had come had been because of Brooks's involvement.

The man was a billionaire, after all. Or rather his father was. Maybe he was too. She didn't know and she didn't care. He'd broken her heart, and months later she still wasn't over him. And she wondered if she would ever get over him. They'd been together for four months. And apart for a little over seven. She should be over him by now. At least throwing herself into work had been surprisingly easy. Working kept her busy and kept her mind off him.

As she turned away from the ambulance pulling out of the alley, she nearly ran into Brooks. The man moved like a ghost. And for someone of his size, it was surprising. He was a little over six feet tall, with dark hair and dark eyes, and while he didn't exactly have that brooding thing down, he was still intense and a little bit serious. Once upon a time, she'd loved to make him laugh. But that was over. Everything between them was over.

She just needed to remind herself of that when he was standing right in front of her with those sad eyes.

"Do you need a ride home?" he asked quietly.

She resisted the urge to snort, because it would be rude. And he *had* saved her. Even if she was hurt and angry at him, she was still grateful for tonight. "No. But thank you." There, that was civil enough.

"I'll follow you home." There was no give in his voice and she didn't like his tone.

But she kept her expression neutral and pleasant. Something she'd learned to do at a young age. "That's not necessary. That guy was likely homeless, and trying to mug me was a crime of opportunity." It wasn't as if she had any enemies. She was a freaking wedding planner. And while some brides might get a little manic, they weren't homicidal.

He simply lifted one of those broad shoulders and didn't respond one way or another. Instead, he reached into his coat pocket and pulled out a card. It said *Redemption Harbor Consulting* on the front, along with his name underneath it and his cell phone number. She flipped it over. Nothing else was on the back. Plain and to the point. "My number is on there. Call me if you ever need anything, day or night. It doesn't matter what time."

She resisted the urge to ask him what this consulting company was all about. As far as she knew, he ran his family's ranch and everything that entailed. So even though she was desperately curious about this consulting business, she bit back all questions as she tucked the card in her pocket. It wasn't as if she was going to call him, but ripping it up and throwing it in his face seemed a bit extreme and immature. Even if it would have given her a short-lived pleasure. "Sure."

His expression turned wry. "I'll take that 'sure' as a 'no way in hell would I call you even if I was on fire.'"

Despite herself, a short laugh escaped. She quickly cut it off and cleared her throat. "Well, unless the police need anything else from me, I'm heading home."

He didn't look away from her, didn't glance back at his detective friend standing by his car. No, Brooks's attention was all on her. It was unnerving to be under that kind of scrutiny.

"You look good," Brooks said quietly.

How could she respond to that? She certainly wasn't going to return the compliment, even if it was true. He *always* looked good. The first time they'd met, he'd stolen her breath. Then, not long after that, he'd stolen her heart—then broken it. She shoved her hands in her pocket and said, "Thanks again for what you did."

He looked as if he wanted to say more, but instead nodded, his jaw tightening. Then he glanced over at his friend. "I'll stay here until she locks up."

"Sounds good. Ms. Cooper, I'll be in contact with you," Detective Hernandez said before getting into his car.

She turned her attention back to Brooks and had to steel herself as she looked at him. "I would tell you that it's unnecessary for you to stay until I lock up, but I know it's probably useless."

"It is useless." Brooks fell in step with her as she headed toward the back door.

She needed to save a few files on her laptop then pack up her purse and she was more than ready to head home. Since she didn't have any meetings tomorrow—gah, today—she was planning on catching up on sleep. And she had some dinner thing with her sister's fiancé's family. Not wedding related, just a family thing, and her sister wanted her to be there. Since Emma was her only family—or the only family that mattered—she would be there. And she couldn't look like a zombie either.

Without bothering to make small talk, she quickly shut everything down before turning off most of the lights. Brooks simply stood near the back hallway, silent and sexy. She wondered what was going on in his head, then cursed her curiosity. She shouldn't care and hated that she did. He was not hers to worry about anymore.

But him showing up tonight and giving her that sincere apology... She wasn't sure how to process it. She certainly wasn't giving him another chance. Not that he'd actually asked for one.

Once she'd finished everything, she set the alarm by the back door and stepped outside with him, her purse heavy at her side. She really needed to clean the thing out.

"At least you have a security system," he grumbled.

"Seriously? You're going to give me grief now?"

"What the hell were you thinking, coming back here so late? And why are you parking back here?" Muted anger and another emotion she couldn't define laced his words.

After what had happened earlier, she didn't have much of an argument. But that was beside the point. "I think I make my own decisions and don't answer to you."

"Are you at least carrying pepper spray?"

She had the pepper spray he'd given her tucked into her purse. Normally she carried it with her anytime she came out back after dark. But she wasn't going to tell him that. Instead, she pulled her keys out as they reached her car, a four-door, boring sedan that she hoped she could get a few more years out of. Though considering the sounds it was making lately, that wasn't likely. "In case you're still thinking about it, you seriously don't have to follow me home. It's overkill." She wasn't his to take care of.

"Can I take you out for coffee this week? So we can talk?" His words were quiet, his expression serious.

She wanted to say yes so badly. But she knew if she did, she would be one step closer to forgiving him. And nothing good would come of letting him back in her life. He'd shown her how little he thought of her. When he'd basically called her a whore, it had cut deep. There was so much she wanted to say to him too. But she'd learned the hard way how to cut a toxic person out of her life. Not that Brooks was necessarily toxic, but she wasn't opening herself up to the way he'd made her feel again. "No." She pressed the key fob and slid into the driver's seat without giving him another glance.

Even as she pulled out of the parking lot, she refused to look at her rearview mirror. She didn't want to see him. Tonight had completely tilted her world on its axis. Seeing him gave her a rush of wonderful, sexy memories—right up until the end. When her world had crashed around her.

Soon enough, she'd get her equilibrium back. Unfortunately, it felt as if she was starting at square one in her attempt to get over him.

* * *

As he drove down the nearly deserted two-lane highway, Gage glanced at the screen of his cell phone, ready to dismiss whoever was calling him at two in the morning on New Year's Eve, until he saw that it was Nova, the new executive assistant for Redemption Harbor Consulting, aka "the voice." She'd been working with them the past couple months and he loved her snark.

The first conversation he'd ever had with her, she'd hung up on him. Deservedly so. And he'd been hooked on her sexy, sultry voice even before he'd met her. But she worked with them and he was one of the cofounders. There was too much of a power imbalance for him to ever hit on her. Of course, if she ever showed an ounce of interest, he might change his mind, but he wasn't going to head down that path.

Still, he couldn't stop the increase of his heart rate when he saw her name. "Hey," he said, picking up on the second ring.

"Hey, sorry I never made it to the party tonight. I'd planned to but got stuck at this stupid country club thing. My friend is sick and can't find her purse or keys. I was supposed to be the designated driver but I can't drive without keys. And..." She cleared her throat. "I hate to ask, but would you be able to pick us up? I can't get a cab or an Uber tonight. It's too busy everywhere. And all of my friends have been drinking. I figured you'd be a safe bet for being sober."

"Of course." Already on his way home, Gage definitely didn't mind making a detour to pick her up. "Where exactly are you at the country club?" Because he knew where the place was, but it was vast, on a hundred acres.

"In the main building, in the women's restroom on the first floor. As soon as you step inside the main lobby, make a left and it's the first restroom on the right. If you text me when you get here, I'll meet you."

"All right. Everything okay?" Because something about her tone bothered him. Nova was smart, beautiful—and a smartass. And she hadn't made one snarky comment tonight. That was what was bothering him, he realized.

"Yeah. Just been a long night." A short pause. "Thank you for doing this. I really appreciate it."

Gage wanted to say more, but didn't. If something was wrong, he'd know soon enough. "Just sit tight. I'll be there soon."

As he headed in her direction, he ignored a few traffic laws and gave exactly zero fucks about it.

Instead of parking or having his vehicle valeted, he left his truck under the overhang. One of the valet guys had told him he couldn't but Gage had slipped him a hundred, and the kid, who couldn't be more than twenty-one, had just grinned and told him to leave it as long as he wanted.

Under any other circumstances, Gage was certain that he wouldn't have been let in, but it was close to two thirty in the morning and whatever shindig had gone down was coming to an end. There were a few stragglers in the hall, men in tuxedos and women in glittery dresses. Some clearly intoxicated; others just looked tired as they made their way to the exit.

As he reached the door that Nova had indicated, he texted her. A few moments later she walked out, looking like a wet dream. Ah, hell. He shouldn't even be noticing. But it was damn hard not to. The shimmering gold dress she had on clung to every one of her curves. And her pouty lips that he'd fantasized about more than he would admit were painted a ruby red. Her dark hair was down in long waves, and he wondered what it would be like to run his fingers through them as he dominated her mouth. In flats she was about five feet nine inches, but tonight she had on heels and had to be at least six feet tall. He was over six feet, so she would fit perfectly against him. Again, not something he should be thinking about.

Relief filled her expression when she saw him. "I'm so sorry to drag you away from the party."

"I was already headed home." He'd only had a couple beers earlier in the night, and even if it was New Year's Eve, he'd still be working tomorrow. There were a few things he needed to check on regarding some of their working intel.

"Seriously? Or are you just saying that to make me feel better?"

"I would tell you that to make you feel better, but I actually am telling the truth. Savage and Olivia are officially engaged, by the way."

Her luscious mouth spread into a grin. "Good for them. I wondered how long he'd be able to hold off." Before he could respond, she continued, "My friend is passed out in here. I'm going to need some help getting her to your truck."

Alarm instantly slid through his veins. "Do we need to take her to the hospital?"

"No." She rolled her eyes. "She's just a lightweight. Normally she doesn't drink much, but her ex-boyfriend was here with his new fiancée and I guess it hit her hard. So she downed three glasses of champagne in quick succession—without having eaten in the past few hours. But I'll be staying with her tonight and checking on her anyway."

It didn't take him long to carry her friend to his truck. The woman was actually lucid, and giggly, by the time he strapped her into the back seat. Nova carried both of their coats and her own purse, but her friend's purse was still missing.

"Should I take you to your place?"

"No...gah, yes. Because we don't have her keys," she said as if just realizing that.

When she shivered, he turned the heater on higher. "What's your address?"

She gave him a sly look, her dark eyes narrowed. "Are you telling me that you, hacker extraordinaire, don't have my address?"

"No. Don't get me wrong, I could easily find it without having to hack anything." All he would have to do was look at her resume and company file.

"Good answer." She gave him her address, which he plugged into his GPS.

He was familiar enough with the area she'd given him but not sure of the exact street. "So you didn't have a date tonight?" His voice sounded normal enough as he asked.

She snorted in a very Nova-like manner. "Hell no. I didn't even want to go to this thing, but Jennifer insisted. She didn't realize that her ex was going to be there."

He wasn't sure about her "hell no" response to having a date. Because she was one of the most beautiful women he'd ever seen. But more than that, she was funny and real. Why *wouldn't* she have been on a date? As far as he knew, she wasn't dating anyone and had no interest. They'd gone out a few times as friends in the last two months and she was checked out everywhere. He didn't think she was oblivious to it, but a woman as stunning as her would have learned to filter out second glances and lingering looks. Or he assumed.

"I'm bummed that I missed Olivia and Savage getting engaged," she continued. "What else did I miss tonight?"

"Nothing... Look, you sounded weird earlier on the phone. Are you sure everything is okay?" It would bother him until he knew for sure, so he just flat out asked her.

Sighing, she fiddled with the vents of the heater. "Yes. Just some jerk offered us a ride home if I would perform...a service for him. With my mouth. Jackass," she muttered. "After that, I called you."

It took him all of a second to understand what she meant and raw rage surged through him. "Who?"

She blinked. "Who... Wait, you want his name?"

"Yes."

"Ah, *no.* Because you look a little like you want to throttle someone right now. It's not a big deal. He was just a random asshole."

It was a big deal, but he didn't push it. For how he felt, he could easily rip said random asshole's life apart for telling Nova she could give him a blowjob. And even Gage knew that was psychotic. But what kind of asshole wouldn't give a woman in need a ride home just because it was the right thing to do? He already knew the answer to that, because there were far too many assholes in the world.

"Hey," Jennifer slurred from the back seat. "You think Taco Bell is still open?" she asked, before slumping back against the seat, snoring softly.

Next to him, Nova snickered. "Or maybe KFC," she murmured, loud enough for only him to hear.

"Did you just quote Will Ferrell?"

She laughed and laid her head back against the headrest. "I can quote most of his movies. And I'm not even embarrassed."

If it was possible, he adored her even more now. She wasn't from Redemption Harbor originally, not like him. But she'd been basically recruited by Skye so he had no doubt that she could be trusted. What he'd learned over the past couple months was that she used to be an analyst for the CIA—which was how she'd met Skye and Colt, two of the other founders of Redemption Harbor Consulting. She'd hated her job and had quickly found work in the private sector instead. But after a bad experience with her former boss, she'd quickly jumped at the opportunity of a new job and a new city. And it seemed as if she'd settled in very quickly, already making new friends. She was outgoing and friendly, whereas he was not. Another reminder that even if she was interested in him, they were too different.

"If you ever want to do a movie marathon at Brooks's place, he's got that movie theater room."

"Yeah I heard about that from Valencia. She thinks it's the coolest thing ever." Valencia, Olivia's six-year-old daughter, had quickly stolen everyone's hearts, including Nova's. "And speaking of, did you know that Skye was teaching her to pick locks? Or more importantly, does Olivia know?"

He glanced over at her as he pulled up to a red light. "I did *not* know. And I'm not going to be the one to tell Olivia."

Nova laughed again, the sound music to his ears. She was way out of his league, and even if they didn't work together, he wouldn't ask her out. He was just glad that she didn't have a boyfriend or someone he had to see her with. He actually didn't even want to think about how that would feel because sooner or later someone would scoop her up. They would be stupid not to.

When his phone buzzed on the center console, indicating an incoming text, he nodded at it. "Will you check that text?" he asked before giving her the code. Normally he only received texts this late if it was work—and an emergency.

"Ooh, giving me your cell phone code was very brave." She picked it up and swiped her fingers across the screen. "It's Brooks, and it's a group text. He apologized for leaving the party so abruptly. He just wanted to let everyone know that he's okay."

"Thanks."

"So...what happened? Why did he leave?"

"I'm not sure." But Gage had a pretty good idea it had to do with a woman named Darcy. A woman's name that he'd only very recently learned by being in the same room as Brooks and his dad during a very awkward conversation. He'd wanted to ask Brooks about her, but had decided not to push.

"You're totally holding back."

He glanced at her as he turned down her street. She lived in a fairly new subdivision that consisted of houses and town-homes.

"Oh, the GPS is weird here. Turn left at this street and we'll get there quicker."

Gage didn't necessarily want to get to her house quicker, but did as she said. "I'm not holding anything back."

"You're such a liar."

He glanced at her. "Why are you so sure?"

"Your face does this weird thing when you're lying."

"I'm not technically lying, but okay, I have an idea why Brooks left the party abruptly." And he wouldn't be sharing it with Nova or anyone.

"Well duh, it's because of a woman."

He glanced at her again.

"What?" she asked.

"How did you come to that conclusion?"

She shrugged and his gaze automatically flicked to the smooth, creamy expanse of her arm and shoulder. Seriously, her shoulder turned him on. He had issues. "He's been kind of distracted ever since I started working for you guys. And..."

"What?"

"I don't want to say. Because it will sound like I was snooping or eavesdropping, but I wasn't," she tacked on.

"Come on."

"Fine. But you have to promise not to say anything to anyone. I don't consider this gossip since it's you."

He wasn't sure how to respond to that. "Okay."

"Say you promise," she said as he steered into her driveway.

He bit back a laugh. "Yes, I promise I won't say anything."

"I stopped by his office a month ago to bring him something, I can't even remember what, and heard him ordering flowers. Who does that over the phone anyway? I'm surprised he didn't just do it online, but yeah, I heard him ordering flowers for a woman. And when he started to give the text for the card, it was an apology. I hurried away before I could hear too much, but he was clearly sending flowers to a woman and apologizing for something. I can't even imagine Brooks doing something wrong. He's all cowboy charm and niceness."

Gage felt a strange pang inside him at the way she talked about Brooks. It wasn't romantic, but all the same it still bothered him. "So what's this thing I do with my face?" He didn't want to talk about Brooks anymore.

She snorted. "I'm not telling you because then you'll stop doing it." Then she glanced in the back seat and sighed. "Jen is probably going to have a hangover tomorrow morning. And I'm going to be the lucky one who gets to drive her back to the country club to search for her purse."

"You're a good friend."

"She is too," Nova said. "Tonight was just a bad night for her."

"Come on, I'll help you get her inside." Gage helped Jennifer out of the back seat and thankfully the woman seemed more sleepy than anything else because she was able to walk on her own—for the most part. She used Gage's forearm to steady herself as they headed up the front steps to Nova's place.

Her townhome was two stories and not actually connected by walls to her neighbors, but there was no yard space. He laughed when he saw the little welcome flag at the bottom of the steps. It said "Welcome to the Nut House."

As he followed Nova inside, he frowned when he didn't hear the telltale sound of a security system beeping. Shutting the door behind them, he said, "Did you forget to set your alarm system?"

She flipped on the light in the foyer. "I don't actually have one yet. I keep putting it off."

He didn't like the thought of that at all, even if this was a safe area. It wasn't like he had a say in the matter, but he still didn't like it. "Do you need help with anything else?"

"Nah, but thank you again for picking us up."

"Yes, thank you," her friend slurred. "Normally I don't drink so much and I'm sorry your first impression of me is this." Or he was pretty sure that was what she said. Then Jennifer continued, "Now I'm going to go throw up and go to bed."

Nova just shook her head as her friend stumbled down a short hallway.

"I'm going to ask you something and if you say no, it's okay," Gage said.

Nova straightened, her expression shifting slightly. "Okay." She looked almost wary.

"Since you don't have a security system, I want to do a sweep of your house before I leave. Which, yes, I know you probably think is insane. But with what we do, I'm not going to be able to sleep tonight without checking out your place. So it's actually a selfish request."

Her body language completely changed, her mouth falling open slightly. "Are you serious right now?"

"Yes. And...I'm going to insist you get a security system installed. The company will pay for it. It's standard for new employees." Okay, that was total bullshit since she was the only new employee other than the founders. They weren't even a year old. And they operated in shades of gray. Their consulting company was more or less a cover. They helped people who needed it and couldn't afford to go to the police or law enforcement. It was actually how Savage had met Olivia in the first place. She'd come to Skye, her college best friend, because she'd been threatened and blackmailed. And there was no way she could go to the cops.

For a moment, he thought he'd pissed Nova off. But then she let out a light laugh and held out her arm like Vanna White. "Go knock yourself out. But stay out of my underwear drawer."

He snorted and headed toward the nearby stairs. "No promises."

"We're going to talk about that whole security system thing later," she called after him.

She could talk about it all she wanted, but it was happening. He had the most intense urge to protect her. He wasn't stupid—he knew nothing would ever happen between them. But that didn't matter. He was still going to look out for her.

CHAPTER FOUR

—Why does life have to be so complicated?—

Two days later

Darcy stepped out of her office as she heard the telltale jingle of the front door of her shop being opened. She had an appointment scheduled early in the morning with a couple. Potential new clients who wanted to get married very soon. They'd just gotten engaged and were looking to fast-track something.

Which was something she could definitely do.

She smiled at the man and woman as she covered the distance of her shop to greet them. Her place was basically a display of wedding dresses from designers and boutiques she worked exclusively with, examples of cakes and pastries from the bakery she worked with, and she had an entire wall of display boards featuring weddings she'd planned. "Hi, I'm Darcy Cooper. You guys must be Olivia and Zac?"

The petite Asian woman smiled easily and nodded. Her fiancé nodded briefly, and while his expression wasn't unfriendly, it also wasn't approachable. He had more of a neutral expression as he glanced around her place. His stance was similar to one Brooks took whenever entering a new place—*Damn it.* No thinking about him today.

"Thank you so much for meeting with us on such short notice," Olivia said. "I'm in the process of moving to Redemption Harbor with my daughter so we'll be planning a wedding and finding a place to live at the same time." She shot the tall man next to her a sideways glance and said, "Unless we decide to move our wedding date to the end of the year?"

The man just softly snorted and wrapped an arm around her shoulders, pulling her close. "Nope. You're going to be my wife as soon as possible." He leaned down and murmured something to Olivia that Darcy couldn't hear. Whatever it was, it made the other woman smile.

Darcy's heart melted a little. "I'm going to go ahead and lock the front door," she said. "I don't normally get much foot traffic this early, but just in case, I don't want any interruptions of our meeting." She wouldn't even be open officially for another few hours, which was why she normally scheduled meetings with potential new clients early. No interruptions. "Can I get you guys something to drink? Sparkling water, regular water, coffee, cappuccino or latte?" she asked as she moved to the front door.

"Coffee would be great," Olivia said.

"Coffee," Zac murmured as well.

"Great, just give me a few minutes, then. Feel free to look around or make yourself comfortable in the seating area." She motioned with her arm to the three couches in one corner of the shop. She'd chosen the furniture specifically, the navy blue tufted couches feminine but comfortable enough to fit anyone. There were also ivory throw pillows, shimmery blankets, and a crystal chandelier overhead, giving the area a whimsical feel. It had been made for function and comfort. She wanted people feeling good enough to talk about everything they wanted, and a stuffy, conference room-type setting would have been too boring for people planning such a big life event.

A few minutes later she carried in a tray with a fresh coffee carafe, complete with cream, sugar and three mugs—and of course pastries. When meeting with new clients, she always had samples from the bakery she used for weddings. If a client had already decided on a bakery, then she did what the client wanted, but for the most part, ninety percent of the couples she'd worked with had used Cora's Cakes.

As Zac began pouring coffee for the three of them before she could even try, she sat down across from the couple. "So you're moving to Redemption Harbor?"

"Yes, it's something we're really excited about," Olivia answered. "Zac is actually from here so I'm the one moving."

"It's a wonderful place." Darcy had moved here with her mom and sister when she'd just been ten and she loved it. Never wanted to move anywhere else, if possible. They made small talk for a few more minutes before Darcy said, "Since your wedding will be taking place so quickly, finding a dress and a venue will be very important."

"Oh, we actually have a venue," Olivia said.

"That's great. Where?" She hoped it was a place she'd already worked with before. That would make things a lot easier for her, but at the same time, she was always open to making new contacts and expanding her business.

Zac cleared his throat. "Some friends of ours were married at the Alexander Ranch. And I'm friends with the owner. We'd like to get married there. It's open any time in the next couple months."

It took Darcy a few seconds to understand what he meant. "The Alexander Ranch? As in, the estate owned by Brooks Alexander?" *What the heck?*

"Yes. He actually recommended you to us. Said you were the best. Since we're business partners, I trust him."

Olivia elbowed her fiancé playfully. "They're more than just business partners. They've been best friends since they were teenagers."

Zac Savage. Darcy hadn't even put the two together when she'd first read Olivia's email. But she recognized the name. Brooks had talked about him often when Darcy and Brooks had been together, usually just calling him Savage. Which was why she hadn't made the connection. He'd been overseas doing...something. She wasn't sure what, as Brooks had been vague about the man's job. Something to do with the government.

Even though she felt beyond awkward that this man was best friends with her ex, she wasn't going to turn down work because of something personal. Especially since it wouldn't interfere with her job. Sure, she might have to see Brooks a couple times if he was in the wedding, but their contact would be limited. And, okay, being able to add a wedding at the *Alexander Ranch* to her portfolio was incredible. As far as she knew, they'd never done any weddings out there. Well, obviously they'd done one, if Olivia and Zac's friends had gotten married there, but it definitely wasn't open to the public. This could be *huge* for her business, to be able to add that to her portfolio.

She smiled warmly, not having to fake it. These two seemed nice and, well, she'd just have to deal with Brooks's involvement. "Well that's great, then. That's a huge thing off your list. Next, we'll talk about wedding dresses..."

She spent the next hour with the couple and could clearly see the love between the two of them. And even though Zac seemed intimidating, it was obvious how much he loved the woman next to him—and her daughter, Valencia, who would be the flower girl. Whenever he talked about her, his entire countenance changed and he actually looked nice. Maybe not teddy bear soft, but definitely approachable.

By the time they'd finished going over everything, she knew she was officially hired before they'd even said it. Sure, she might have been recommended by Brooks, but she could tell enough about these two that they hadn't been completely decided until now. Which was smart. They would be working with her and needed to like and trust her.

"You've given us a lot of information but I feel a lot saner now. The thought of planning a wedding and finding a house at the same time was daunting, but not so much anymore." Olivia stood as she spoke, Zac standing with her.

Darcy followed suit and smiled at the two of them. "My job is to make sure this is a fairly painless process for you. Please take your time deciding if you'd like to work with me—"

"We would," Olivia said even as Zac nodded. "And given our time frame, it sounds as if I need to start looking at dresses and figure out who we'll use as a caterer."

"You're in luck, I have a couple tastings already set up next week. I can add you to one of them."

"Perfect. I'll get in touch with you later about the exact dates and our schedule."

She started to respond but stopped as she heard a little knock. Turning around, she saw her sister standing behind the glass door, holding her own fiancé's hand. Emma waved at her, smiling and shivering a little. Her sister had a key, but had probably left it at home. Darcy waved back then turned to face the couple. "That's my sister. I'll introduce you guys to her and her fiancé. They're actually scheduled to get married in less than a week."

"Maybe she can give me some advice," Olivia said, laughing lightly.

Darcy opened the door and let the other couple in. And though it was probably her imagination, as she made introductions, Zac looked at Peter as if he knew him. But Peter didn't give any indication that they'd ever met. Darcy was probably imagining it anyway; she didn't know Zac and the man was difficult to read, regardless.

The two couples made small talk for a few minutes before Olivia and Zac left. Once they were gone, Darcy left the door unlocked. Technically she didn't open until a little later, but she wouldn't say no to any foot traffic today.

"They seem nice," Emma said as Peter headed to the back, no doubt to get coffee for the two of them. "New clients?"

"Yes." She glanced over her shoulder before turning back to her sister. Darcy figured that Emma would tell Peter anyway, but she liked the illusion of privacy right now. "Brooks recommended me to them. Apparently Zac works with him."

Her sister's eyes widened. "Are you serious? That's crazy, especially after all the horrible things he said to you."

Darcy bit her bottom lip. She still hadn't told her sister about what had happened the other night. Mainly because she hadn't wanted to talk about the almost mugging. Her sister had enough on her plate right now. But she rarely kept secrets from her sister and she wasn't going to start now. "I sort of ran into him on New Year's Eve."

"What? And this is the first I'm hearing of it!" The words were more a shouted statement as opposed to a question. "Wait, you were working though."

Darcy winced. "Okay, let's take it down about ten notches. And yes, I was working. He stopped by and..." She winced again, internally this time, because she knew what was coming. "Don't freak out, but I was almost mugged. I was taking some stuff out to the trash when this random guy with a knife demanded all my money. Brooks had stopped by to apologize about what he said to me. I found out later that was why he'd come by, but anyway, he stopped the mugging. The police were called and it was a whole big thing."

Her sister stared at her in pure shock. "How did you keep this from me for two whole days?"

Peter chose that moment to join them, passing a mug of coffee to her sister, fixed just the way she liked it. Darcy really did like him. He treated her sister like a princess. Then he handed the other mug to Darcy. Because that was just the kind of guy he was. Thoughtful of everyone. She was so happy for her sister. "What's going on?" he asked.

"Oh nothing." Emma's tone was slightly sarcastic. "Just that Darcy was almost mugged on New Year's Eve. And her ex-boyfriend showed up and saved her. The freaking police were called and everything. Oh my God, obviously you're okay, right? Did the man hurt you?" Emma looked her up and down as if checking for hidden wounds.

"Yes, I'm fine. I just didn't want to bother you with this. You've had so much on your plate lately."

"For the record, you can always bother me with anything. And it's not a bother anyway." Emma looked dangerously close to tears, which made Darcy feel shitty.

She was the big sister, used to looking out for Emma. Still, she should have told her.

Even Peter frowned at her. "Darcy, come on, that's serious. You should have told us."

"Okay, you guys are right. But everything turned out okay. I guess the guy was out on probation and he very clearly broke it, so he's going back to jail. I don't have to testify or anything."

"So...Brooks apologized?" Emma asked after a long moment. Her sister had adored Brooks. She'd been just as shocked as Darcy when he'd assumed the worst of Darcy.

"Yes. And he wants to have coffee and talk more." That definitely wasn't happening.

"When are you meeting him?" Emma took a sip of her coffee and sighed in appreciation.

"Ah, I'm not. There's nothing to say."

"Darcy—"

"Come on, Em." Peter shook his head. "Let it go. Should I tell your sister why we're here?" His tone was resigned.

And when Emma's expression mirrored his, Darcy had a feeling she knew exactly what her sister was going to say even before she said it. Okay, maybe not exactly, but Peter's father had likely changed the guest list or decided he wanted to use a new caterer—again—or come up with something else insane for her to do. Maybe he'd decided that he wanted a peacock as a ring bearer. It was the weirdest thing: Peter's father seemed to have more interest in this wedding than either Peter or Emma. The two of them would have eloped if it was up to them, but apparently his father wanted a whole big thing, complete with people invited who neither Peter nor Emma even knew.

"Well…Peter's dad wants to move the rehearsal dinner to his estate. Instead of using Eat Pray Love as the venue, we want them to cater instead. Since they're already catering for the big day…" Emma lifted her shoulders.

Which meant Darcy needed to call and smooth things over with the owner, Mr. Singh, tell them they'd be catering the rehearsal dinner as well as the wedding, and figure out all the new logistics. "I'm surprised you came to tell me in person," she said dryly.

Emma laughed. "I thought about texting you, but Peter of course is the voice of reason."

"I really am sorry about my dad." He shook his head. "I think he's so used to micromanaging every aspect of his businesses that he's taken to treating this as a business deal or something."

"It's okay, trust me. I'll make sure this is taken care of." And Peter's dad, who was footing the bill for the wedding, would simply pay for the changes. Even if it was a pain in the butt to deal with, everyone would still be paid accordingly.

And hey, dealing with all of this wedding insanity kept her mind off Brooks. Sort of. Because for the past two days, the man had consumed her mind. She'd tried desperately to shut him out, but when she was home alone at night—or in the shower—he invaded her mind. The handsome jackass.

* * *

Brooks looked over at the door as Savage and Olivia stepped inside the conference room where he was reading over some files Gage had sent him. He was surprised to see Olivia with Savage. He knew she didn't have any contracts right now. She worked for a boutique security firm, breaking into places that had hired them and demonstrating all of their weaknesses. She'd taken a break for the next two months as she got Valencia settled in Redemption Harbor, found a new place to live, and planned a wedding. Regardless, she didn't work here, and rarely stopped by.

He shoved back his chair and stood, stretching his legs. "Hey guys, what's up?"

"We just met your ex-girlfriend," Olivia said, plopping down into one of the swivel chairs.

He flicked a glance at Savage. Of course his best friend would have told Olivia about Darcy.

Savage simply shrugged. "She's nice."

"She's adorable," Olivia said. "Seriously, how on earth did you screw things up with her?"

"I didn't tell her all the details," Savage murmured, taking a seat next to her.

"Who's adorable?" Skye asked as she stepped into the room, a Hot Pocket in her hand. That woman was always eating.

"Brooks's ex-girlfriend. She's going to be our new wedding planner," Olivia supplied helpfully.

"Ex-girlfriend? This is the first I've heard of you dating anyone." Skye sat directly on the table as opposed to one of the chairs and crossed her legs as she munched on her food. Her auburn hair was pulled back into a tight braid and she looked like she normally did, ready to kick someone's ass.

"She's as cute as a button. I want to put her in my pocket and carry her around," Olivia continued.

"Coming from you—someone also as cute as a button—I've gotta see this woman." Skye took another bite of her food. "Why'd you guys break up?"

"Oh my God, this is why I don't tell you people anything," Brooks muttered. Then he glared at Savage, who'd told Olivia about Brooks's past with Darcy in the first place. "You got anything to say?"

Savage just stretched back in his seat, sliding his hands behind his head. "Not about that. But Darcy's sister is engaged to Peter Markov—son of Semyon Markov."

Brooks paused, watching his friend carefully for a moment. Savage wouldn't joke about something like that anyway. Still… "Are you sure?"

"Yes. We met them as we were leaving her shop this morning. 'Them' being Emma and Peter."

That was beyond interesting. During their Miami job, the one in which they'd saved Olivia's ass from blackmail—though she'd done a lot of the heavy lifting herself—they'd discovered a flash drive with a lot of information on various criminals worldwide. Anything with concrete proof of crimes they'd anonymously turned over to the FBI and DEA. But there had been more than a few files they'd kept for themselves. Basically as a backup should they ever end up in hot water with a government agency. Because there were far too many government officials in those files. Semyon Markov didn't work for the government—but he had contacts with men and women at various agencies, and he'd allegedly done some deals with a man named Alexei Kuznetsov.

The file on Markov had been new, because the now-dead man who'd started it had been in the data-gathering stages. It was unclear what he thought he might find, but clear enough that Markov was involved in some dirty shit. Drugs, skin trade, the kind of stuff Brooks and his people would shut down. And his loose link to Kuznetsov—a criminal they planned to bring down—was enough that their crew would be looking into Markov.

Knowing that Darcy might soon be related to the man had Brooks tensing. He'd always been protective of her and now was no different. Maybe even worse. Because he had no right to feel possessive, protective. Well, he was going to look out for her whether she liked it or not.

"Have you gone to Gage yet?" Brooks asked. Gage was a hacker, to put it mildly. He'd been headhunted by some of the most prolific tech companies in the country. And most of the government agencies.

Savage shook his head. "Not yet. He's in his office working on something. I just wanted to let you know first. Do you know how long Darcy's sister has been with Peter?"

"I knew she was dating someone when I was with Darcy, but I never met the guy." Brooks and Darcy had been so wrapped up in each other all those months ago. All their spare time had been just the two of them. He hadn't been interested in double-dating or any of that shit. Thankfully neither had Darcy. "I knew his name was Peter. His last name was never

brought up. Not that it would have registered back then."
They hadn't started their consulting business yet and hadn't
known about that blackmail file. Savage had still been doing
contract work for the CIA, Colt had been working directly for
the CIA, Gage had been in Seattle working for a big firm, and
Brooks hadn't even known Skye back then—hell, a lot had
changed in the last seven months.

"So you guys broke up when?" Savage asked, a slight bite
to his words.

Probably because Brooks hadn't told him about Darcy until after they'd broken up. "Right before Colt headed off to
Mexico." To save their friend Mary Grace, who'd been kidnapped by a Mexican cartel but was presumed dead by the rest
of the world. Oh yeah, life had been a roller coaster the past
year.

"Okay, so roughly seven months ago. And if they were together while you were with Darcy, that puts Emma and Peter
together at least eleven months."

"Yeah, so?" Brooks wasn't sure where Savage was going
with this.

"I'm just thinking out loud… And I'm guessing that Darcy
has access to the Markov mansion." Savage frowned, looking
off into space for a moment.

"Whatever you're thinking, stop right there. She won't
even talk to me. And even if she was talking to me, I sure as
hell wouldn't ask her to go into his house on a recon mission.
She's a wedding planner." He would never put her in danger.

Olivia frowned at Savage, clearly shocked he would sug-
gest something like that.

Savage raised his hands, palms up. "I know! I wasn't sug-
gesting that. I'm just thinking out loud, I swear. We've been
gathering intel on the guy, and I haven't seen anything in
Gage's file about Markov's son or said son's fiancée. But if

Emma Cooper is marrying him, there's a good chance that she and Darcy will end up as notes, at least, in some government file. Because if the FBI doesn't have Markov in their sights yet—"

"They will soon enough." Brooks settled down, leaning against the table now. Anyone remotely connected to the Markovs could become targets for the government as well. He didn't like that at all.

"While this is all very interesting," Skye said, wiping her hands off on the napkin her Hot Pocket had been wrapped in, "I came in here to let you guys know that Colt and I got a job in Oregon. A quickie. One we'll be able to actually put on the books."

"When do you guys head out?" Brooks asked, glad to not be talking about Darcy anymore. He was already twisted up over her to the point of distraction. He'd called her and texted her to check in on her after New Year's, but he'd gotten radio silence.

"Tonight. Colt's at home packing."

"You let him pack for you?" Olivia's tone was dubious.

"Hell yeah. He packs better than I do. And as long as he doesn't forget our weapons, I'm good."

Brooks leaned back as they continued talking, trying not to think about Darcy. And failing. Seeing her two days ago in person had shaken him to his core. How many times had he wished he could go back in time and pull his head out of his ass?

What the hell had he been thinking? How had he even *thought* she would have taken that money? Unfortunately, he knew the answer to that. She wouldn't have been the first woman to. He shelved that thought. Because there were more important things to think about. Now that he knew she had a loose tie to the Markov family, he couldn't ignore that.

He narrowed his gaze at Savage, who was watching Olivia with complete adoration as she talked to Skye. Brooks knew his friend would do anything for Olivia.

Something he could understand. It didn't matter that Darcy wasn't his anymore. Now that he knew she was soon going to be linked to the Markov family, he wasn't sure what to do. There was no way he could tell Darcy what they knew about Semyon Markov either. Not now. She had no trust in Brooks, and for all he knew, even if he did tell her, she would go right back to her sister—who could tell Peter Markov. And they had no idea if Peter was involved with his father.

If he was, then Emma Cooper could be marrying into a criminal empire. And Darcy would be related to them. There wasn't much he could do about that now, but he would certainly be digging deeper into the Markov family.

CHAPTER FIVE

—Today sucks.—

Darcy dropped her purse onto the center island of Se-myon Markov's kitchen. Peter's father was a little intim-idating but he'd always been welcoming to her and her sister. He'd told Darcy more than once that he wished he had an-other son for her to marry. Because she was such a "good girl."

She nearly snorted at the thought. He was definitely an old-school type of man. She couldn't say for certain but he seemed to view women in certain ways: good girls or not-good girls. It was so archaic and yes, insulting, but she took it with a grain of salt. Besides, he wasn't *her* father-in-law to-be. She figured after this wedding, she'd only see him a couple times a year. Maybe at some holidays.

Opening her purse, she pulled out her folder for the Mar-kov-Cooper wedding. After going over a few things, she took out the catering menu from the restaurant they were origi-nally supposed to have their rehearsal dinner at. The menu was slightly different than the one at the restaurant, some-thing Mr. Markov likely hadn't thought of. No, he just liked to make decisions and expected things to happen his way. It was a pattern she'd seen with extremely wealthy people, and while she tried not to judge, oh sweet Lord, it was annoying.

Mr. Markov had told her that he'd be here at seven and normally he was very prompt—often early. Which was why she'd arrived at six thirty.

61

She pulled a water bottle from the refrigerator and took a sip. When she'd first started planning this wedding, it had felt weird being here on her own. But in the last few months, she'd been here so often to meet with him about changed details that she almost felt at home. Not completely. This place was huge and beautiful. Not the kind of place she ever saw herself living in. But he'd insisted that she feel at home here. That any food or drinks she wanted while she was here were hers. So it only felt a little weird taking water from his refrigerator.

When she heard the sound of male voices, she set her water bottle down on the counter and headed in that direction. She'd been waved in by security at the front gate so Mr. Markov would likely know she was here. But she hadn't wanted to wait in his office.

Her ballerina flats were quiet against the tile, then the wood floors as she made her way down different hallways. Traditional, kind of stuffy art hung on the walls. Mostly boring scenes from nature. Some by artists she very clearly recognized. But she didn't think they were originals. Who knew, though.

As she neared his office door, she saw that it was partially open. She wondered if she should knock or just text him instead to let him know she was here.

"For the second time, you shouldn't even be here. You know that Semyon doesn't like you here, *detective*," the male voice snarled. Ice crystallized in her veins when she heard the sound of Oleg Polzin's voice inside the office.

The man was in his thirties, handsome enough, but there was something in his eyes that set her on edge. He worked closely with Mr. Markov when he was in town, but thankfully he seemed to travel a lot. She wasn't sure what he did, but she was sure that she shouldn't be in a room alone with him. He'd never looked at her sister the way he looked at her—as if he was imagining her naked and under his control. Ugh. Even so, she'd mentioned her feelings to Emma.

And to her surprise, Emma said she felt the same way about him. She said that Peter had told her never to be alone with him. That in itself was scary. It also made her question why Mr. Markov worked with him. But that was none of her business. And as soon as this wedding was over, she hoped to never see Polzin again. Or at least only once or twice a year. And always with someone else around. He was the only reason she hated that her sister was marrying into the Markov family, and she kept secretly hoping Mr. Markov would fire him.

She paused, wondering if she should even knock now. At the sound of another voice, she took a step back. It was one she vaguely recognized but it wasn't Mr. Markov.

Stanton Turner. A detective she'd met the other night. He'd stopped by to talk to Detective Hernandez after the mugging. They hadn't spoken directly, but his voice was raspy and distinctive. He'd had a runny nose so she'd assumed he was sick. Maybe she should just wait in the kitchen after all. Neither of them could help her, and she didn't want to talk to Polzin anyway.

"Well too bad. He hasn't returned my calls," the detective snarled. "And we're a week away from...finishing it."

It? Darcy paused, feeling a little bad for eavesdropping.

"Are you getting cold feet?" Once again, ice dripped from Polzin's voice. The man was like a snake, slithering around.

Shivers rolled through her at his tone. She'd never heard him talk like that before. The way he'd looked at her, as if he was always undressing her with his eyes, put her on edge. If he'd ever spoken this way, she probably would have run in the other direction.

"No. Of course not."

"Are you certain? Because not everyone can stomach hurting kids." There was a certain gleeful note in his voice now that said he would have no problem doing such a thing.

Her palms went clammy. Hurting children? What were they talking about? And why was a *detective* with him?

"I'm not getting cold feet. I just want to make sure everything is in place. If I'm going to do this—"

"If?"

"I'm doing this. I just meant that I better get paid. I want half of my fee up front. I'm doing more than just looking away this time. I'm going to have to plant evidence. I could get caught. I could lose everything. Because the fire department will be called in this time too. Maybe even the Feds. A bombing of this magnitude—"

"Shut the fuck up. You wired?"

"What—"

There was a brief scuffling sound and she wondered if Polzin was attacking Stanton. Or maybe just patting him down. Either way, she'd heard enough and felt sick to her stomach. She couldn't be caught in this hallway. There was no telling what they would do to her. Not after she'd overheard them talk about a *bombing*. And hurting children.

She had to tell someone what she'd heard. But first she had to get out of here. As she started to move down the hallway, she heard a sound near the end of it. It could be nothing, but more likely it was Mr. Markov. Oh God, was he involved in this? Of course he was—they'd been talking about him, in *his* office.

Bile rose in her throat as she tried to digest everything and keep calm. Instead of heading down the way she'd come, she ducked into the nearest room. A bedroom. Leaving the door cracked open slightly so that she was still hidden, she paused and watched as Mr. Markov strode down the hallway toward his office with confidence.

Yep, she definitely had to get out of here. But she wasn't certain she could make it from the doorway to the end of the hallway without being seen. There was every chance in the world that one of those men would step out and see her.

Shoving back the growing panic spiraling through her, she hurried to the French doors. They were locked, so she unlocked one and eased it open. No alarm sounded so she stepped out onto a small stone patio and locked the door behind her before shutting it. She couldn't leave any proof that she'd been here.

Of course if she'd had her phone, she could have at least called someone, but she'd left it on the kitchen counter. Thankfully she was on the first floor and was familiar enough with the grounds that she could easily make it to the kitchen.

Heart pounding, she took off across the backyard, sticking to the shadows near the house and avoiding the pool, which was brightly lit up despite not being in use this time of year. At each window, she paused and peeked inside to make sure no one would see her. Most of them were covered. She knew that there were security cameras on the property, but she didn't think they were this close to the house. It was a risk she would have to take anyway. Because she couldn't just hang out in a guest room.

When she made it to the side door that led to a room right off the kitchen, she nearly collapsed in relief when it opened. Ducking inside, she glanced around quickly. She was alone. Without wasting a second, she hurried to the kitchen. Her stuff was still there and looked untouched.

Even though every instinct inside her told her to *run*, if she did that, it would look strange. And she wasn't sure who to turn to at this point. It was a giant risk to stay here, but if she left now, after security had already seen her—and Mr. Markov no doubt knew she was here—there would be questions. No, she needed to have his meeting with him and act as normal as possible. She wasn't sure how she was going to do that without throwing up, but somehow she had to keep it together.

As soon as she could, she was going to tell someone that she was here. So she sat down at the center island and quickly texted her sister, letting her know that she was at Mr. Markov's house, going over the new menu. Then she chugged half of the water bottle, feeling parched and a little out of control. As she set it down, Mr. Markov stepped into the room, moving like a wraith.

"Darcy, you're here." His voice was neutral enough, not the normal jovial tone she was used to. *Oh, God.* Did he know she'd overheard them talking?

She smiled and hoped it looked natural. "I thought I'd get here early since you're always so punctual." She let out a short laugh and hoped it didn't sound strained. Because she felt as if he could see her every thought, and knew what she'd heard.

"I hope I didn't keep you waiting long."

"No. I had a chance to go through some emails anyway." She tried to smile again but couldn't make her mouth work properly. She wasn't cut out for this.

"Is everything okay?" he asked quietly, concern in his voice. Or maybe it was simply concern for himself.

Darcy realized that she would never be able to hide all her emotions from this man. So she decided to tell a half-truth. Wincing, she said, "Normally I wouldn't talk about my personal life with a client, but soon you'll be family. I recently ran into my ex and it kind of threw me off. Our breakup wasn't pretty. I guess…I'm still trying to deal with it. He called earlier and…" She trailed off, letting out a light laugh. "Sorry for over sharing. This won't affect my work or anything. I'm just having a bad day. That's all. I'm embarrassed you even noticed."

"Ah." Sighing, he stepped farther into the room and patted her on the back. She resisted the urge to flinch away. "Don't worry. Any man who let you go is a fool." He patted her again in a paternal manner, then pulled out the seat next to her, a modicum of relief in his expression.

She wasn't sure how she was going to get through meeting with him, not when her heart was racing out of control. But if she wanted to survive, she'd better keep it together. "Enough about that. Let's talk about this menu. The catering menu is slightly different than the restaurant one. Which is better for you. They have some great options."

Just like that, he was in business mode. Whatever strangeness she'd felt emanating from him only minutes before was gone. So he was convinced that she'd been in here the whole time, that she'd heard nothing. But that didn't mean he couldn't check security cameras. What if he caught her racing around the back of his house? She had no way of knowing if the cameras were on or... *No. Stop.* She had to stop thinking about that and focus on the present. As soon as she was done, she would leave and figure out what to do.

She certainly couldn't call the police. Not when she didn't know who could be trusted. That man she'd heard talking was definitely a detective. And she'd specifically heard him say "I'm doing more than just looking away this time. I'm going to have to plant evidence." That was very, very bad.

She could call Brooks. Maybe. She knew Zac Savage had worked with him, and at one point had worked for the government. She was pretty sure that it had been in a federal capacity too. He could have contacts to help her. She wasn't even sure what she was going to tell him, but she'd heard enough, and the mention of hurting children and a bombing in the same conversation was terrifying.

She couldn't do *nothing*. So she sat there for the next half hour going over menu options, when all she wanted to do was give in to her flight instinct. To run and never look back.

* * *

Semyon looked up from his desk as Oleg stepped into his office, his expression grim. "She's gone."

"I know." And he didn't have time for Oleg's bullshit tonight. He had too much work to do. His only living son was getting married and he was dealing with something even bigger. Taking out the man he hated more than anything was proving to be the biggest challenge of his life.

He was up to the task, however. His enemy would never see it coming. He'd had nothing growing up on the streets of Chicago. Semyon had clawed his way to where he was. And no one would take it away from him. Especially since his enemy had already taken so much from him. The man had to pay.

"You should let me follow her." Oleg's voice was clipped.

"You're being paranoid—and stupid. You never should have let Turner in this house," he snapped.

"It wasn't me—"

"No excuses. At least you were smart enough to turn off the security feeds." No evidence of the detective ever being here. He would have erased it anyway, but it was better to have not existed at all. He'd already talked to the security guard on duty at the front gate. The man wouldn't make the mistake of letting Turner in again. "Have you turned them back on?"

"I will. I wanted to talk to you first about Darcy." Oleg's tone bothered Semyon but he ignored it for now.

Soon enough he was probably going to have to cut Oleg loose. He would be merciful—a bullet in the back of the head. But his own son had complained about Oleg enough and he didn't like the way his second-in-command looked at Emma or Darcy. Semyon didn't think Oleg would ever do anything about it, but Semyon knew the other man's predilections. For now, however, he needed Oleg. There weren't many in his organization who he trusted to get their hands quite so dirty. Oleg didn't balk at any of his requests. Right now, he needed a man like that. "What about her?"

"She shouldn't be allowed to have free rein here."

"I asked her here. And last time I checked, this is my house." He stood as he spoke, his anger growing even as he told himself to keep his annoyance under control.

"I know," Oleg said, taking a small step back. He held up his hands in mock surrender. "But what if she'd seen the detective?"

He lifted a shoulder. "So what if she had? You let me worry about my family and you worry about our business. And I better not hear that you're bothering her." He lowered his voice, taking on the deadly edge Oleg was familiar with. Semyon might need the other man right now but soon enough Oleg would be expendable. He tried not to get his hands too dirty—that was what he had Oleg for—but he had in the past. And he would again now if necessary. Eliminating Alexei Kuznetsov was worth it.

"I just think it wouldn't hurt to keep an eye on her."

Semyon clenched his jaw, refusing to explain himself again. He had a feeling he understood what this was about. Oleg was interested in Darcy but she'd made it clear she didn't care for him. The woman couldn't hide her emotions. Which was why he'd been temporarily worried when he'd found her in the kitchen, her expression stressed. But he believed her explanation, especially since he'd heard his soon-to-be daughter-in-law talking about Darcy and her ex-boyfriend with Peter. He made a mental note to find out more about the other man.

What kind of fool let a good girl like Darcy get away? He nearly shook his head. The world was full of whores but Darcy and Emma were the right type of women—hard-working, smart and not sluts. He was glad his son had met someone like Emma. Soon he hoped they would give him grandchildren. He wanted to have someone to leave everything to.

His oldest son and wife had been murdered because of Kuznetsov. He wouldn't lose Peter too. It was why he needed to kill Kuznetsov. And he couldn't be suspected of it. No, he had to make sure Kuznetsov's allies and men had someone to blame. Which was what he was working on. Once the man was dead, Semyon planned to move more and more of his businesses to the legal side of things. Paying taxes, becoming respectable. That was the legacy he wanted for his family.

"Fine. I'll put a man on her." A lie that should appease Oleg for now. He didn't like appeasing him at all, but he hadn't gotten where he was by not listening to his instincts. And lately Oleg had been pushing him. He should bend a little bit. Soon enough, the other man would be dead anyway.

CHAPTER SIX

— I'm going to put an out of order sticker on my
forehead and call it a day.—

Sitting in a booth at Dancing Dragon, Darcy tried to remain
calm, but her heart rate seemed to be permanently higher,
a staccato rhythm in her chest that simply wouldn't slow
down. She hadn't been able to sleep much last night, tossing
and turning as she went over her options. She'd tried to
google Semyon Markov but hadn't found much. Just some articles related to business and other references to individuals
who weren't him.

She'd also looked up that detective, Stanton Turner, and
had found more on him. Nothing very useful, however. She
knew that she needed to tell someone what she'd heard, but
she had to find the right person. Even though she didn't want
to reach out to Brooks, she figured he might be the best bet.
He'd known that other detective, Hernandez. What if the detective was dirty too? She might be angry at Brooks, but she
had no doubt he was an honest man. But that didn't mean his
contacts and friends were.

As Olivia and Zac approached the table, she forced herself
to smile. They'd asked her to meet them at this restaurant to
go over a few things. Since their wedding was being fast-tracked, they'd jumped straight to the final stages of most
wedding planning. As she slid out of the booth to greet them,
she knocked over her glass of water.

It happened in slow motion, and though she tried to stop it, she was a jittery mess. It clanked against the table and as it rolled off, she bent to grab it but Zac was faster. He moved like a ninja, snapping it out of the air before it could hit the floor. There was still water everywhere, but at least no broken glass.

"I'm so sorry," she said, her voice trembling. Oh God, she couldn't have a breakdown now. Maybe she shouldn't have taken this meeting at all. She was still reeling from everything she'd heard last night. And she couldn't even tell her sister because she didn't want to inadvertently put Emma in danger. Darcy didn't trust Peter now and knew her sister wouldn't be able to keep a secret from him. The only thing she knew was that the men last night said something would be happening in a week. *A week.* She had to figure out who she could trust.

"It's no big deal," Olivia said, reaching for the napkins.

Zac murmured the same but watched her carefully. Avoiding his gaze, Darcy grabbed some napkins as well and started cleaning up. Or tried to. Zac took over for the two of them. By the time he'd finished, their server had arrived and gathered the wet napkins.

Laughing nervously, she sat across from them. "I promise not to spill anything else this morning."

"Is everything okay?" Zac asked, his tone neutral with a slight thread of concern. It was the most emotion she'd read off him so far.

She nodded out of habit. "Yes, of course. I think I just need more coffee." Another nervous laugh. "But I'm ready to get down to business if you are." She set her binder on the large table to the right of her.

Olivia nodded, smiling. "The main thing I want to get taken care of is my bridesmaids dresses. One of the women is out of town now but will be back soon—and fair warning, she'll be difficult. She hates wearing dresses, but it's happening. Overall, I don't want everyone to look exactly alike either. There should be some freedom in their styles."

Before Darcy could respond, an attractive Asian man stepped up to the table. In dark slacks, a white button-down shirt and with a pretty-boy face, he smiled easily at them, even winking at Olivia. Zac's expression turned slightly dark.

The man spoke in a language Darcy didn't understand as he focused on Olivia.

Olivia shook her head. "I still don't speak Korean, Hwan." Her voice was dry. "But if you want to learn ASL, I'll teach you."

Hwan laughed, the sound rich. "My mom will teach you Korean and you can teach me ASL."

Savage let out a growl. An actual growl.

Hwan, clearly unfazed, continued, "Good to see you guys again. Though I'm sad Skye isn't with you."

"Are you really sad?" Olivia's voice was teasing. "Last time she almost demolished your entire buffet."

"It's worth it to see her eat. I don't know where she puts it all. Anyway, I just wanted to stop by and let you know that today is on the house." When Olivia went to protest, he waved his hand in the air. "It's not up for discussion. It's on me. Your server will be here in a moment." Then he gave Zac what Darcy could only describe as a cheeky grin and left.

"One day…" Zac trailed off, shaking his head.

"He only does it to get under your skin. He's just a big ole flirt," said Olivia.

"You're the *only* one he ever flirts with."

Darcy smiled at their banter and glanced out the window into the parking lot. Was it her imagination, or had that SUV across the street been following her this morning? She'd seen it earlier, then it had disappeared as she'd pulled into the parking lot of Dancing Dragon. It could be a different vehicle, but there was a little red and white sticker in the top left corner that made it distinguishable. But...she was pretty sure that was a diving sticker or something.

When she felt Olivia's gentle hand on her own, she nearly jumped out of her skin—and was glad they didn't have any more drinks on the table, because she would have certainly knocked another one over. Oh God, they were totally going to fire her if she kept this up. She was acting like a shaky mess.

Before anyone could say anything, their server arrived and took their order. Despite what she'd said about needing more coffee, she ordered water. She didn't need anything else to make her jittery.

Once they were alone, Zac leaned forward, placing his forearms on the table. "Okay, I'm going to be blunt. Something is wrong. Is it personal? Or is this something else? Because you're pale and look *scared*."

Was she really that transparent? She opened her mouth once, then snapped it shut. She couldn't tell them. Could she? She knew that Zac used to work for the government. At least according to Brooks. Maybe Zac would have contacts. Brooks had always been vague on the details, but right now Zac and Olivia both were looking at her like they wanted to help her.

She looked around once, then whispered, "I'm in trouble. Sort of. I heard something I wasn't supposed to. But...there's no way you'll be able to help me." She shouldn't have even said as much as she had. What the hell was she thinking? She needed to find someone in law enforcement she knew wasn't dirty. But...how would she know?

Zac's expression was neutral. "Try me."

She paused, glancing between the two of them. They looked so sincere and she was certain that they *thought* they could help her. She doubted they could, but... "Brooks mentioned that you used to work for the government. You might know someone I could talk to." The words came out in a rush before she could stop herself.

He nodded, looking thoughtful. "So this is something that needs law enforcement?"

"Yes."

"Then why not go to the cops?"

Swallowing hard, she could feel the color drain from her face. She felt clammy and shaky as she glanced out the window. The SUV was still there. It was too far away to see inside and the tint was too dark anyway. For all she knew, it was empty and she was being a paranoid freak. "I know at least one person involved with what I overheard is a cop," she whispered, looking back at the two of them. There was no one remotely close enough to them to overhear but she whispered anyway.

Olivia cleared her throat delicately. "Zac and I met because I was being blackmailed by someone, and I couldn't go to the police for various reasons. He helped me. Zac and Redemption Harbor Consulting saved my life."

Oh. Darcy took a moment to digest the woman's words. Sincere and truthful.

She glanced over her shoulder. No one was in the two booths directly behind them. And no one else was close enough to overhear. "The men I heard were talking about a bomb—and hurting kids," Darcy said in a rush. "In a week's time." As soon as the words were out, she felt as if a weight had been lifted.

Zac went still in a sort of preternatural way. It was scary. "Who?" The word was covered in ice.

She paused as their server returned to refill their drinks. It seemed to take an interminably long time, the seconds ticking by. When the woman was gone, Darcy shoved out a breath. "Fair warning, before I tell you anything, I think these people are dangerous. In fact, I'm pretty sure I was followed here. I could just be paranoid, but my instinct is telling me that someone followed me this morning. It was just a feeling I had, like I was being watched."

Zac leaned back against the booth then, the picture of relaxation as he wrapped his arm around Olivia—who also looked calm. "Open the binder next to you and look down at it. Act as if you're reading something and tell us who you heard talking," he said quietly.

She did as he said, her fingers only trembling slightly as she flipped it open in front of her. He didn't think she was crazy, at least. "My sister is marrying a man named Peter Markov. Oh right, you met them both. Anyway, his father is wealthy. I'm not completely sure what he does, something to do with real estate maybe. He's rich, to put it bluntly. Over the last few months, he's completely taken over their wedding. I chalked it up to a sort of neurosis on his part. He likes to micromanage everything."

It drove her sister a little crazy but Emma was keeping quiet because she loved Peter.

Darcy continued. "In that time, I've been given basically free access to his house—ah, his mansion. He's got great security, including a security guard at a gate at the front of his driveway." She cleared her throat again and took a sip of her water as she looked at them. "I can't keep looking at this folder, it will look weird."

Zac nodded once. "Just go on." His smile was still in place, easy and relaxed.

"Anyway, I went there last night to meet him. He knew I was coming. But I was early because sometimes he's early and it makes it easier to just get stuff out of the way. And I'm rambling. Okay, so I got there early and I heard voices coming from his office. The door wasn't completely closed but I started to knock and realized that it wasn't him inside. It was a man who works for him." She couldn't fight off the shudder that overtook her.

"Who?"

"His name is Oleg Polzin. He's always given me the creeps. My sister too. He's never touched us or done anything wrong per se, but..."

"You're trusting your instinct again," Olivia said. "He's just a creep."

Darcy nodded. Most women had a creep-o-meter firmly in place. Not all women listened to theirs, but she did. "Yes. Put it this way, I would never let myself be alone in the same room with him. I heard him talking to someone. It was a voice that I recognized. It's random too."

She quickly relayed the rest of the conversation she'd overheard between Oleg and the detective she'd met on New Year's after almost being mugged. By the time she'd finished, she wasn't trembling as much. If anything, she felt stronger, and famished. Like she could eat half of that buffet. Telling someone had lifted the heavy weight pushing against her shoulders.

When she was finished she said, "Are you sure you guys can really help?" She would understand if they couldn't. She'd just dropped a bomb of information on them. There was no way—

"Yes. This is what we do." Zac's tone was matter-of-fact.

"It feels weird not calling the cops."

He nodded in understanding. "We might eventually involve the Feds. But maybe not officially. If we bring them in now based on just what you've heard, they have to play things a certain way, follow certain rules. Get warrants. We don't." There was an edge to his tone now. "We'll rip their lives apart. And if we can't find anything, we can give an anonymous tip to a couple Feds who will definitely look into Polzin, Turner and Markov. Nothing that will fall back on you."

She wasn't sure at all what they would be able to do about this whole thing, but they both seemed positive they should be able to dig up information. She just wanted to make sure the bombing never happened, and that no children got hurt. She got sick just thinking about it.

"How often are you at his house?" Savage asked.

"All the time. And the rehearsal dinner will be at his mansion. But I'm seriously over there all the time, so if you need me to get into his office—"

"No!" It was said almost, well, savagely. "You're not going to be doing any recon or anything that puts you remotely in danger. We'll just want to know anytime you're over there for your own protection. We're here to help *you*. Everyone with our company is well trained. You know Brooks, so you must know that."

It felt weird to be talking about him, but she nodded. Brooks had military experience and was an all-around badass. She hadn't actually known that when she'd first met him— she'd thought he was a sweet, charming cowboy. After getting to know him and hearing some of his stories, she could guess how trained he really was. "Will Brooks be involved in this...whatever this is?"

"Is that going to be a problem?" Zac's tone was mild.

"Of course not. Right now, this isn't about me. It's about..." She wasn't even sure. Darcy shook her head slightly. "I'm just worried about what might happen. This not knowing who might be targeted is terrifying." Because the stuff she saw on the news every day told her how very dark the world could be.

"For now, you're going to live your life like normal. But we're going to have to check out your house and sweep your vehicle to make sure your conversations aren't being bugged."

She blinked. *Uh, what?* "Are you serious?"

"Yes. If you thought you were being followed, there's a good chance you were. Maybe you're just being paranoid, but I've learned to never ignore my instinct. You shouldn't either. Since we're your clients, it will be easy for you to meet with us and have everything look normal. A dress shop is the perfect cover. Can you set something up tomorrow for Olivia?"

When she nodded, he continued.

"Good. I can have someone check your car out while we're inside, make sure your vehicle doesn't have a tracker or something on it."

She nodded even as bile rose in her throat. This felt very real and very scary. She hated feeling out of control, and right now she felt trapped in a whirlwind. Still, she found her voice. "What else are you going to do?"

"Rip apart Polzin's life. And Stanton's. And Markov's."

"What about my sister's fiancé?" Because Darcy had no idea if he was involved in any of this. She didn't want to think that Peter could be, but what if he was? *Oh, God.*

"We'll dig deep. If he is, we'll find out." The promise in his voice was deadly.

She simply nodded because she couldn't find her voice anymore. Their server chose that moment to arrive with their food and though nerves skittered through her, she still picked up her fork and tried to act normal. As if she hadn't heard two men talking about hurting kids and...maybe bombing something. As if she hadn't just trusted virtual strangers with the knowledge. Somehow, she managed to take a few bites, though the food was like cardboard going down. She thought she'd been starved but actually eating was another matter.

After a few minutes of eating in silence, she set her fork down. "So, I feel weird talking about this now, but if we *are* meeting at the dress shop, you should be there to actually shop for your dress." No need to waste the opportunity.

Olivia smiled. "Oh, I plan to try on dresses. And hopefully get one picked out. I'm a very decisive person."

Something perfect in a bride, as far as Darcy was concerned. "Good. I've also brought some things for you to go over regarding band versus DJ and things like that. These are the things that you can narrow down easily and then point me in the right direction." It felt beyond strange to be talking about wedding stuff after their earlier conversation, but this was why they'd agreed to meet in the first place. She'd just ended up spilling her guts to them.

"Sounds good to me. We want this to be as simple as possible. And trust me when I say that Zac will be able to help you. I wasn't kidding when I said he saved my life."

Darcy had a lot of questions about that, but didn't bother asking. If they became friends, Olivia would share the details. For now, all she really cared about was finding out what those men had been talking about—and stopping them before anyone got hurt.

CHAPTER SEVEN

—There is nothing quite as complicated as family.—

Brooks slammed his fist into the punching bag, barely registering the sensation. Sweat poured down his face and body as he expended the energy pulsing through him. Now that he knew how badly he'd screwed up, he was consumed with what he'd done to Darcy. He couldn't sleep, and didn't care about eating.

No, the only thing he cared about was Darcy.

Shifting on his feet, he hit the bag over and over, pummeling it with his fists in an attempt to release the anger inside him. Not long ago they'd installed a gym at the consulting building and though he rarely used it, now he was glad it was here. He normally got his workout on the ranch, with his horses, but more and more he'd shifted into taking jobs with the consulting company.

He hadn't even realized something was missing from his life. Other than Darcy. But apart from her, he'd been satisfied. His work was honest and he enjoyed it. It was more than he'd hoped for when he'd gotten out of the Marines. He hadn't been sure he'd be able to transition back to civilian life. But the ranch had made it possible—if not easy.

Then he'd started working with Colt, Skye, Gage, Leighton and Savage. And they were really helping people. People who couldn't otherwise afford to help themselves. Or if they could actually afford it, they couldn't go to the cops. Even if they occasionally—often—operated outside the law, it felt good.

When he paused to grab his water bottle, movement from the corner of his eye made him turn.

Savage and Gage strode into the room like two forces of nature. Gage's expression was neutral but there was a grimness about Savage. He'd been best friends with the man for a long time so it was easy enough to read him.

Brooks hadn't realized he'd moved but suddenly he was standing in front of them. "What's wrong?"

"I'm going to tell you something and you're going to remain calm. You're not going to rush out of here like a jackass," Savage said quietly.

Energy pumped through Brooks. There was no need to even add that kind of disclaimer unless something was wrong. He nodded, but there was only one thing he had to ask first. He figured Savage would have told him, but just in case… "Is anyone hurt?"

"No."

"Fine. I won't storm out of here." *Unless something has happened to Darcy*, he added silently. No one, not even Savage, would stop him if that was the case.

"Olivia and I had a meeting with Darcy this morning about wedding stuff," Savage started.

Brooks was silent as Savage gave him a rundown of their morning and everything Darcy had told them. Savage had been right to forewarn him. Because he *did* want to storm out of here and go to her. But he wasn't going to. If someone was watching her, he didn't want to put her in danger. But they were definitely going to be sweeping her place and finding out if she was being followed as she suspected. And they didn't need to wait until later to check her place out.

"So Markov is dirtier than we imagined," Brooks finally said.

Savage nodded. "It would appear so."

"We already had a file started on Markov," Gage said. "But you already know that. It's my number one priority right now. With Skye and Colt gone on that other job, this is going to be our only focus right now."

Normally they divvied up duties diplomatically, but it was clear what they'd be working on. He'd never been personally involved with someone on a job before—and wouldn't be taking a back seat just because he was this time. "We need to make sure Darcy and her sister are safe. What do you know about Peter Markov?"

"I'm still looking into him," Gage said. "He doesn't seem to have any financial ties at all to his father. No properties, no accounts, nothing."

But that didn't mean anything. "What are we going to do about keeping Darcy safe?" Brooks hated the very idea of her being near Markov or anyone who worked with him, but he also knew it wasn't avoidable. Not without raising suspicion.

"I'm still working on that," Savage said. "However, there's something we can get started on in just a few hours. I want to search Turner's house."

The detective. "I'm going with you." That wasn't even up for discussion.

Savage nodded. "I figured. I also think you should talk to Hernandez, and casually bring up Detective Turner, see what you can find out about him. Is there any way you think Hernandez is dirty?"

Brooks's first instinct was to say no, he truly didn't think Hernandez was dirty. If he had, he wouldn't have called the man when Darcy was almost mugged. But right now, with Darcy in potential danger, he wasn't going to trust anyone but his closest friends. The people who had always had his back. "I don't think so. But I won't pull on that string unless absolutely necessary. If I bring up Turner it might seem strange."

"Yeah, let's shelve it, then. Listen...I hate to even bring this up, but your father runs in the same circle as Semyon Markov. From what Gage has been able to find out about that wedding rehearsal and wedding, it's huge. More than just people who are friends with the bride and groom. Which lines up with what Darcy told us. Apparently Markov has taken over their wedding and is inviting an insane amount of people."

"You want to see if my father can somehow get an invitation?"

Savage shrugged. "If not get an invitation, at least reach out to him, maybe on some bullshit business proposal. If we can get in his house without having to break in, that would be ideal."

"I'm going to be hacking his computers anyway," Gage added. As if that was ever in question.

Brooks had a lot of issues with his dad. Douglas Alexander hadn't exactly been an absentee father, but he hadn't been the best father. The man was now trying to make up for it. It was as if he'd had an epiphany—or a knock in the head—in the last year, and wasn't remotely the same man who had raised Brooks. The man who'd gone through wives and girlfriends, only caring about outward appearances. Now, his father was smitten over Olivia's friend and former nanny, Martina Cruz. A woman much closer to his age and more appropriate for him than all the others. But she was giving him a run for his money, thankfully. Brooks's dad didn't need anything handed to him. "Yeah, I can talk to him."

"Good. Go grab a shower and we'll meet in the conference room. We'll start going over the details of everything."

"Okay," he said, picking up a hand towel from the neatly stacked pile near the door. Before he'd taken more than three steps, Savage's voice stopped him.

"Don't call her." A soft order with an edge to it. Savage had never spoken to him like that before, never flat out told him what to do.

He wanted to snarl at his best friend and tell him to screw off. Instead, he didn't say anything at all, just left the room. He deserved a medal for not calling her. Hell, for not rushing over to see her right now. But doing so would be stupid. If someone was watching her, she needed to be living her life as normally as possible. Which meant she lived it without him in it.

And he would never put her in danger.

* * *

Dust kicked up on the long dirt road as Brooks drove his four-wheeler toward the house his father was staying at on their property. Technically the whole estate belonged to Brooks because his father had given it to him, but his father had use of it. He'd spent the last decade—maybe longer—in Florida. Brooks hadn't been counting. As soon as he'd been old enough, he'd joined the Marine Corps. To his surprise, his father had actually been proud.

Now Douglas Alexander had moved back to Redemption Harbor and was apparently staying for good. Of course, Brooks would believe it when he saw it. He wasn't certain he bought into this whole "changed man" thing.

Which was why he hated coming here in the first place. He and his father did well enough if they didn't have to talk to each other.

He parked in front of the small, one-story ranch house near where the foreman lived, and got out. He'd called ahead, and had been surprised when his father had said he was home.

Glancing up, he realized it would likely snow tonight. The scent of it was in the air. By the time he reached the front door, it'd swung open.

Wordlessly, his father stepped back and he stepped inside. Brooks hadn't been out here since his father had moved in. He knew the foreman's wife had kept this place up since it had remained empty for years. It looked mostly the same. Dark wood floors, ranch-themed decorations, and heavy leather furniture.

"Everything okay?" his dad asked, shutting the door behind him.

Brooks always felt awkward around his father. He shoved his hands in his pockets. "Yeah. But I need to ask you for a favor." Something he hated doing more than anything.

His father raised an eyebrow, his dark eyes showing surprise. "It must be something big. Because I know you wouldn't be out here otherwise. Come on, get some coffee."

Gritting his teeth, Brooks followed after him, his own cowboy boots thudding against the hardwood floor in tune with his father's. He watched as his father started the Bunn. "So how are things with you and Martina?" There, he could be civil.

His father snorted and pulled down two coffee mugs. It didn't matter that it was afternoon, coffee was what his father drank. Brooks too, if he was being honest. "She doesn't give a shit about my money. And she wants me to be emotionally available."

Now Brooks snorted and sat down at the center island. "I hear she's been spending time with Colt's dad," Brooks said, mainly to be an asshole. Though it was true. But Brooks was pretty sure Martina and Colt Senior—aka Senior— were just friends.

"You really want to bring that up when you're asking me for a favor?" His father's voice was dry as he leaned against the counter, crossing his arms over his chest.

From the time Brooks was about twelve, people had commented on how much the two of them looked alike. Nope, there would never be any denying that the two of them were related. Dark hair, dark eyes, and according to Olivia, he was "Hollywood handsome." Brooks wished that she was the only one who ever said that to him. He lifted a shoulder at his father's question and couldn't fight the small smile tugging at his lips. "Just seems ironic that after all these years, the first woman you really like can't be bought."

Okay, he was definitely into asshole territory but he didn't much care. His father was going to do the favor no matter what he said. And Brooks needed to get some stuff off his chest.

"I deserved that," his father finally said. "I'm sorry I wasn't a better father. Or a better man."

Brooks stared at him in stunned silence. He'd just meant to poke him a little—he hadn't been expecting this. "Why now? Why are you here, trying to…whatever you're trying to do between us?"

"I would like to have a relationship with you. I know that might not be possible. When your mom died—"

"Nope. We're not doing this." He simply couldn't deal with it. Brooks might have wanted to get some stuff off his chest but he didn't want to talk about his mother. It was time to get down to the reason he'd come here in the first place. "Do you know a man named Semyon Markov?"

His father nodded slowly. "Yes. I don't do business with him."

"Why not?" The reason was important to Brooks.

"I don't trust him. I've heard rumors he's embedded with Alexei Kuznetsov—and I definitely don't trust *him*. And before you ask why, he's into running drugs, people, nasty shit. He's not a good man. And I'm not saying that I am, but my business is all legal. Mostly." His lips curved up slightly at the last word.

"Will you reach out to Markov anyway? Make it look by chance? Don't push him to do business, just..."

"What?"

Brooks weighed his options. It did him no good to keep this from his father. It would be better if he knew everything going into this. "Darcy's sister is getting married to his son. Darcy's planning their wedding. She overheard something she shouldn't have. No one knows that she did. We want to get into Semyon Markov's house. The wedding is at his estate."

"So you want me to get an invitation to his house?"

"Yes. For the wedding or before. During the wedding would be ideal, though I guarantee security will be hyped up then, so maybe before." And the wedding was soon.

"Is Darcy planning Savage and Olivia's wedding?"

"Yes."

He nodded once. "I can do it."

All right, then. "How will you reach out to him?"

His father paused, thinking. "Do you have a schedule? If not, I can have one of my assistants look into the man."

Even though his father claimed that he'd retired, he still had a hand in multiple businesses and relied on a few assistants. Though one in particular had been with him for decades. Brooks actually liked Roger. "No. The fewer people who know about this, the better. I'll get his schedule."

"You mean Gage will."

Brooks half-smiled. "Exactly."

"So have you and Darcy made up?"

He definitely didn't want to talk about this with his father. Especially since he was the one who had offered her a couple million to walk away from him. But his father hadn't been the one who'd treated her like garbage. Well, he had, but it was different. "No."

"Why not?"

"She doesn't care what I have to say."

"How did you end things with her?"

"Not well." And he regretted it deeply.

"So what have you done since you found out you were wrong to make it up to her?"

Brooks shrugged awkwardly. *Nope.* Not having this conversation either. "It doesn't matter."

"Just don't give her gifts or bullshit like that. That's the kind of stuff the old me would have done. Don't follow in my footsteps."

Brooks paused, digesting his father's words. "I sent her flowers."

"Ah."

"Did you ever apologize to her?" He'd never asked his father. Never talked to him about Darcy after that day he'd learned the truth. Because that was their MO. They buried shit deep and never talked about it again. The cowboy way.

"Yes. In person."

"When?"

"Right after our conversation in your office, around Thanksgiving."

Hell. His father certainly hadn't wasted time—unlike Brooks. He rubbed a hand over the back of his neck. Darcy hadn't told him his father had come by. Not that Brooks would have expected her to. She hadn't wanted to exchange two words with him. It had been clear she'd just wanted him out of her space. "Did she accept it?"

"More or less. Called me a couple names. She's…feisty. And real." There was a note in his father's voice Brooks couldn't read. Respect, maybe.

And despite his personal vow to keep all the past between them buried, he found himself asking, "Was my mother 'real'?"

"Yes. She was the most authentic woman I've ever met. When she died…something in me died. Or I thought it did. I went down a dark hole. One I never really climbed out of. Not until recently. Last year, I came home to find Claire screwing some guy. Our pool guy, maybe." He let out a derisive snort as he shook his head. "It was so cliché. I didn't care. As I walked out of our bedroom, I saw myself in the mirror in the hallway and I didn't like what I saw. I knew your mother wouldn't have liked me—no, she would have loathed me."

Brooks remained still and silent as his father took a sip of coffee. Part of him wanted to get up and walk out, but his father almost never talked about his mother. He'd gleaned some information about her over the years, mostly from letters he'd found between his father and her, and from pictures. But pictures only told a certain story. The old foreman, Terry, had told Brooks stories before he'd retired. Stories Brooks had been sure were lies to make a young boy happy. Or at least exaggerations. Because he couldn't reconcile the stories with the man he knew as a father. Maybe there'd been some truth in them after all.

"Your mother was…wonderful." His father's eyes looked surprisingly glassy.

Brooks looked away.

"She would have been pissed I let you join the Marines. Well, pissed and proud."

"You couldn't have stopped me," Brooks said quietly.

"I know. She wouldn't have wanted to either. But you would have been her baby forever."

"Why did you never talk about her before?" Brooks had to know. Because growing up, his father had said almost zero about her.

"It hurt too much." His father turned away then, his back ramrod straight. "When she died, I wished it had been me. She would have been a whole lot better at parenting. Would have known how to be a parent. Truth be told, the only reason I didn't put a bullet in my head back then was because of you."

Brooks straightened as he digested the words. This was... *What?*

Clearing his throat, his father turned back to him. "I made a lot of mistakes with you. A lot of mistakes in general. I'm sorry. I should have been a better father. I should have been there for you. Instead, I drowned myself in my own pain. In women who could never, ever hope to compete with the memory of your mother. I disrespected her memory and I...I'm afraid I've ruined things with you and me beyond repair."

"You haven't." The words were out before Brooks could think about them. For so long he'd thought he'd hated his father. But the last couple months had shown him a different side to the man.

His father straightened a little, looking surprised.

Yeah, well, Brooks was surprised too. "I'm not saying..." He didn't know how to finish. Because he hadn't forgiven his father for everything. "You were a shitty parent. But you gave me more than most kids could dream of. I had everything I could need." Everything except a present parent. But Brooks was pragmatic enough to understand that he'd had a hell of a privileged life. Still did.

"Not everything."

Brooks didn't respond. Wasn't sure he knew how at this point. For the first time...ever, he wondered if he maybe had a chance at a relationship with his father. Standing, he cleared his throat. "I've got to go. Got some stuff to take care of." Namely, breaking into Detective Turner's house.

His father nodded, then blurted, "I've been in therapy."

"What?" Since Thanksgiving of last year, Brooks had felt as if he'd stepped into an alternate reality. Now he was certain of it—because his father thought any type of psychology was "jackassery" and that "shrinks" were overpaid assholes.

"Yep. Have been since before the divorce. I might have been wrong about shrinks." His father grunted. "One of them anyway."

"Okay, then." Brooks definitely did *not* know what to say to that. "Call me if you make contact with Markov."

His father looked as if he wanted to say more, but simply nodded.

Brooks left, wondering what the hell had just happened. Maybe in this alternate reality he had a shot with Darcy. A chance to fix the past—and claim the woman he'd never stopped loving.

CHAPTER EIGHT

—Keep the faith. Things will get better.—

Brooks slid into one of the only open booths at his friend Mercer Jackson's pizza joint. Mercer had played in the NFL years ago, but retired so he and his wife—Mary Grace, the love of Mercer's life and also a kick-ass doctor—could start a family. Now Mercer had everything he'd ever wanted: married to his childhood sweetheart; a sweet baby girl; and a home in the place they'd grown up in.

Mercer sat in the booth opposite him, his smile easy and relaxed. "Hey man, what're you doing here in the middle of the week?"

"I'm headed back to the office, but thought I'd stop by and say hey." And also, he was ninety-nine percent sure he'd been followed. Not by a pro, that was for certain. He'd noticed a red car—red!—tailing him not long after he'd left the ranch. So instead of heading to the warehouse they'd converted into their office building, he'd come to see Mercer. Mercer wasn't part of the consulting business, but he was family in all the ways that counted.

"Hmm. What's up? You seem weird today."

"You can't ever let anything go, huh?" Brooks muttered.

Leaning back, Mercer stretched an arm out on the seat, practically taking up the whole damn bench as he watched Brooks thoughtfully. "You're at my restaurant. So no."

Out of the "original seven," as Brooks sometimes thought of them, Mercer had always been the "dad" of the group. He had his shit together. Hell, he'd known he was going to marry Mary Grace when he was about fifteen. And he'd made sure everyone else knew it too. "It's just been a weird day, that's all."

"Weird as in your ex-girlfriend is planning Savage's wedding?" Mercer grinned at Brooks's no doubt surprised expression. "Gage told me."

"Not that kind of weird. I... My dad just told me a bunch of shit. Even talked about my mom."

Mercer's eyes widened. "Oh."

"Yeah, oh. I don't want to talk about it. Also, I'm pretty sure I was followed here. Don't make it obvious, but about four booths behind me." And way out of earshot. "Single woman, dark hair pulled back in a ponytail. Sitting solo." He hadn't looked at her directly when she'd come in, but she had on jeans, boots, a button-down flannel shirt under her thick jacket. The jacket was puffy and she might be hiding a weapon under it, but there was no way to tell. She looked young, too, like she should be in college. And pretty small under that big jacket. He didn't consider her a real threat to his safety though.

"Think it's related to a job?"

"I don't know." Mercer and Mary Grace didn't work with them, but they knew the full extent of what went on at Redemption Harbor Consulting. "Skye and Colt are out of town on a job, and the one we're working on...I don't know."

"You want me to snap a picture of her?"

Brooks gave him a *get real* look, because he'd already taken a few of her with his own phone. And he'd be sure to check out her license plate when he left. "I've seen her before. I didn't realize it at first but I saw her over Christmas when I was out buying presents." He was good with faces, and for some reason, seeing her walk into the restaurant had triggered the memory of seeing her back during the holidays. The only reason he remembered was because she'd looked at him as if she knew him, almost like she wanted to talk to him. Then she'd gotten a scared rabbit look on her face and disappeared among a bunch of shoppers and he'd never seen her again. Not until today.

"Could be a coincidence. Redemption Harbor is a decent-sized place."

"I know." But he didn't think so. He always trusted his gut. "How's the baby?"

"Perfect." Mercer grinned, always the proud parent. "So you gonna order anything or did you just come by to take up one of my tables during my busiest time?"

He placed a hand over his heart. "That's cold, man."

His friend shrugged. "I've got another mouth to feed now."

Brooks grinned. "I'll take a couple pizzas to go. And a Greek salad." He planned to bring them to the office for those still in town. Nova—their new admin assistant—wasn't a huge fan of pizza, but she did love the salads here.

"Only two?"

"Skye's out of town." That woman ate more than any of them. Of course, she also ran ten miles every morning. For fun.

Mercer laughed lightly. "All right." Standing, he patted Brooks on the shoulder once. "Everything will work itself out. Have faith."

This right here was why he'd really come to see Mercer. He could easily have lost his tail. And he would when he left here. He'd just wanted to see his friend. Mercer always knew what to say. Even if it wasn't true, because right about now, Brooks wasn't sure how *anything* was going to work out. Not with Darcy anyway.

But he'd damn sure make certain she was safe. In just a couple hours he planned to break into Detective Turner's house and find any potential evidence against him. Even if he didn't find anything, Brooks would be planting listening devices inside—top of the line. They'd be keeping an eye on this man no matter what.

When he was done there, he was going to see Darcy. Because he couldn't stay away any longer.

* * *

"You're sure the security system is disabled?" Brooks asked through his earpiece. Plastered against the back wall of Detective Turner's house, he already knew the answer but still wanted to double-check before he made his next move. A civilian security system was no match for Gage's hacking skills.

"I'm going to pretend you *didn't* say that." There was a bit of derision in Gage's voice.

It was an hour after dark, and most people would be sitting down to dinner or doing homework with their kids or whatever the hell people with families did. He would have preferred to break in at three in the morning, but this was second-best only because they knew Turner was at work. "Just checking. It's my ass on the line."

Gage snorted. "Seriously, like you can't take him out if he comes home early?"

Okay, that was fair. The Marine Corps had spent a lot of money making sure he knew how to be invisible and kill. But the whole point of this mission was to get in and out completely undetected, and with no collateral damage. No one could know he'd been here. If Turner got on to the fact that someone was looking into him, he'd report it to Polzin or Markov. Right now, they had the element of surprise in that they knew Markov was up to something. Brooks wanted to keep it that way.

Gage had offered to do the break-in, but Brooks had insisted. This job was personal for him. And he didn't care that it was. Not that he doubted Gage's abilities, but whatever. He was doing this. The fact that Darcy had overheard those guys talking, had been in Markov's house, been in danger... No, this was on Brooks. She might not want to talk to him, but he was still going to protect her any way he could.

It took about thirty seconds to pick the lock on the back door. Child's play. Gloved hand on the doorknob, he turned it slowly. They knew for a fact he was at work, but they hadn't been able to garner if he was dating anyone. It didn't seem so, going on his phone records or email messages, but if the guy was working with Markov, it was likely he had burner phones. So they didn't know everything about him.

There was a soft *beep beep beep* as he opened the door, and an electronic message that said "back door open." Shit. Gage had disabled the actual alarm but if someone was here, they'd heard the electronic message. "Did you hear that?"

"Yeah."

Heart rate slightly accelerated, he stepped farther inside and shut the door behind him. Turner had left a few lights on so he didn't even need to turn on his flashlight. "It's quiet." But he would do a full sweep to check for any signs of life. He wouldn't make a rookie mistake now.

Moving quickly, he scanned the living room, kitchen, dining room, half bathroom and hurried upstairs. Two bedrooms and one bathroom. All empty of life.

The second bedroom had been turned into an office. Bingo. "I'm at his desk." Brooks quickly turned on the man's laptop. "It's password-protected." They'd figured it would be. He quickly plugged in the device that Gage had given him.

Seven minutes later, he'd cracked the password. Next he downloaded all of the files to the flash drive he'd brought. "You ready to take over?" he asked Gage. Gage could have already taken over remotely, but they'd wanted someone in the house to do an actual search.

"Yes. Go do what you have to do." Gage's voice was clipped, as it normally was when he was working.

The most obvious place to search for anything would be the detective's bedroom. So he started there. Brooks had no idea what he was looking for, but if there was anything incriminating, he was going to find it. He looked in the vents and any potential hiding spots. There were two safes, one a small one for handguns. Unlocked and empty, because the detective would have his firearm with him. The other one was a wall safe in his closet. Not super high-tech, but he also couldn't open it himself. Not without tools and he would most certainly damage it. "There's a safe."

"We'll come back for it," Gage said.

Meaning they'd bring Olivia into this since she was a professional safecracker. Of course, that was if Savage was okay with it. Brooks wasn't certain how his best friend would feel about it. "Okay." He snapped a couple pictures of it so they could look up the type later.

After searching the bedroom, he found a roll of cash in the false bottom of a cheap-looking vase. He also found a burner phone and downloaded the contents of it in case they could use it. Returning to the office, he started rummaging through the file cabinet but didn't find anything interesting. Mostly just bills and records of personal purchases or warranties. "I'm going to start planting the bugs now," he murmured, already moving into action.

They had to be careful where they placed everything in case the detective periodically swept his house. So he planted one in the living room—in a small clock on the fireplace mantel—one on top of a dusty cabinet in the kitchen and of course he placed them in Turner's office and bedroom.

"Someone's pulling into the driveway. Can't tell if it's him. It's not a black and white." Gage's voice was calm.

"Shit. I've got to close the laptop." Everything had to be exactly as it had been when Turner had left. There was no room for error.

"All right. I'm done anyway. Hurry up and get the hell out of there. Someone's getting out of—yep, it's him." Gage was in an SUV across the street and would need to leave soon anyway. "Looks like he's leaving his vehicle running. Maybe he's just stopping home for a second," Gage added. "I'm going to turn the alarm system back on. There aren't any motion sensors, so you can move freely."

"Got it." Brooks would meet Gage a couple streets over and use the backyard as an escape route. At least that was the plan. He was silent as he raced back up the stairs. After turning the laptop off and easing it shut, he heard the front door open, and this time instead of the three beeps, there was a message telling whoever had opened the door to disengage the alarm.

Brooks didn't love this situation, but right now the smartest move was to find a place to hide. Since his options were limited, he ducked into the adjoining bathroom and stepped into the master bedroom even as he heard footsteps hurrying up the stairs.

Just as the bedroom door opened, Brooks slid underneath the bed. Forcing his heart rate and breathing to remain steady—something he'd learned in scout sniper school—he listened as Turner moved around the bedroom. The closet door opened. There was a slight shuffling sound. Then five beeps. The safe opened. Moments later, the door shut and Turner retreated from the room. Not long after that, footsteps descended down the stairs.

Easing out from his hiding place, Brooks stood, brushing the remnants of dust off him. On silent feet, he moved toward the door.

Footsteps pounded back up the stairs.

Shit.

No time to dive under the bed.

He stepped into the bathroom and moved behind the navy blue shower curtain without making a sound. He might be able to control his heart rate, but all his muscles tensed as he prepared to attack. They might not want Turner to know anyone had been in his home, but it might be unavoidable.

Brooks didn't move for his weapon—his hands were as deadly as any pistol. And he didn't want to kill the man anyway. If necessary, he would just incapacitate him.

The light flipped on and—he heard a zipper. Then...oh hell. The guy was peeing.

Remaining still, this time Brooks waited until Turner left and he heard the sound of the alarm being set. Once the front door closed, he shoved out a breath.

"You okay?" Gage asked in his ear.

"Yeah. I'm going to do one more sweep of his place though. Where are you?"

"A children's park across the street. He's leaving. And I'm turning the alarm off again."

Brooks was glad he did another sweep of the house, because he found a tablet on the kitchen counter that hadn't been there when he'd done his first sweep. Turner must've brought it in with him.

"I ran the information on that girl," Gage said as Brooks turned the tablet on.

"Who?"

"The girl from the diner."

Oh, right. "Anything interesting?" Mercer had ended up giving him her name—which he'd taken from her credit card when she'd paid. It appeared to be her real name, as it matched up with the name linked to the license plate on her car.

"Not really. She's in college. Twenty-two, no boyfriend that I can tell, about to graduate. Attended on a full scholarship. Really smart. She's about to start veterinary school this summer here in Redemption Harbor. And she's originally from Florida."

He paused at that. "Where?"

"Jupiter."

Huh. He filed the information away to deal with later. "I can't get into this tablet."

"Give me a sec." Gage was silent, but Brooks could hear the faint click of his keyboard. "I'm in. Go ahead and get out of there. I can shut the tablet off remotely."

"Done." Brooks exited the back door and used the cover of darkness as he hurried across the backyard. When he jumped the fence, a sensor light went off and a nearby dog started barking.

Picking up his pace, he raced across the lawn and into the front yard of the neighbor behind Turner. Instead of running, because that would draw attention to himself, he simply shoved his hands in his jacket pocket and strolled down the sidewalk as if he was just out for an evening walk.

No one bothered him—or even looked outside because of the barking dog. It was too damn cold to be outside anyway. Most people would be inside with their families and wouldn't even register the sound of a dog barking, especially if it was common.

When he reached the end of the street, a dark SUV pulled up next to him. Gage opened the driver's side door and then jumped into the passenger seat. "You drive, I'm going to work."

Brooks hopped in. "Any news from Leighton?" Leighton was doing recon of Oleg Polzin's home—in a much ritzier neighborhood.

"Yeah. Says Polzin's place will be a lot harder to break into. The guy's got security cameras and an upgraded system. I can hack the actual system but the thing is, he'll know someone messed with it. Markov has a similar system."

And the whole point of breaking into these places was to remain undetected so they wouldn't give themselves away.

"Plus," Gage said, "Leighton thinks Polzin might be under surveillance. He's not sure if it's government or someone else."

They couldn't afford to be seen by the FBI, DEA or whoever. "I'm going to see Darcy tonight," Brooks said abruptly.

"I'm not your fucking guardian," Gage said without looking up from his laptop, no rancor in his voice.

Some of the tenseness in Brooks's shoulders eased as he headed back to their warehouse. He didn't answer to anyone. And going to see Darcy wouldn't put her in danger. He was her ex-boyfriend. Him visiting was easily explainable to anyone who might be watching her. And he simply couldn't stay away any longer. He'd apologized once but he needed to make this right.

He just wasn't certain he knew how.

CHAPTER NINE

—I'm not giving up on us.—

Brooks parked his truck in Darcy's driveway, glad to see her lights on inside. He definitely should have called first, but it would have given her an excuse to tell him not to come over.

He wasn't putting off scanning her place for listening devices any longer. Savage had warned her to be careful about what she said at home, and Brooks knew she was smart. She wouldn't be telling anyone else what she'd overheard. But he still wanted to check.

More than that, he simply wanted to see her, to show her how much he'd missed her, how important she was to him. He'd come prepared, at least. Grabbing the takeout boxes from the passenger seat, he slid out of his truck. There was a light dusting of snow over everything, including the little gnomes on the three steps leading up to her porch. He'd given her one of them, and was surprised she'd kept it.

After knocking on the door, he stood back and waited until the porch light came on. There was a long pause, and for a moment he thought she might ignore him entirely. Then he heard the soft snick of the door being unlocked.

Darcy opened the door, giving him a wary look. Wearing black leggings and a black and white formfitting sweater, as always she looked good enough to eat. God, he'd been such a fool.

"What are you doing here?" She wrapped her arms around herself.

"I figured you hadn't eaten, so I brought you food." He lifted up the boxes with the distinctive logo from Mercer's pizza place.

She lifted an eyebrow, but some of the tension seemed to ease from her shoulders. "Ham and pineapple?"

"Of course." It was her favorite.

Surprising him, she stepped back and motioned for him to come in. So he did. For some reason he was surprised that everything looked the same. It seemed as if they'd been separated for an eternity. To his left, her living room was warm and inviting. Her laptop was open on the buttercream couch and a shimmery blue blanket was pooled on the left end, no doubt where she'd been stretched out, computer in her lap.

As she shut the door behind him, he held up a note card that read, *Need to scan your place for listening devices. I'll start in the kitchen. Keep conversation normal and make sure all the blinds are shut.* She had a security system, so he felt it was unlikely her place was bugged, but this was a necessary precaution.

She nodded, as if she'd expected this. He knew that Savage had told her this would happen eventually—which was likely the only reason she let Brooks inside her house so easily.

"You look great," he said as they stepped into her kitchen.

She made a noncommittal sound as she went to her refrigerator. She opened the stainless steel door and he wasn't surprised to see only water, yogurt, and a takeout container of likely old food in there. "I can offer you water or water," she said, laughing slightly. "Oh, I actually have some red wine in the pantry."

"Water is fine." He set the bag down, and while she started getting plates out he hooked his jacket behind one of the high-backed chairs at the island and pulled out the scanning wand.

"Business seems to have taken off." That was banal enough conversation for anyone potentially listening.

"I'm working crazy hours, but it's worth it."

He stepped into her laundry room, which was right off the kitchen, and grabbed a small ladder she kept there. He was going to start at the top and work down. "I heard about your sister getting married. That's great." God, he hated making conversation like this. Especially when all he wanted to do was pull her into his arms, kiss her senseless, and remind her how good they'd been together.

She made another noncommittal sound as she poured herself a glass of wine. Then she pulled out a bottle of water and set it in front of the plate for him. He would eat later, however.

"When you're done with your pizza, I made sure they tossed in extra of the tiramisu you like." He nodded at the lone white bag next to the pizza boxes.

Darcy glared at him as she sat down at the center island. "Wasn't that thoughtful of you."

Oh yeah, she was annoyed with him, likely because he was in her personal space—and she hadn't forgiven him.

"Have you dated anyone since we broke up?" he asked abruptly. In case someone was listening, he knew she wouldn't argue with him.

She paused in opening up one of the boxes, her eyes widening as she looked at him. He continued his scan, but met her gaze dead-on.

"I'm not sure how that's any of your business." She gave a haughty little sniff before pulling out a piece of pizza. She let out a moan as she inhaled the rich scent and he felt that sound go straight to his cock.

"It's not. But for the record, I haven't been with anyone since you."

She snorted before taking a bite—and letting out another moan he was certain she did just to drive him crazy. Probably not, but that was what he was telling himself. When she made little sounds like that all he could think about was the many, many times she'd come apart in his arms—or against his face.

Hell. He needed to stop thinking about that. Uncomfortably, he shifted on his feet. "You don't believe me?"

"Doesn't matter what I believe. I thought I knew you and then it turned out you're just another jackass." She paused, set her pizza down. "Did you know your dad came to see me again?"

"I just found that out today."

"It's weird. I want to not like him, but I know *why* he offered me that money. He was doing it to protect you from gold diggers. He was worried about you. Of course, he went about it in the completely wrong way, but that I can understand. Your assumption about me is what I honestly don't understand." Now there was no anger. Just...confusion and pain.

Brooks was silent for a few minutes as he continued his scan, digesting her words. "I have no excuse for what I did. I was wrong."

Without responding, she turned on the CD player/iPod docking station on her counter. No surprise, Frank Sinatra started singing a moment later.

When he was almost completely finished with the room, and she'd polished off a couple pieces of pizza, he said, "After I got out of the Marine Corps, I was pretty serious with someone."

If she was surprised by his sudden statement, she didn't show it. Setting her food down, she nodded. "I remember."

He'd told her a little about his previous relationship, but had left out one very big detail. Darcy's expression was hard to read as she watched him. "I thought I was in love. Looking back, I know it wasn't remotely that." The only reason he understood that now was because of Darcy. "My dad offered her a couple million to walk away from me."

Darcy blinked, understanding immediately. "She took the money."

He nodded and set the wand down on the island. He wasn't hungry, but he opened the water bottle and downed half of it. Just being in her kitchen, being around Darcy, it brought back so many memories. They'd made love right here on the island—and on the damn floor. Pretty much every surface of her house. He'd had her pinned up against her refrigerator once, completely naked, her dark hair wild around her face as he'd thrust into her over and over. Until they'd both come so hard they'd collapsed on the floor in a heap of tangled limbs—and gone another round once they'd caught their breath.

"I'm sorry," she said softly.

The sound of her voice pulled him back to reality. Sighing, he pulled out the seat next to her. "I'm not. I dodged a bullet with her. I would have realized sooner or later the type of person she was, but I was blinded and..." He cleared his throat, not wanting to open up that can of emotional worms. Looking back, he'd just been searching for someone to drown out his pain. He'd lost too many friends overseas, and transitioning back to civilian life had been hard. That being the understatement of the century. He'd found the wrong someone and latched onto her, trying to fill the void. Like a fool.

"And...what?" Darcy pushed.

He was done talking about his ex. Brooks didn't want to talk about that anyway. "Nothing."

Darcy tightened her jaw and slid her plate forward on the granite countertop. Brooks had absolutely blindsided her by showing up. Then he'd finally started opening up to her, telling her about what happened with his ex. Only to stop. Just like always. Back when they'd been together, she'd never pushed him, even though getting him to open up emotionally had been like pulling teeth. She'd chalked it up to that just being his personality, and everything he'd been through in the Marines. But he wasn't getting a pass now. "No way. You don't get off that easily."

His head tilted to the side ever so slightly, his confusion clear. His dark hair was a little longer than it had been when they'd been together. Nothing else about him had changed. His dimple wasn't visible now. No, she only got to see that when he smiled. And it was annoyingly sexy and adorable at the same time.

Gah, she wanted to punch him for that damn dimple. It was what had sucked her in in the first place. He'd smiled at her and she'd absolutely melted. It had been at the drugstore, of all ridiculous places. He'd been picking up a prescription for one of the men he worked with and she'd been getting chocolate because she'd had a craving. He'd started talking to her in the checkout line, smiled that smile, and she'd been a goner. He'd asked her for coffee right then and there—and she'd said yes. She'd had no clue who he was. Even when she'd learned his full name, she'd never put two and two together, that he was a billionaire's son. Was a billionaire himself.

"What are you talking about?" he asked.

She took a deep breath. "When we were together, I used to let you off the hook whenever you shut down. Now you show up out of the blue, bringing me dinner and you're being all sweet. Then you start to open up and just when it's getting interesting, you shut down. *No.* Keep going."

She didn't care if he'd come by tonight to do a sweep of her house for listening devices or whatever might be planted here, she was going to take advantage of having him as a captive audience. It didn't matter that she tried to tell herself she didn't want to see him anymore—it was such garbage. She'd never gotten any closure after they broke up. And the word closure was kind of stupid when it came to relationships, but there it was.

"You were blindsided and...what?" she pressed.

"That was it. I was blindsided and reacted poorly." His words were clipped.

So that was how it was going to be. Rolling her eyes, she stood and picked up her plate. She wasn't going to push him for any other sort of conversation or emotional clarity. As she reached the sink, without turning around, she said, "If you're referring to reacting poorly to me, I wouldn't exactly put it like that. You reacted like a jackass."

He let out a short curse and the chair moved against the tile. A few seconds later he was at her side. She set the plate in the sink and turned to face him—and was suddenly very aware of how close they were. He was tall—well over six feet—and she was pretty average in height. Tonight, she just had on thick, comfortable socks because it was freezing out. It put her at a disadvantage in the height department. But she placed her hands on her hips and stared up at him.

He stared down at her, his dark eyes pleading. "You're right. And I'm sorry. I'll keep saying it until you forgive me."

She watched him for a long moment, a swell of emotions ricocheting through her. "I *do* forgive you, Brooks. It's not even what you said to me, though that really hurt. It's the fact that you actually believed I would take the money. I simply can't understand that. I thought you knew me, saw the real me. Instead you lumped me in with someone like your ex."

His dark eyes filled with the pain mirrored inside her. She resisted the urge to reach out and comfort him. Barely. It was hard, because even if she wanted to deny it, she still cared about him.

Finally, he spoke. "Can we at least try to be friends? I miss you."

Okay, she hadn't been expecting that. It was childish or just plain stupid that she was disappointed that he wasn't fighting harder to win her back. But that was what she wanted, right? Saying no to his request felt too bitchy, and the truth was she missed him as well. They'd had a lot of fun together. "Only if you're the type of friend who lets me go horseback riding for free at his ranch," she said lightly, trying to ease the tension between them.

He seemed surprised by her answer but then his mouth curved up and that stupidly sexy dimple was back. Damn, she missed that dimple. "Anytime you want."

Looking up at him, she thought about how easy it would be to lean up on tiptoe, close the distance between them, and ravage his mouth. Because *that* would be smart. He would let her, too, and would take over in an instant. He'd always been like that, all dominating and possessive. And she'd loved it. Even thinking about the way he'd taken charge with her in the past, simply had to have her sometimes, not caring if they might get caught, sent a rush of heat between her legs.

He would have her pinned up against the counter or her fridge or any flat surface in record time. She could read it in the tense lines of his body and see how much he still wanted her in those dark eyes. But making an ill-advised decision because of simple lust would be stupid. Her own mother had married a man she'd fallen madly, desperately in love with, only to be tossed over for someone shinier when Darcy and Emma were young. She wouldn't lump Brooks in the same category as her father, but...they didn't need to do something they'd only regret. It would just cause more heartache down the road.

She could forgive him, but she wasn't going to let him back into her life. Not as more than friends, anyway.

Clearing her throat, she looked away and slid to the side, needing some distance between them. As she moved, he moved with her until her back was up against the counter.

Oh so slowly, he placed his hands on either side of her, his gaze pinned to hers. He stared at her as if she was the only thing in the world that mattered. And she was only human. She melted inside, damn him.

Though she tried not to, she inhaled deeply and was consumed with the earthy, spicy scent of him. He smelled like the outdoors. All raw masculinity and sex she wanted to roll around in. If someone could bottle that scent, they'd make a fortune. More heat rushed between her legs and she cursed her physical reaction. Being this close to him when he was looking at her as if he could devour her, well, it was no wonder she was getting turned on. It took all her restraint not to reach for him, bury her face against his chest and simply inhale.

For a long moment, she couldn't even breathe—wouldn't let herself. They just watched each other and she wondered what the hell was going on in his head.

When he shifted slightly and finally stepped back, she blinked as if coming out of a haze. He held up a card for her and it took way too long for her fuzzy brain to emerge from the "fog of Brooks" to read it.

I need a reason to be here so I can scan the rest of your place.

Wow, he'd really come prepared. She nodded, disappointed that the intense moment between them was over, while simultaneously relieved she'd be getting space from him.

"I'm having an issue with my plumbing. Do you mind if I take a shower here before I leave?" he asked.

As excuses went, it was kind of lame. If someone listening knew who Brooks was, it was pretty doubtful that one of the five or six or however many bathrooms he had at his place weren't working. There were a few more believable scenarios for him to be here as a friend, but since he'd gone in that direction, she said, "Of course. You know where everything is."

His gaze dropped to her mouth for a long moment. "I do." Something about the way he said that made her wonder if he was remembering the many times they'd been naked together in her shower.

Because she certainly was. It was hard to forget the sensation of being pinned up against the slick tiles as he thrust into her over and over, his thick length as he stretched her... *No. No, no, no.* She turned away from him and started cleaning up the kitchen, definitely needing distance from him now.

Luckily he didn't say anything else, just hurried upstairs with that wand. She figured he'd start the shower and start scanning each room while the water ran. Luckily her place was small so it shouldn't take him too long.

When her cell phone pinged that she had a text, she glanced at the screen. It was a message from her sister, wanting to know what she was doing tonight. She thought about telling Emma that Brooks was here, but knew *that* would open up a conversation she didn't want to have.

Especially since she couldn't tell her sister why Brooks was really here. And at that reminder, ice crept through her veins. She really hoped he didn't find anything in her place. Even if he didn't, she was still worried. Darcy knew that Brooks and his friends were working on figuring out what Markov, Polzin and that detective might be up to, but it didn't ease her fear much. She wanted to be doing more, but wasn't sure what that might be. And she hated that she couldn't tell her sister anything. But that wasn't an option.

When she heard the shower start upstairs, a sudden thought of Brooks naked with water running down his hard, bare pecs and thick, muscular legs made her jolt slightly. It wasn't as if he was actually upstairs naked. But her imagination was running away with her. She shook herself. There was no time for that nonsense. They were just friends now. Even thinking that felt sad and wrong. She wasn't sure she could ever be just friends with him. No, she'd probably always want more. Which made her a fool for even contemplating his whole "let's be friends" thing.

When her phone pinged again, a vendor this time, she locked up thoughts of Brooks and responded. She was simply going to have to deal with him for right now. Soon enough, her life would hopefully go back to normal and he wouldn't be in it. So why did that make her feel so sad?

CHAPTER TEN

—Some people just need a pat on the back.
Right off a cliff.—

Brooks rubbed a hand over his face as he, Gage, and Leighton all looked at the screens Gage had pulled up. Blueprints found on Detective Turner's computer.

Each blueprint was that of a school. An elementary school, a middle school, and a high school.

"An elementary school," Leighton muttered, disgust in his voice.

Brooks simply nodded in agreement, feeling nauseous. He'd seen and done more than he wanted to think about overseas. Whenever kids were involved... He tightened his jaw. They had a chance to do something before anyone was hurt. But he didn't think this was something they could handle alone. And he wasn't afraid to admit their crew had limits. "We need to bring in the Feds on this."

To his surprise, Gage nodded as Leighton said, "I agree."

Okay, then. They were all in agreement. Brooks didn't want to bring Darcy into this or let the Feds know how they'd come across this information. "We need to find a way to give them this information anonymously." The only problem was, the FBI had a lot of resources. Giving them something anonymously could prove difficult. Eventually Darcy would be questioned, as would her sister. At least Emma didn't know anything. But Darcy was a terrible liar and they would see right through her.

"I might know a way around that," Leighton said. "I've got a contact with the FBI."

"Since when?" Brooks asked.

"Woman I worked with in Iraq," was the brief answer. There was a flicker of something in his gaze, but the man had been like a ghost the last year. Impossible to read.

Brooks waited for him to continue and when he didn't, said, "You trust her?"

"With my life." No hesitation.

That would have to be good enough for now. "You trust her to keep Darcy out of anything?"

Leighton nodded, his expression neutral. "I'll talk to her, make sure that before I give her anything, Darcy is protected."

"Good. If she goes back on her word..." Brooks didn't have to finish. The threat was clear. And he didn't give a shit that he was indirectly threatening a federal agent. If someone got Darcy hurt or put her in the line of fire, all bets were off. She was his to protect. From any and all threats.

When Leighton took a surprisingly menacing step toward him, Gage jumped up. "Leighton's word is good, dude. Come on."

Brooks stared at his childhood friend for a long moment, wondering at Leighton's relationship with this unnamed FBI agent, and feeling like a jackass. "I'm sorry," he muttered. "I'm twisted up over Darcy." No reason to deny it.

The tension in Leighton's shoulders eased. "I get it."

Brooks wondered if he did indeed get it. His friend had been a shadow of his former self since moving back to Redemption Harbor. He'd assumed it had been because of something that happened overseas but...maybe it was because of a woman.

"We need to visit some of the schools," Gage said, cutting through his thoughts. "At least get some eyes on the ground, do some recon… See if anything is already in place." Anything meaning an explosive device.

Because there was no telling how long the FBI would take to respond to the information. Brooks didn't think it would take long, but just in case, they needed to be able to find out if the places had any after-hours visitors. "What's that?" he asked, pointing to one of the minimized files.

Gage clicked on it and a flyer for a carnival popped up. Brooks frowned, looking at it. "That carnival is the same day as Markov's son's wedding." It could mean nothing, but was worth noting.

"If he is going to attack a school, his son's wedding gives him the perfect alibi." Leighton's voice was as grim as his expression.

They were all silent for a moment. Then Brooks said, "Savage and Olivia should be able to get in to see the elementary school. All they have to do is ask to tour it. Then Savage can break in later and add cameras."

Gage nodded. "We can split up who breaks into the others after dark. Anyone have a preference?"

Brooks and Leighton both shook their heads, and Brooks said, "I'm headed out soon." Savage and Olivia had a tasting with a potential caterer and Darcy had set it up so that they would run into Emma and Peter again—and this time Peter's father would be there. Apparently he wanted to talk to the caterer in person before the rehearsal dinner. Brooks was using the opportunity to meet the guy in person, and to plant a listening device in his vehicle if possible.

He also had another reason for going—one that was sure to piss Darcy off, but he didn't care. The night Markov had questioned her, Darcy told him that she'd recently broken up with her boyfriend. Brooks wanted to get some face time and make it clear they were now back together. So his presence around her any time in the future wouldn't look weird if Markov was watching her. Brooks hadn't run this by Darcy yet, but it was happening.

He would just ask for forgiveness later.

"Keep your earpiece in. Let me know if you need anything," Gage said to him. Then he turned to Leighton. "You ready?"

Leighton nodded. "Yeah. Let's get everything together so I know what I'll be giving her."

They didn't need Brooks anymore, so he left. It was time to see Darcy.

* * *

Darcy pulled out of her driveway, heading to work. It felt weird going to work in light of everything that was going on, but what else was she going to do? She had to trust that Brooks and his company were handling things. So far, he was being transparent. Or she assumed he was. He'd promised that he would keep her updated with any news. After he'd scanned her place last night, she felt a little better that no one was listening in on her conversations. And he'd told her that his friend would be monitoring her security system to make sure no one tried to break into her place. It was a little strange to think his hacker friend could even do that, but she now felt freer to talk to Brooks or anyone from Redemption Harbor Consulting if they called.

Now she had to head to the shop, deal with some administrative stuff and after that she would be meeting with Zac and Olivia, who would be talking to a potential caterer—the same one Peter and Emma were using. Since they'd asked, she'd also scheduled a meeting with Semyon and the caterer around the same time. Semyon wanted to talk to the owner of the restaurant—again—about Friday night's rehearsal dinner. It had been easy enough to schedule their meetings close together.

Though they hadn't said why, Zac and Olivia had been pretty adamant that the two meetings be almost overlapping. She wasn't certain if they wanted to meet Mr. Markov or more likely plant some kind of tracking or listening device on him. Or maybe his car? Even thinking about stuff like that made her head hurt. She liked to read mystery novels, but all of this was so far out of her wheelhouse. Whatever the reason, she didn't care. She just wanted to stop whatever he had planned.

As she pulled out of her neighborhood, she had that strange feeling that she was being followed again. Just like she'd felt the day she went to Dancing Dragon to meet Zac and Olivia. Since her place wasn't bugged, she wondered if she was being paranoid. Her schedule was predictable and boring—so anyone watching her wouldn't even need to follow her. Not really. Almost every morning, she stopped at her shop before meeting with potential clients or dealing with various vendors.

As she contemplated whether or not she should call Brooks and tell him about her paranoia, her phone rang. When she saw that it was her sister, she slid her Bluetooth in. "How's the bride-to-be?"

"Thinking about eloping," her sister said laughingly.

"Uh oh. What's wrong?" This wasn't the first time her sister had not-quite-jokingly said that.

"Nothing. I just don't understand why Peter's father is insistent on making this a huge production." Now Emma sounded serious. "God, you and I barely have any family. And Peter and I would have been happy with a small ceremony and an equally small reception. I just looked at the guest list and it's grown *again*. He keeps inviting people and neither of us know who they are."

Darcy was careful with her words. "What does Peter say?"

"He's just as annoyed as me. But he feels bad saying anything since his dad is spending so much money on our wedding. And I feel bad too, like I'm being ungrateful. It's just...this thing is a whole production neither of us want—and didn't ask for."

"I'm sorry," she said.

"Sometimes I wonder if this wedding is more about showing off his money than anything. Then I feel horrible for even having that thought."

Darcy'd had the exact same thought, but didn't say it aloud. She was simply here to listen to her sister vent. She had her own issues with Mr. Markov now that had nothing to do with his ostentatiousness. "Well, I might have something that will make you feel better. Cora texted me some pictures of what the final cake will look like. It's stunning." Darcy looked in the rearview mirror as she turned onto the ramp to get on the highway. She only had a few exits to go to get to work. No one was behind her and she chastised herself for being so paranoid earlier.

"Forward them to me!"

"I will as soon as I get to work. So, other than the insanity of your soon-to-be father-in-law, how are you really doing?" Darcy had everything well in hand for her sister. The dress, caterer, flowers and every little detail were as under control as possible. There would be some hitches on the actual wedding day, but that was normal, and they would be tiny.

"I'm good, just trying not to stress out. I'll be glad when this whole thing is over and Peter and I can move on. More than anything, I'm looking forward to the honeymoon."

Darcy started to respond as she pulled off on the next exit. As she pressed on the brakes, nothing happened.

Oh, God! She pressed again. Nothing. "My brakes aren't working!"

"What?"

"I'm getting off on exit forty-three and my brakes aren't working!" Darcy was shouting, couldn't begin to keep the panic out of her voice. Clutching the wheel tightly, her heart jumped into her throat as she gained speed going downhill.

She was vaguely aware of her sister saying something in her Bluetooth, but couldn't focus on anything other than staying in control. Two cars were at the stoplight at the end of the exit. The third lane that veered to the right was a yield lane. She hadn't planned on going that way but it was her only choice unless she wanted to crash into one of the sitting vehicles.

Her palms were damp against the wheel as she veered to the right. Her little car didn't slow down at all as she merged into the lane. There was an oncoming slew of cars from the other direction, and she had no choice but to cut them off.

Horns blasted as she merged into the new lane. The next light was green at least so she kept up with the flow of traffic and at the next four-way, she made a sharp right turn. Her car fishtailed slightly as she tried to get it under control. And as she passed a Lowe's parking lot, she made another sharp jerk of her wheel.

"What's happening?" her sister shouted.

Darcy rattled off the location of where she was—not that her sister could do anything about it. No one could. She was going to have to crash her car. It was the only way to stop and she wasn't going to risk running into someone else.

"I'm calling the cops!" her sister shouted again before the line went dead.

Thankfully the parking lot wasn't full, so she steered her car to the very back where it neighbored an abandoned gas station. Her car jerked violently as she ran over a pothole, but it was slowing down second by second. Still gripping the wheel tightly, she made a left turn into the gas station parking lot.

Oh God, the emergency brake!

She yanked on it and couldn't stop trembling as she jolted to a stop. She was okay.

By the time she finished shaking, two police cars were pulling into the parking lot. Swallowing hard, she tried to shift the gears but it didn't work. So she stopped the ignition and got out of her car—and couldn't stop shivering. And it had nothing to do with the cold.

What had happened was a lot less climactic than she'd expected, and for that she was grateful. Her heart was still racing wildly at the thought of what could have happened. What if she'd been on the highway and had to stop? She wouldn't have been able to, and anything could have happened. A multicar pileup, or she could have flipped over a guardrail... She was going to make herself sick if she kept thinking of all the what-ifs.

Both officers were out of their vehicles and moving toward her at a fast clip. Despite the fact that she wasn't sure who she could trust in the local police department, she still felt grateful to the man and woman who had just arrived.

"Ma'am, are you okay?" the woman asked.

Darcy nodded as she tried to find her voice. She was definitely in for a long morning. But at least she was alive and unharmed.

For now. What if this hadn't been an accident? Her stomach dropped but she shook the thought off. No, the emergency brake had worked. If someone had been trying to kill her they would have disabled that too. Right?

CHAPTER ELEVEN

—Some days there comes a time that no matter what the question is, the answer is wine.—

Though she felt as if she might come apart at the seams, Darcy thought she was pulling off her "polished and together" look pretty damn well, all things considered. After talking to the police and filing a report—fun times!—riding with the tow truck driver to her mechanic's, then catching a ride to the car rental place with her sister, she'd still managed to make it to her meeting with Mr. Markov and Mr. Singh, the owner of Eat Pray Love Catering.

They were mostly done going over the last few things—which should have been settled months ago. Mr. Singh was a saint, because Darcy knew he had to be annoyed with Mr. Markov but he hadn't said a thing. It was actually the whole reason she was here. Technically she didn't need to be here, but for this particular wedding, she'd been basically running interference with Mr. Markov and...everyone.

Peter had ended up having to pass on coming to this meeting and Darcy had convinced Emma that just dropping her off at the car rental place would be fine—though Emma had wanted to follow her to this meeting. Peter had work today—and Darcy was certain he didn't care enough about the menu anyway—and Emma had been called into work for a last-minute emergency. Since her sister had already picked her up and driven her around earlier, Darcy knew she could use the time to catch up with all the last-minute stuff before the honeymoon.

"I didn't see your little car outside," Mr. Markov said as he approached her where she was sitting at a high-top table by the window.

Though it was cold outside, it was a beautiful day, with a clear blue sky and only a smattering of white clouds. Darcy blinked at his observation, surprised he'd even noticed. Setting her phone down, she said, "Oh, I was in a little fender bender this morning." She decided to downplay it. There was no need to tell him that her brakes had stopped working. Because of the nature of her accident, the police were actually going to do an investigation once they got a report from her mechanic. She wondered if...he'd had anything to do with it. But that seemed insane. Or maybe she was giving him too much credit? She swallowed hard, tried to keep on a pleasant smile.

"Fender bender?"

"Well, I had an issue with my car. I didn't get in an actual accident, but the roads were icy and I had to have it towed." There, that was vague enough. "But luckily that's why I have insurance. I got a rental." She shrugged.

Out of the corner of her eye, she saw Brooks entering the restaurant with Zac and Olivia. He looked good enough to eat, as always. But what the heck was he doing here? After the morning she'd had, she was feeling raw and unsteady. And seeing him after last night, and all that weird tension between them, was a punch to all of her senses. With him around, she always felt safer, and she had the most absurd thought that she missed his hugs. Because whenever he'd had his arms around her, the world had seemed sane.

"Is everything okay?" Mr. Markov asked, concern in his voice as she slid off her stool.

She was having a hard time reconciling who Markov was with the way he treated her and her sister. When she thought of someone as a "bad guy," like from the movies, it was so obvious they were a villain. But he cared about his son, and he'd been so welcoming to her sister and even her. It was disconcerting to think that he might be involved with bombing someplace, hurting people, hurting *children*.

"Oh yes," she said, nodding once toward the door so that he turned to see Zac and Olivia entering. "This is a new couple I'm working with. They're having a rushed wedding. They're just a little earlier than I expected." A big fat lie. They'd showed up right on time.

"It's no problem at all. I'm basically done here anyway, so I'll leave you to it. If you have any issues with your new car, just let me know. I have extras you can use."

"Ah, thank you." Before he could leave, she smiled politely as Zac, Olivia and Brooks approached. To her surprise, Brooks moved in next to her and wrapped an arm around her waist, pulling her close, as if he had every right in the world. What the heck was he doing?

He kissed the top of her forehead. "I hope you don't mind me tagging along, sweetheart," Brooks said, all cowboy charm. "Zac said the tasting was today and I insisted on coming."

Okay, she couldn't elbow him in the ribs without it being obvious, but the thought did cross her mind. "Of course I don't mind." There, that sounded real enough. "Brooks, Zac, Olivia, this is Mr. Markov. He's the father of Peter, who you both met the other day."

Mr. Markov smiled and shook hands with the two men, and nodded politely at Olivia. "You can stop calling me Mr. Markov. We're going to be family soon," he said. "And is this a new boyfriend?" he asked, curious.

Before she could answer, Brooks said, "I'm an old boy-friend who is now a boyfriend again. She finally forgave me for making the biggest mistake of my life."

Darcy resisted the urge to snort. "Mr.... Ah, Semyon, Brooks owns Alexander Ranch. It's where Olivia and Zac will be getting married."

His eyebrows raised slightly and he nodded. "Yes, I've met your father. Just ran into him yesterday, in fact."

Brooks smiled neutrally. "He's just moved back from Flor-ida. He's not sure if he wants to retire or not."

Semyon laughed good-naturedly. "I think he'll say he'll re-tire, then never actually do it. He'd be too bored, if he's any-thing like me."

Brooks turned on the cowboy charm then, laughing lightly. "Too true. Are you leaving now or were you staying for a bit? I just stopped in to see my girl, but was planning to head next door for coffee while they do the tasting. Join me?"

Semyon glanced at his watch, then nodded. "Coffee sounds good."

Well, that was easy enough. She wasn't certain what they had planned, just that Olivia had requested Mr. Markov be here when they arrived. She'd assumed they'd wanted to search his car or whatever. She wasn't sure why Brooks would want to talk to him and couldn't ask now. But she was going to ask later.

Before she could say anything, Brooks completely sur-prised her and brushed his lips over hers. She barely got a taste of him—not that she wanted one—before he pulled back, tak-ing every delicious inch of himself away. Her heart raced out of control even as he left the restaurant, and she turned to the couple. "I didn't realize he was coming."

"Brooks is just full of surprises lately," Zac said mildly.

"Is there anything I need to do?" she whispered.

Zac shook his head. "Other than help us go over our menu options...no."

Well that was...disappointing. But what did she expect? "Okay, I know I'm your wedding planner, but I'm going to need an update soon. Brooks came over last night and...did his thing. But I'm having a hard time sleeping or thinking of anything else other than..." No need to say it out loud.

"We planned to update you tonight," Zac said.

"Oh."

"I realize we've been...quiet with communication, but only two days have passed. I promise we're looking into everything. And it's likely the Feds will have to get involved." Zac said the last part so low she almost didn't hear him.

The Feds? That sounded...serious. Which she knew it was, but it still scared her. She was supposed to not tell her sister about any of this and act normal around Mr. Markov— or Semyon. *Gah.* "That's a lot to take in."

Olivia nodded understandingly. "I think you'll feel better after tonight. Brooks is going to talk to you about everything."

"Okay...then are you guys ready to move on to the fun part of wedding planning?" Anything that involved food was always welcome, and she needed the distraction.

Olivia's eyes lit up. "Yes. I promised my daughter I'd bring her to the cake tasting. I didn't want to bring her today because of..." Yeah, Darcy could guess why. She likely didn't want her daughter anywhere around Semyon Markov. "Anyway, will it be okay if I bring her?"

"Of course. I'm excited to meet her. Is she excited about being the flower girl?"

"Ah, yes. And she's insisting on having her hair sprayed pink for the big day. She wants it to match her dress—which will also be pink. I let her do it once for Halloween and she thinks our wedding is somehow similar to Halloween since everyone is getting dressed up."

"That sounds fun," Darcy said, laughing lightly.

"Really? Not too over the top?"

She shrugged. "She's six."

"That's what I said," Zac said, wrapping his arm around Olivia's shoulders. He kissed the top of her head. "If it makes her happy, I say we let her do it."

Olivia lightly elbowed him. "You're going to spoil her."

"So what?"

Olivia looked at Darcy and raised her eyebrows. "How do I argue with that?"

Smiling at the two of them, Darcy was somehow able to get into work mode and focus for the next hour. Now that she knew they would update her this evening, the band of tension around her chest had loosened somewhat. Even if the Feds were involved, that was probably a good thing. If Mr. Markov and those men were planning something, they had to be stopped.

And despite her issues with Brooks, she still felt better knowing he was directly involved—where her safety was concerned, she did trust him.

* * *

"I think we should bring Nova into this," Savage said as Gage pulled up one of his fake IDs on screen.

Gage eyed the ID critically. He liked to enlarge his handiwork a thousandfold to really get a look at it. And not to be full of himself, but the damn thing was amazing. Savage had asked Gage how he managed to make such perfect copies. Hacking into the DMV—often—was a good start. But he couldn't really explain it. He just had a knack for some things.

Well, a knack and a whole lot of practice. The whole crew had fake IDs courtesy of Gage, including Nova. And all of them were stored offsite as part of their escape plan—if they ever needed to run at a moment's notice. It was unlikely, but life could change on a dime. He knew that firsthand. A year ago, he'd been working a cushy—boring as fuck—job in Seattle. Now he was back in his hometown working in shades of gray. And loving every second of it.

"Bring me into what?" Nova asked, stepping into the conference room. She looked like Gage's personal fantasy come to life, as always. Today she had on a pencil skirt and heels that he'd fantasized about. Okay, he hadn't fantasized about the heels, but about her digging them into his back as he buried his face between her legs. And he felt like a total douche for even thinking about that right now. Or ever. She worked with them. She was an employee. He couldn't hit on her. Couldn't have anything with her. Not that it would matter. The woman was light years out of his league. "Nothing," Gage said.

She lifted an eyebrow. "I know I heard my name."

Savage cleared his throat. "We're looking into something that's a little dangerous—"

"I'm in." She grinned, and just her smile transformed her from beautiful to out of this world gorgeous.

Gage looked away from her because it hurt to watch her sometimes. He focused on what he was doing instead. "You want to be involved in something dangerous?"

"Skye hired me because I wouldn't balk at the gray-area stuff you guys do. Of all people, I understand why it's needed." She did, and she was right. At one time she'd worked for the CIA but had gotten burned out. He wasn't sure what happened at the private company she'd worked for after that, but only because he hadn't wanted to violate her privacy. Still, he was curious. One day he hoped she opened up to him and told him what had happened.

"Your help is not needed." Okay, even he could admit that had come out wrong.

Her eyebrow hiked higher. "And why is that?"

"You're not qualified." He couldn't back down now.

"What exactly am I not qualified for? If you're going to shoot me down, at least tell me what I'm getting shot down for." Of course she wasn't backing down either.

Gage glanced at Savage, who was looking at him strangely. He turned back to Nova. "Savage and I need to discuss it further."

She stared at him for a long moment, her expression unreadable. Finally she nodded at him briskly. Then she smiled warmly at Savage. "I just stopped in here to tell you that I found a place that teaches ASL classes. It's supposed to be really good. You'd mentioned that some of the guys were looking to take extra classes in an actual classroom as opposed to online. I'm signing myself up now. I've emailed you the information but since I knew you were here, I thought I'd let you know."

Savage's soon-to-be daughter was Deaf. She had cochlear implants but didn't always wear her processors and was bilingual. Everyone who worked for Redemption Harbor Consulting—plus their friends Mercer and Mary Grace—was learning ASL. Skye and Savage already knew it, and Gage was learning but wanted to be fully immersed.

"That's great, thanks," Savage said. "Olivia has looked into some local places as well. But there aren't many." His tone was frustrated.

Nova smiled. "I copied her on the email too. Oh, she said you guys had to leave the tasting early because Valencia had an earache. Is everything okay?"

Savage nodded. "Yeah, but we wanted to take her to the doctor."

For a few minutes they talked casually before Nova left, shutting the door behind her.

They had an informal atmosphere here mainly because the only people who worked here were the cofounders—and now Nova.

"What the hell was that?" Savage asked mildly once they were alone.

"What?"

"You seriously want to give her grief or tell her she's not qualified to go on a fake school interview?" Again with the mild tone. "All she'd be doing would be pretending to be a parent looking for a school for her kid. She would go on a tour with you or Leighton. That's it."

Gage didn't feel like explaining himself to anyone. Not where she was concerned. Because he knew his feelings were irrational. "I just think it's better if we have a dividing line with her duties. We can't be pulling Nova into missions."

"I didn't realize an interview was a mission."

"You know what I mean."

"No, not sure that I do. It's not like she's some civilian off the street. She used to be CIA and I know she takes Krav Maga religiously. Not that I think the high school principal or one of the teachers is going to attack her and her fake husband." Savage snorted at the very idea.

Gage still didn't like it. Instead of responding, he said, "Have you talked to Leighton yet?"

"No. He said he should hear back from his Fed friend today. I foresee a meeting tonight or tomorrow."

"I don't want to be the one to tell Skye or Colt that we're bringing in the Feds."

Savage shrugged. "It makes sense to do it this way. They'll see that."

Yeah, true enough. But Gage had seen Skye lose her temper before—because someone stole her food from the company refrigerator—and it wasn't pretty. The woman carried around C4 in her purse and called it "being prepared." And he was just distracting himself with thoughts of anything other than Nova and the way he'd talked to her. He'd been kind of a jackass. Maybe he should apologize. But he still didn't want to bring her in for this or anything mission related.

He also didn't want to further examine why either. Colt and Skye worked together, and Colt had once told him that he trusted Skye to take care of herself. He worried about her, yes, but Colt said that his wife was the most capable person he'd ever met. Gage apparently wasn't as evolved as that because he didn't want Nova in any danger. Ever.

CHAPTER TWELVE

—If you have the moral compass of a pumpkin, own
it. Don't make excuses.—

Brooks tried to contain his temper as he strode back to his
truck. He'd left his coffee meeting with Markov, fully
planning to come back and talk to Darcy—and ream her out
about not telling him about her accident this morning—only
to find out that she, Savage and Olivia had left. Coffee had
gone on way too long, but he'd wanted to give Leighton time
enough to plant a listening device in Markov's vehicle.

Not an easy task when he had his own personal security.
Markov's guys were good, blended in well, but Brooks's training had helped him spot them. Leighton had been able to dis-
tract and avoid them.

He turned on his Bluetooth as he pulled out of the parking
lot and called Savage. "Why the hell did you guys leave?" he
snarled the second Savage answered his phone.

"Ah, this is Olivia."

He winced. "Oh…sorry. Where's Savage?" He'd assumed it
was his best friend when the phone picked up.

"At the office… We recently left the pediatrician's and we
somehow switched phones. I'm going to drop it off to him."

"Is everything okay?"

"Yeah. Valencia has an earache, and because of her cochlear implants I never ignore when she has ear issues."

Brooks felt like a jerk. "Sorry for snapping at you. Are you
sure she's okay?" he asked as he took a left turn. Traffic was

light today and he should be at Darcy's shop in less than ten minutes.

"Yes, I promise. I just like to be careful with her."

"Tell Savage not to worry about calling me back."

"Are you sure?"

"Positive." Brooks had been calling to ask why they left without waiting for him and now he had his answer.

By the time he made it to Darcy's shop he'd worked himself up. He knew he needed to calm down, but when Markov had said something about Darcy being in an accident it had blindsided him. The thought of anything happening to her carved him up inside. He knew he couldn't control everything or look out for her all the time. Even the thought was pure insanity. But he still worried about her.

There was no parking in front of her shop so he parked a couple blocks over. Before Darcy, he'd always been the calm one. Hell, he still was. He wouldn't have been able to be a sniper in the Marine Corps if he'd had any issues. But Darcy brought out all of his protective and possessive instincts. There was no way around it.

The little bell jingled overhead as he stepped inside. Two women were at one of the jewelry displays, looking at necklaces and tiaras. *Seriously, tiaras?* Some people. One of the women, a petite blonde, looked over at him and gave him an inviting smile. He really hoped she wasn't the one getting married.

Ignoring her smile, he scanned the rest of the place. Darcy had done a lot in here and it was impressive. Nice furniture, aesthetically pleasing, this was the type of place that made people feel comfortable but also screamed quality. The black and white photos on the walls of weddings were new. They really added a lot to the place.

As he made his way to the back of the shop, Darcy stepped out of the dressing room area and frowned when she saw him. But then she smiled what he thought of as her "work smile." Pleasant and perfectly polite, but it was missing the warmth he'd once received from her. And he would do anything to get it back.

There was an older Hispanic woman with her, wearing a shimmery gold dress that still had the tags on it. Clearly Darcy was helping her, and her shop was busy enough that he probably should have called first.

Damn it, he needed to start thinking when it came to her. As he inwardly berated himself, Darcy murmured something to the woman next to her and crossed over to him.

She was wearing knee-high boots over black tights and a red sweater dress that hugged all her curves—he wanted to peel it from her body inch by inch. "Is everything okay?" she murmured as she reached him.

"Yes. But I should be asking *you* that. I heard you were in an accident today." And he was seriously annoyed that she hadn't told him this morning. Not that she owed him anything but still, he wished she'd told him. Unable to stop himself, he took one of her hands in his. To his surprise, she didn't pull away.

"It wasn't an accident, not really," she whispered.

"Darcy?" The Hispanic woman she'd been talking to approached them, a tentative smile on her face. "I wasn't trying to eavesdrop, but you were in an accident today? Are you okay?"

Darcy's cheeks flushed an adorable shade of pink. "I'm totally fine. Mrs. Gomez, this is Brooks, my—"

"Boyfriend."

"Oh." The woman's eyes lit up and she assessed Brooks with a critical eye.

"Hopefully soon she'll be my fiancée and make an honest man out of me," he continued, because he was seriously unable to help himself. Darcy was going to kill him later, but it would totally be worth it. They'd already told Markov that they were together, so this was just selling it to everyone else. At least that's what he told himself when he heard Darcy's little gasp of surprise.

"Oh my gosh, isn't that just the sweetest thing," the woman gushed.

"Yes, he is wonderful." There was a hint of acid in Darcy's voice as she said, "Mrs. Gomez, if you can give me just one second, I need to talk to Brooks in my office and I will be right out. But that dress is perfect for you. You're going to be a beautiful mother of the bride."

"Take your time, I'm going to be looking at shoes."

Once they were in her tiny office, Darcy turned to him, hands on her hips. "What the heck was that?"

"First tell me about this accident."

She paused and looked away for a moment. Then she sighed and leaned against her small desk. "My brakes stopped working. The police took a report and my mechanic is going to let them know what he finds. It's not a big deal."

"Are you kidding me?" Somehow he kept his tone even and his voice low. "Your brakes stopped working? That's not normal."

"I know," she finally muttered. "But I have no idea how this would tie into anything else—and the emergency brake worked just fine. Thankfully. If Semyon wanted to kill me, he'd put a bullet in my head. Right? I mean, he wouldn't risk that this brake thing didn't even work. Or if he was going to try to kill me via my car, the emergency brake would have failed too. I didn't want to make a big deal of it until I heard back from my mechanic. My car is freaking *ancient* and the mechanic said something about natural erosion. I thought maybe, I don't know, that had something to do with it. I get it worked on every month, it feels like."

"I can't believe you're still driving that thing." Her little car *was* ancient. He'd actually offered to buy her a new one when they'd been together but she'd simply scoffed at him. Something he should have remembered when he'd accused her of taking a couple million dollars. If she wouldn't take a damn car, she certainly wouldn't have taken any money.

She simply pursed her lips together when he brought up the topic of her car. "So what was that craziness out there about being my fiancé?"

"We've already told Markov I was your boyfriend. Might as well let everyone else know. It needs to sound legit."

She nodded slowly. "I guess that makes sense."

"You're selling dresses and shoes and stuff too?" he asked, curious since she was a wedding planner. He didn't think they did that. And he wanted to smooth things over—by not focusing on how he was telling everyone they were together.

"What... Oh, no. Well, I mean, yes. The dresses, shoes and stuff are from Faith's shop. Since I meet with clients here it only made sense for me to showcase her stuff. And anything I sell for her, I get a commission." She smiled, very pleased with herself. It was a smart move too. "So Zac and Olivia told me that you'd be filling me in on everything tonight?" she asked, her smile fading.

"I am. And you'll be staying at my place, considering your car might have been tampered with."

She pushed up from her desk and her hands went straight to her hips again. "That's weird, it didn't sound like you asked me a question. No, it sounded more like you just gave me an order."

He grinned at her. "I've missed your sass. And...I would like it if you would stay at my place tonight."

She snorted. "No. I have a lot of work to do." Before he could argue, she held up a hand. "But I have a guest room. You can stay with me tonight. I don't have a death wish. If someone wants me dead—then I won't balk at you staying with me. And I'm not saying anyone does! My car is old, Brooks. Anyway, all my work is at my house, and it will be a lot easier to simply get it done there. Plus I have to get up really early tomorrow."

"Fine. I'll also be chauffeuring you around." That wasn't up for discussion. He wasn't letting her out of his sight. Her sister's wedding was Saturday and today was Wednesday, so he understood that she was busy. But there were some things he wouldn't bend on.

"I want to argue with you, but you've got that annoying determined look in your eyes."

"Glad that's covered. Have you eaten anything today?"

She seemed jolted by the change in topic. "Ah, I ate a little at the tasting. By the way, have you talked to Zac or Olivia? Is their little girl okay?"

"It sounds like she will be but I'll let you know."

"I should be done here in about two hours. You're really going to tell me everything?"

"I'll tell you everything we know up to this point. Fair warning, the Feds are definitely going to be involved. One of our guys is talking to someone now. And that means you're probably going to have to talk to them." Brooks had no idea how involved the FBI would be but if they tried to railroad Darcy, he would push back. Hard. "No matter what happens, I've got your back."

"Thank you." She cleared her throat once. "For everything you're doing. Maybe I should have gone straight to the FBI in the first place. But I was scared and…just, I'm really apprecia-tive of everything you and your friends are doing."

"You never have to thank me for anything. But you're wel-come." Reaching out, he cupped her cheek gently and stroked his thumb over her soft skin. Touching her was stupid, but she wasn't pulling away and he couldn't stop himself.

For a moment, her eyes drifted shut and she leaned into his touch.

Just like that, his body reacted. *Hell.* What he wouldn't give to be able to pull her into his arms, to hoist her up onto her desk and—

Her eyes snapped open and she stepped back suddenly. Her cheeks flushed and she wouldn't meet his gaze. "I need to get back out there. Are you going to stick around, or just meet me here in two hours?"

"I won't bother you here at work, but I won't be far." No way in hell. He hadn't been kidding when he'd told Mrs. Gomez he hoped that Darcy would soon be his fiancée. He wanted her as his wife.

His love for her had never died. When he thought she'd betrayed him, he'd hated her, but he'd also never been able to get her out of his head. And knowing that she'd never done a damn thing wrong, that she hadn't taken that money, well, he couldn't deny that he still loved her. He wanted her forever. Too bad for him, the feeling wasn't mutual. Yet.

Because he was still determined to win back the woman who'd stolen his heart.

* * *

Semyon unrolled the physical blueprint of the building they would be bombing on Saturday morning. He felt a twinge of conscience about what he was going to do, but not enough to stop. This was the only way to bring Kuznetsov down.

And he'd been so careful in his planning. Only a select few knew about it. His inner circle—and even if he didn't completely trust Oleg, he trusted the man at least to keep this quiet. Because if Oleg talked, he would incriminate himself. This had been in the works long enough that if Oleg told Kuznetsov, the other man would know Oleg was part of it.

When Semyon heard the door to the office open, he turned. Oleg stepped inside and nodded once at him. "Kuznetsov is in town. He just checked into his hotel. One of the staff informed me."

"Good." So far everything was going according to plan. Later tonight, Semyon would go pay respects to Kuznetsov, and while he was in the man's hotel room, he would swipe bomb residue everywhere he could. Because after Saturday, he would point the Feds in Kuznetsov's direction. Anonymously, of course. The bomb residue wouldn't be meant to incriminate Kuznetsov, but someone else in the man's organization—because Semyon planned on killing Kuznetsov. He just couldn't take credit for it or have anyone suspect him. That would defeat the purpose of everything. "How is everything looking?" he asked.

"Everything is still a go for Friday night. I'll get everything set up at the school and we'll be good to go Saturday."

"Good," he said again, looking back at the blueprints. He'd gone old-school for this job. He had nothing saved to his computer, nothing online to link him to any aspect of this job—nothing in this house or his office. Except the blueprints, of course, but he would dispose of those soon. Stanton might have something at his house, but that was on him. And Semyon planned to take care of that problem soon enough.

He'd used the detective in the past, paying him to lose evidence or let Semyon know when prisoners would be transported. And he'd used him to get access to the schools and their blueprints. He hadn't wanted to get his hands dirty—or show up on any potential CCTVs down at the courthouse—and he definitely hadn't wanted to show up on any security cameras near or at the target sites. Stanton thought they would be using him to plant evidence, but Semyon could do that himself.

"Do we need Stanton anymore?" he asked.

Oleg paused, thinking. Then he shook his head. "I'll be handling everything myself Friday night. And you'll be dealing with planting evidence. No...we can tie up that end now if you'd like?"

Semyon mentally went over everything they had left to do. Yes, it was time to cut Stanton loose. "Can you do it tonight?"

"Yes. How should I do it?"

Making it appear accidental would be difficult and not worth the risk. "Is he working today?"

"Yes. He should get off..." Oleg glanced at his watch. "In an hour, give or take."

Semyon had learned that detectives put in regular enough hours unless they were working a big case. It would be too difficult to get Stanton pulled out for a regular call, so that was out. He was a detective, not an officer who rode the streets. He was only called out for investigations—and usually with a partner. It seemed luck was on his side tonight.

"Follow him when he leaves the station, then. Does he still stop at that Quick Stop for lottery tickets?"

Oleg snorted in derision.

Semyon agreed. He didn't understand why anyone bothered with those things. "Good. Kill him and whoever else is at the Quick Stop. Make it look like a robbery." He knew Oleg would take and dispose of the security feeds if there were any so he didn't bother telling him to. "Once you're done, head to his house." He wanted to tell Oleg to burn it to the ground, but that would be too suspicious. "Do a sweep of his place. Take anything that might link back to us." There shouldn't be anything there, but just in case.

Oleg nodded once, but instead of leaving immediately as Semyon had expected, he continued. "I know you said that you put someone on the wedding planner, but I wanted to let you know I saw her with some man today. He looked like trouble."

This again? Perhaps Oleg's fascination with Darcy was greater than he'd realized. "What did the man look like?" After Oleg told him, Semyon said, "That's her boyfriend. They're back together. So why don't you stop wasting both of our time and go do your job."

Oleg's eyes narrowed. "What boyfriend?"

Semyon stared at the man for a long moment, unable to believe he was seriously asking him instead of doing his damn job. "Don't worry about things that don't matter. When we bring Kuznetsov down, we'll have complete freedom." As it was, Semyon unfortunately answered to Kuznetsov. They weren't linked in the way the Italians were, not like the mob on TV, but it was the same concept.

He had to pay his dues. Literally.

He wanted to get out from under Kuznetsov's thumb, to be free. More than that...this was personal. Kuznetsov had taken from him long ago. He would pay for what he'd done. And there was no walking away from this life. "And you want to worry about some woman? What's the matter with you?"

Oleg's expression was defiant. "She thinks she's too good for me."

Darcy *was* too good for Oleg, but Semyon didn't say that. They were too damn close to pulling this thing off to risk ruffling egos now. "Let's finish this job and worry about her later, yes?" Or in reality, he'd kill Oleg.

Finally, Oleg nodded.

"How are things looking with Dimitri?" The man they planned to frame for the bombings and Kuznetsov's murder. He was one of Kuznetsov's men—and Semyon knew that Kuznetsov had hurt someone close to Dimitri, giving the man a motive to hurt Kuznetsov.

Not only that but Dimitri had links to people at each potential bomb site, which was how Semyon had chosen the potential targets in the first place. The Feds would have to dig, but they'd eventually uncover Dimitri's "motive" of wanting to kill everyone he believed had wronged him in life. Dimitri would be arrested for the mass murders—and then killed by someone tied to Kuznetsov. That part was still up in the air, but knowing Kuznetsov's men, he had almost no doubt that Dimitri would die soon after.

Oleg nodded. "Good. I've got the laptop to plant with his manifesto and a search history of how to make bombs. It's all buried sufficiently so the Feds will have to dig for it."

Perfect. That would make things all the more believable. Running a hand over his face as Oleg left, Semyon sat on the edge of the desk. The blueprints wrinkled slightly as he moved. For a moment, doubt crept in, allowing him to contemplate what he was doing.

But no, this had to be done. He needed to be free. Because if he wasn't free, his family wouldn't be. His oldest son and wife had been killed by Kuznetsov. Not directly, of course, but it had been on his orders. And Kuznetsov had no idea that Semyon knew.

When he'd been a young man and first starting out, he'd resisted being recruited by Kuznetsov. Then when his wife and son had been killed by a business rival—allegedly—Semyon had massacred him and his entire family.

Kuznetsov had convinced Semyon that the only way he would have insulation from others would be to join forces, to become part of his organization. A decade later, Semyon found out the truth, that Kuznetsov had ordered the death of his family to bring him in line. It was only by chance that Peter hadn't been with his wife and other son that day. And Peter had no idea the real reason they'd been killed or even what Semyon did for a living.

Semyon was patient, cunning, and would soon get what he wanted. His only son would be free to live his life. Not that Peter even knew his life was in a constant state of danger. Because if Semyon's treachery was ever discovered, what was left of his family would be destroyed. Which was why he couldn't simply put a bullet in Kuznetsov's head. Not only couldn't he be even remotely suspected of this, he had to be a potential victim as well.

Sighing, he pushed up from his seat. He only allowed himself a few minutes of doubt before his resolve kicked in.

Now it was time to go face the beast in his hotel room. And start putting this whole thing into motion. He'd been planning it for a very long time, had been waiting to find the right person to blame for everything. Now Semyon had someone. And everything else had fallen into place.

He patted his jacket pocket once. His gloves, with their explosive residue, would do his job for him. He would make sure every surface possible was covered in it. And no one would be the wiser. Then on Saturday, when Kuznetsov came to his son's wedding, he would make sure the man's vehicle was rigged with the same explosives as the school.

Semyon would make sure Kuznetsov died. Then he would detonate the explosives Oleg would set in Semyon's own vehicle. It would be made to look as if he'd been targeted too. Dimitri would eventually be blamed for killing everyone, and Kuznetsov just one of many he'd wanted to kill in his quest for revenge.

The only thing that mattered was that Semyon looked like a victim. That he walked away and Kuznetsov didn't.

CHAPTER THIRTEEN

—Not to brag, but I don't even need alcohol to make
really bad decisions.—

Darcy set her purse and laptop bag on her counter. Trying
to ignore the huge cowboy behind her would be impossible. And he was staying for the night...apparently. After the
day she'd had, she was actually fine with it. It was just going
to be weird having him under her roof again.

Because he wouldn't be in her bed, he would be in the
guest room. Where he belonged. At least that was what she
tried to tell herself. The truth was, she wouldn't mind having
him in her bed again. But no. No, no, no. For...reasons.

She mentally shook herself as she turned to face him. He
was pulling out the takeout boxes. He'd picked her up from
work, and she'd found that he'd already gotten takeout for
them. Because of course he knew she had no food here. She
rarely did.

What he'd done was thoughtful and so typical Brooks. At
least typical of the Brooks she'd fallen for. Not the Brooks
who'd morphed into a huge jackass and broken her heart. But
that wasn't something she was going to think about right
now.

"How does water sound? Or do you want wine?" she asked.

"Water works."

"So...what's going on?" she asked as she grabbed them both
bottles of water. His friend Gage was monitoring her security
system so she knew that they were free to speak. No one had

come near her house, which was a good sign. And another reason she didn't think someone had actually tampered with her brakes. "Don't leave anything out. You mentioned something about a federal agent earlier. What's going on with that?" It was hard to believe that only a couple days ago she'd overheard a conversation that had changed her life. It felt as if eons had stretched on since then. Probably because she couldn't sleep or concentrate.

"Leighton, one of the cofounders of our company, is meeting with a federal agent tomorrow. *Early* morning. It was the earliest she could get down here. We'll know more then." He pulled out plates and silverware for them.

And she realized that he was done. "Is that it?"

"Truthfully, I think they've already started doing more work than the agent is letting on. With the urgency of the situation, with kids in danger... When we meet tomorrow they'll have already put people on all the schools." He sounded so certain.

She let out a small breath of relief. "What else? You said you were going to fill me in on everything."

He shrugged. "We've been keeping an eye on Markov Senior, Detective Turner, and Polzin. The cop is definitely dirty." Brooks paused, frowning as he watched her. Even as he frowned, the man looked ridiculously sexy. Dressed casually today, he had on jeans, a worn pair of boots, a pullover sweater, and he'd hung his thick jacket by the front door. She was surprised he hadn't worn his Stetson. Just as well, because she loved it on him. "Turner has some blueprints in his house of three schools. All local. And we've found some interesting financial records linked back to him."

"How do you know he has blueprints in his house?"

Brooks simply raised an eyebrow.

"You broke in?"

He didn't respond, and that was answer enough in itself.

"I don't want you getting in trouble...or putting yourself in danger."

Brooks snorted softly. "Trust me, I wasn't in any danger." He said it with complete confidence.

Well that was interesting. She hadn't realized he knew how to break into places. "What kind of work does your consulting company do exactly?" She'd never really gotten an answer on that. She'd just been so happy to have someone to help that she hadn't pushed.

"When I've got an engagement ring on your finger, I'll tell you." He was so matter-of-fact. As if what he'd just said was *normal*.

"Brooks!" He had to stop saying stuff like that. It was insane. And...she liked it. Which made *her* insane. Because he couldn't be serious.

He simply nodded at the sesame chicken he'd put on her plate. "Eat up. I know you must be starving."

Since she didn't remotely want to talk about the "engagement ring on your finger" comment, she sat down and moved her plate in front of her. It was impossible to ignore his incredibly sexy presence, however. And his stupid "engagement ring" talk. Oh my God, what was wrong with her? She had to stop thinking about it. Even if he was serious, that ship had sailed.

Time to focus on other insanity. "So...you said that I will most likely have to talk to a federal agent." She knew she wasn't asking a question, she just wanted to confirm. Because the very thought of that made her nauseous. She'd known that was a possibility from the very beginning, but it was still scary to think about. All she'd really done was overhear a conversation. She had no *evidence* of anything. And she lived in the real world. Just because she *said* she'd heard something didn't mean anything would happen or anyone would believe her. Justice for victims of crimes seemed to be a very rare thing indeed. All she had to do was turn on the news or look at social media for proof of that.

"It's possible—probable. Like I said, I'll be with you when and if that happens. I won't let them put you in any compromising position or in danger."

She gave him a soft smile. "Yeah, I know that. Thank you."

"I'm serious." He looked so earnest that it warmed her insides.

"I know. Whatever has gone down between us before...I do know that about you."

"Darcy—"

"Don't. If you're going to apologize again, don't. Please." When he didn't continue, she did. "Look, I know you're sorry. And I was being sincere when I said I forgive you. Let's just work on being friends again," she said softly. Apparently she was a walking contradiction. She knew that attempting to be friends with him was stupid. But she really *had* missed his friendship on top of everything else. Before she could contemplate anything else, they had to get back to the place where they trusted each other. Meaning, *she* had to trust *him* again. And she wasn't there yet. She wasn't sure she ever would be.

"Okay." His tone was quiet as he turned back to his food. "I've missed watching zombies with you on Sunday nights," he said a moment later.

Despite her confused emotions, the comment made her laugh. No matter her work schedule, or how early he had to get up on Mondays, Sunday nights had been their zombie night. "I've tried watching it with Emma, but it's definitely not the same. She closes her eyes pretty much the entire show. It's ridiculous." And it also made her laugh. Because her sister had no problem watching dark crime shows but anything with zombies? Forget about it.

"How's she doing with the wedding?"

"Really good. I hate not being able to talk to her about anything. It's weird." Because since they were little, Darcy and Emma had always shared everything with each other. But this past week, Darcy had been keeping things to herself. Worry that her sister would be marrying into a criminal family was eating away at Darcy.

"Did you tell her about me?"

"What do you mean?"

"Well, today we let her soon-to-be father-in-law know that you have a new boyfriend. Did you warn her?"

"Oh, crap. Nope. I'm surprised I haven't heard from her yet." As if on cue, Darcy's cell phone rang from her purse a few feet away. And she recognized the ring tone as her sister's. "That's her. I'm just going to ignore that for now."

He grinned at her, revealing one of those sexy little dimples, and her insides melted all over again. She was such a goner for him. No matter how much she tried to tell herself that she didn't want to get her heart broken again, she was pretty sure that if she let him go, it was going to stay broken no matter what. But deep down, she knew they needed to rebuild trust. She couldn't just jump into something with him.

* * *

A couple hours later Darcy jerked to a halt as she entered her living room. Brooks had moved her coffee table and was doing push-ups right there on the rug, over and over.

God, look at the man. Sweat glistened on his arms and back and she wondered how long he'd been at it. Of course he wasn't wearing a shirt, showcasing all of that bare, gorgeous skin. Skin she'd run her fingers and mouth over countless times.

What the heck was he doing? Well, it was obvious what he was doing, but... Why was he doing it in here? She started to step back out of the room when he looked over and saw her.

Giving her that charming cowboy smile, he slowly eased up to a standing position. It was as if he was moving in slow motion, all for her benefit. As if he was doing it intentionally to drive her crazy. Had it gotten hot in here?

"Sorry for using your living room. There's a lot more room in here than the guest room."

"It's fine." More than fine, she thought as her gaze trailed down his bare chest, to his eight-pack, right down to his belt. Damn it, she did not need to be staring at him like this. "Do you want a shirt?" she blurted. Then she inwardly winced. *Way to be smooth.*

His lips kicked up in a wicked grin. He patted his washboard stomach. "No, I'm good."

She stared at him for a long moment. Then she turned on her heel and headed to the kitchen. She couldn't be in the same room with him when he was half naked. But no surprise, he followed her.

"Is everything okay?" he asked as she started pouring herself a glass of water. And it wasn't her imagination, he was definitely grinning at her as if he knew she was flustered. Of course he did. She wasn't hiding it well and he was walking, talking sex. Heat rushed between her legs and she forced her gaze to remain on his face. "You're being obnoxious," she snapped, leaning against the countertop—she needed something to steady her.

Slowly he ran a hand down his stomach. "How's that?"

"Stop, seriously. You know exactly what you're doing."

He lifted one of his big, broad shoulders and grinned. God that grin was panty-melting. "Do I?"

"Yes. You prancing around here half naked is...distracting." That being an understatement.

His grin only faded a little. "I do not prance."

She snorted.

"So, you like what you see?" he asked, his voice dropping an octave into pure sin and sex territory.

"I'm not feeding your ego." *Of course* she liked what she saw. She had a pulse, was heterosexual, and she was single. How could she not appreciate all of that?

He closed the distance between them. "Well I certainly like what I see. I've missed you, Darcy." Gone was the sweet, teasing cowboy. In his place was the intense, raw, sexual Brooks. The man who'd swept her off her feet. Now he was watching her with that possessive intensity she'd never fully gotten used to. It had always made her feel off-balance.

She swallowed hard and put a hand on his chest. *Oh...no.* Why had she done that? She automatically ran her fingers down the hard planes, as if she had every right to. Then froze.

"You can touch me anywhere you'd like," he murmured.

Darcy started to pull her hand back. She really did. But apparently her body had decided to stop listening to her brain. "We...can't..." She wasn't really sure what she planned to say.

Not when he started oh so slowly lowering his head toward hers.

She should really stop this. For reasons she couldn't remember. Especially when his spicy, masculine scent was overwhelming her. She felt almost lightheaded as his lips brushed over hers.

Moaning, she arched into him, not caring that he was just a little bit sweaty. If anything, that sparked something wild inside her. The feel of him against her fingertips made it hard to think of anything else. She raked her fingertips over his chest, down his stomach and back up again, greedy to touch him everywhere.

For months, she'd missed this. Missed him. She'd *grieved* for what they'd lost. Because it had been ripped away from her in an instant, completely pulling the rug out from under her. Now he was right in front of her and she didn't have the strength to push him away anymore.

His kiss went from just the barest touch to devouring her. His tongue teased against hers as he hoisted her up onto the counter. The way he kissed was as if he was starving. For her.

She spread her thighs, giving him more room to plaster himself against her. She couldn't get enough of him. Moaning again as he gently sucked her bottom lip between his teeth, she clutched onto him.

His big body was vibrating with energy as she traced her fingers over the width of his shoulders. Seven, almost eight months without him had been horrible. And she could admit that she'd listened for any tidbits of gossip about him. But of course there were none. He didn't even have any social media accounts. She'd been far too curious if he'd taken up with someone else and had been glad when she'd heard nothing.

When he'd admitted that he hadn't been with anyone since her, it had shifted something inside her. Opened her up more to the idea of...them. Because despite the way things had ended between them, she'd never gotten over him. She still remembered the sweet, dedicated boyfriend who'd actually listened to her when she talked, who remembered exactly how she liked her coffee, who always opened doors for her, who'd been a cheeseball on Sundays with her, watching their favorite television show and getting just as into it as she did. And right now, that was all she wanted to remember. She didn't want to think of anything else as he nibbled a path along her jaw.

She opened her legs wider for him, needing to get closer. That wasn't happening unless they lost their clothes. While she might be a little off-kilter tonight, she hadn't completely lost her head.

Maybe.

Because when he slid his hand up her leg, she was reconsidering everything. She'd taken off her sweater dress and tights earlier. Now, freshly showered, she had on leggings and a T-shirt that said *Keep Calm, I'm the Wedding Planner*, given to her by a client—

"Oh," she whispered as he continued going higher and higher, sliding his hand up her shirt. He stopped right at her ribs, his big hand spanning her waist.

"I want to make you come." His words were harsh and unsteady against her ear as he bit down on her earlobe.

She loved the way he said exactly what he wanted. He'd always been like that. And he wanted to make her come?

For a long moment, they were frozen like that, his face buried against her neck, her fingers linked behind his neck, and the only thing she could hear was her heart pounding in her ears. "I think..." Words escaped her as she tried to finish her thought. Him making her come sounded like the best idea ever. Her body craved his touch on a level that made her tremble.

"You think that sounds like a good idea?" He leaned back slightly so he could look at her.

"It sounds like a very bad one." Because it would just confuse things between them. As if them kissing right now *wasn't* confusing.

"Very bad can be really damn good." His gaze dropped to her mouth and another rush of heat flooded between her legs.

She hadn't bothered with a bra—because she didn't need one—and right now her nipples were hard points against her T-shirt. The friction as she took a deep, steadying breath sent a frisson of awareness rolling through her. It wouldn't take much to make her come right now. "Brooks—"

He groaned and let his head roll back for a moment. "Love it when you say my name." Then his eyes were on hers again, pinning her place.

She couldn't have moved if she wanted to. Which she didn't.

His hand crept higher and she hitched in a breath when he cupped one of her breasts. Oh, hell. She was definitely done. When he gently strummed his thumb over her already hard nipple, she made an incomprehensible sound at the pure pleasure shooting through her.

He was barely touching her and she was ready to come apart in his arms. It was simply because she hadn't had sex since Brooks. *Right.* She couldn't even swallow her own lie.

"Let this be about you. I just want to feel you coming around my...fingers." He sounded desperate for it.

Which was insanely hot. "Brooks."

"Say my name again." His words came out all growly and raspy.

Her cheeks flamed at his words. This was the only time he ever lost control. Normally he was the laid-back, steady cowboy. Except when they were getting intimate. Then it was like he lost all vestiges of civility. He loved talking dirty to her—and she ate it up. She might not return the dirty talk, but he didn't mind. "Brooks," she whispered again.

And when his other hand moved to the band of her leggings, her inner muscles tightened around nothing. She could already feel him touching her, cupping her—then he was.

His slid his hand down the front of her panties until he was cupping her mound, his middle finger lying lazily against her clit. "I've missed touching you. Missed the way you look when you come."

He had to stop saying *come*. "I've missed you too." Missed everything about him. But she couldn't find all the words to tell him how she'd missed waking up in the mornings to him. Missed the way he'd surprise her in the shower. Missed...him. Just Brooks.

Slowly, he slid his hand down a little farther. "You're so wet."

"Hmm," was all she could manage as she brushed her lips over his.

He shuddered at the gentle kiss and began strumming her clit. Methodically and perfectly; he hadn't forgotten how she liked to be touched. Clearly.

She bit his bottom lip as her body shook from the pleasure spiraling out to all her nerve endings. It was too much and not enough. And maybe tomorrow she would regret this but for now she was going to take this pleasure. Then she wanted to give it back to him.

But first... She bit down again, harder this time. He groaned into her mouth, rolling his hips against her, simulating sex even as he strummed her clit. Teasing her over and over, her inner muscles tightening with each stroke. She was so damn close.

He crushed his mouth to hers, taking over in that dominating way of his, right before he slid two fingers inside her— and pushed her over the edge.

He held his fingers inside her and kept teasing her clit, the sensation too much for her to show any restraint as her climax slammed through her.

Her head fell back as pleasure punched through her, spiraling out to all her nerve endings until she felt like she wasn't in control of her body anymore. She wanted to climb right out of her skin and get as close to him as possible, to feel all that rock-hard body against hers. She wanted to rub up against him like a cat in heat and feel no shame.

Her inner walls convulsed around his fingers as she came down from her high. Feeling sated and as if her body was made of noodles, she brought her hands up to his face and cupped his cheeks. He didn't have a smug or satisfied look on his face. Well, he did look satisfied, but mainly he just looked sexy as he leaned down to nibble at her lips.

When he withdrew his hand, she immediately felt the loss. And when he sucked his fingers into his mouth, her cheeks heated to epic proportions.

"Just like I remember," he murmured.

That was just like she remembered as well. Perfect.

Wanting to give him as much pleasure as he'd given her, she reached for the button on his jeans but he clasped her wrists and held them at her sides on the counter. The sensation of being slightly restrained made her inner muscles clench again. He'd tied her up before and she'd loved it. Something she'd never even considered before him, but he'd made her throw all of her inhibitions out the window.

"That was just about you."

"I want it to be about both of us." She tugged slightly, even knowing he wouldn't let go.

"It will be about both of us once you commit to me," he murmured, his gaze falling to her lips.

Annoyance snapped to life inside her. "What is that? Some kind of sexual blackmail?"

He snorted at her questions. "No blackmail. I'm just saying, until we're together—for real—my body is off-limits."

She barked out a laugh at the ridiculousness of his words. "Fine. Mine is off-limits as of this point as well."

"I can have you begging for it." His voice dropped dangerously low, a hint of seduction in his dark eyes.

"And I can have you begging for it too." She tugged her hands free and grasped the hem of her shirt, lifting it up and off.

If he thought she was just going to fall into a puddle at his feet, well, he was mostly right about that. But he wanted her as much as she wanted him. She was going to remind him of that.

"Fuck." The word sounded savage.

Cool air rushed over her hard nipples and she resisted the urge to cover up. He'd literally just made her climax and had seen her naked countless times. "Still want to play this game?"

"I don't want any games." He pinned her with his eyes.

"I'm not playing," she whispered as the mood went from heated to...she wasn't quite sure. "But I'm not ready to commit to anything right now. We're just...getting to know each other again."

"I know everything I need to know about you."

Do you really? she wanted to ask. Because once upon a time he'd assumed the worst of her, had made it clear he didn't know her at all. Yes, he'd apologized, but that was just words. She knew more than most how useless words could be.

Feeling far too vulnerable all of a sudden, she wrapped her arms around herself. She wasn't sure what to say.

Abruptly he stepped back. "I'm going to do a sweep of the house one more time."

It was just an excuse to get away from her because he'd already locked down her house earlier—and her alarm system was on. But clearly, he wanted distance. She did too, so she didn't call him back.

Once he was gone, she sucked in a deep breath, able to actually breathe again. Things had gone from zero to sixty in a second and she wasn't sure how she felt about anything right now. The one thing she was sure of: she definitely wouldn't be sleeping tonight.

Not with Brooks in the room next to hers.

CHAPTER FOURTEEN

—I'm more confused than a chameleon in a bag of
Skittles.—

Brooks practically jackknifed up when a slender form stepped into the guest bedroom doorway, then he immediately settled down. "Everything okay?" At two in the morning, there was no reason for Darcy to be here. Unless she wanted sex, and he was pretty sure that was off the table. For now, anyway.

He was still reeling from the way she'd come apart in his arms earlier, the feel of her muscles tightening around his fingers as she came for him.

She hovered in the entrance, still wearing the yoga pants and T-shirt from before. "Yeah." Moonlight from the hallway illuminated her enough that he could see every tense line of her body. A body he'd seen naked too many times to count. Too many and not enough. Because they should be tangled together right now.

"Want to come in?"

"Yeah." But she still didn't move.

He tugged the covers down on the side opposite him. "I won't bite." Unless she asked.

Laughing under her breath, she stepped inside, slowly and tentatively. "I'm... I can't sleep. I keep thinking about your meeting tomorrow with that agent and wondering what it means for...well, me and my sister and Peter. And then I feel selfish for having those thoughts when there might be a bomb somewhere even as I'm saying this."

"Come on." He motioned toward the bed and, to his surprise, she slid right in next to him and laid her head on his shoulder. He closed his arms around her tightly.

It was surreal to be holding her like this. Surreal and as perfect as he remembered.

"I'm sorry you can't sleep," he said quietly. "Your worries are normal." Hell, she wouldn't be human if she wasn't concerned.

"I know. Doesn't help me any."

They were both quiet for a long time, something he didn't mind. He'd spent years in the Marine Corps, and many of those he'd been alone or with his spotter, out wherever they'd been sent behind enemy lines. The quiet soothed him. So did having Darcy pressed against him.

"When did you start sleeping with clothes on?" Darcy murmured, taking him off guard. Curled up against him, she smelled like sunshine and strawberries.

"Why? Hoping to get a peek of the goods?"

She just snorted and pinched his side.

He'd worn a shirt and boxers since he was here to keep her safe. If her house was infiltrated, he didn't want to get into hand-to-hand combat with his dick hanging out. "I didn't want to disrespect you," was all he said. When she didn't say anything else, he continued, "I had a weird conversation with my dad yesterday."

"Yeah?"

Of all people, she knew about his strained relationship with his father. Her relationship with hers was a lot worse. Try nonexistent. "Yeah. It was...strange. I feel like he wants to be friends now. Or maybe not friends, but make up for lost time or something. He even started talking about my...mom."

"Wow. How do you feel about all that?"

He wasn't used to talking about his emotions. There didn't seem to be much use in doing so, but something Darcy had said about him shutting her out made him realize that there were some things he *did* need to talk to her about. If he had a chance in hell of ever getting her back, he needed to put himself all out there. She was worth it. "Honestly, I don't know. If someone had asked me that a year ago, I probably would have brushed it off. And I probably would have shut him down. But he's sincere. That much I know."

"Then I hope you let him in."

"Have you heard from your father lately?" When he'd been with Darcy, her father had reached out to her and asked for an introduction to Brooks. Darcy had shut him down cold. And it had taken all of Brooks's restraint not to reach out himself to the man and kick his ass.

"Unfortunately, yes. He's got some serious nerve."

Brooks stiffened slightly, already knowing what she said was going to annoy him. Her father was a waste of space. "What did he want?"

"He said that Emma wouldn't answer his calls and he wanted to know how his girls were doing." She gave a tired, brittle laugh. "He wasn't even subtle about it. He wanted to know about the man she was marrying and why he hadn't been invited to the wedding. Then..."

"What?"

"When I told him to stop bothering me, he got in a dig about me losing you. About how I couldn't even hold on to... Well, whatever. He's an asshole. But what I don't understand is why he even bothers. He married into a wealthy family. He got what he wanted. He made it clear he wanted nothing to do with my mom or Emma and me years ago."

Brooks was quiet for a moment then said, "He got fired from his job a year ago. Something to do with sexual harassment. They cut him loose fast. Now his wife keeps him on a short leash. He's on an *allowance.*" The thought made Brooks laugh.

Darcy sat up and stared at him. There was enough moonlight streaming through the slat blinds that he could see the nuance of her expression. "How on earth could you know that?"

"I looked into him." And he wasn't going to apologize for it.

She blinked once. "Why?"

"You want the truth?"

"Yes," she said slowly, pushing away from him slightly.

"The stories you told me about him pissed me off. What kind of man abandons his family for something 'better' and then turns his back completely on his own children?" Brooks's dad might have been an absentee father but he'd never abandoned him, and he'd made sure that Brooks had anything he could possibly want. And now that he was an adult, he could see that his father had been grieving. Not that he was making excuses for him, but he understood the difference. "I'd planned to see if there was anything I could do to make him suffer financially." Brooks knew it was a totally shitty thing to do, and he didn't care. "But it turned out he was a piece of shit and got himself fired all on his own. But I did call a few companies in his industry and blackballed him. Not that I really needed to. They wouldn't have touched him after the scandal he caused at his former company."

She blinked once. "I...really want to kiss you."

His cock jolted to life at that. "I won't stop you."

Shaking her head, she laid it back down on his chest and snuggled up against him. "That's just asking for trouble."

He bunched the covers at his waist, covering his erection as best he could. Hell, he was in bed with Darcy. How could he not be hard? Especially when he'd made her come only a couple hours ago, could still taste her on his tongue. Okay maybe not, but it was fresh in his mind.

"Thank you, for what you did. I feel super mean for even saying thank you, but…"

"He's not a good man. Karma caught up to him all on its own."

"Sexual harassment?" she asked a few minutes later.

"Yeah." Brooks wouldn't give her the details unless she asked.

Thankfully she didn't. He didn't want to talk about her piece-of-shit father. He wanted to talk about them, but…he realized she'd dozed off.

Even though he'd wanted to keep talking to her, he couldn't help but laugh a little. He shouldn't be surprised. She'd once told him that whenever she was in bed with him, in his arms, she felt safer than she'd ever felt.

He should have remembered that—should have treasured what he'd had when he'd had it. Sighing, he pulled her closer and closed his own eyes. If he wanted to be on his game in a few hours, he needed sleep.

* * *

Brooks didn't want to leave Darcy at all, but knew he had to. Because he was going to be there for that meeting with the Fed.

Leaning against the countertop in her kitchen, Darcy lifted her coffee mug to her lips. For a moment his gaze dipped to her mouth but then he managed to focus.

"I hate leaving you."

Her lips curved up the slightest bit. "I'm seriously fine."

"Have you heard back from your mechanic yet?" he asked, even though he knew the answer.

"Unless he called me in the last ten minutes, no." She set her mug down but still kept her distance from him. "I'm going to be at the Markov residence all day. Which isn't the best thing in the world, but I'm not afraid to be there—especially since you told me that Semyon was truly concerned about my car issues."

Brooks didn't respond, though it was true. Gage had been listening to all of Markov's conversations in his vehicle via the planted listening device, and Markov wasn't behind Darcy's car troubles. That much was clear.

She continued. "The rehearsal dinner is tomorrow so the place will be packed with people setting up. I'm going to be safe, surrounded by tons of people—witnesses."

"I still don't like what happened with your car."

"I don't like it either. But I have a rental and it's only a year old. A lot nicer than my car."

"Keep your phone on you all day."

She lifted an eyebrow, at his tone, no doubt.

"*Please* keep it on you."

Her mouth curved up, making him wish he could capture it with his own, tease his tongue past her lips... "I will. And the same goes for you. If you learn anything new, I want to know about it."

He set his own mug down and rounded the island top. "I'll contact you as soon as I can." Despite the lingering tension in the air, he reached out and gently wrapped his fingers around one of her hips.

She set her fingers against his chest. "What are you doing?" she whispered.

"Nothing. Just wanted to touch you before I left."

"When you say stuff like that, you drive me crazy."

"Good crazy?"

Sighing, she set her forehead against his chest and mumbled, "Yes."

He inwardly grinned and kissed the top of her head. "I'll call you soon."

Stepping back, she nodded, her expression unreadable.

The drive to the rented office where they were meeting the Fed didn't take long. Leighton had thought it best that they meet somewhere neutral, and since Brooks owned a couple commercial buildings that weren't currently in use—while waiting for updates and renovations—they'd chosen a place close to the harbor. The last time it had been rented out, it had been a café.

Some of the tables were still there, which was all they needed to have this discussion. Brooks recognized Gage's truck as he pulled up. And there was a plain black four-door sedan with a Virginia license plate—definitely the Fed's.

The little bell above the door was still in place so when he stepped inside, it jingled. Leighton leaned against the dusty glass-front countertop. Gage was sitting at one of the small square tables, his laptop open, and a woman who didn't look like most Feds he knew was swiping her fingers across her cell phone at warp speed.

She looked up when she saw him enter, nodded once, and returned to her phone. Her jet-black hair was pulled back into a bun at her neck and she had on cargo pants, a button-down, cargo-style shirt in the same pale green, and boots. After a moment, she shoved her phone in her back pocket and turned to look at all of them, hands on her hips. "I'm going to get straight to the point. I just got off a long flight, and I know who you are," she said, nodding again at Brooks, "so I don't need an introduction. And—"

"This is Special Agent Hazel Blake," Leighton said dryly. "She won the personality of the year award three years running when we served together."

Hazel just snorted, but her expression softened slightly as she looked at Leighton.

Brooks frowned. The ban on women in combat—in the Marines—hadn't been lifted until a few years ago. "You two served together?"

Leighton nodded. "She provided CAS for us more than once."

Close Air Support. That meant she'd been a Cobra pilot. He nodded once at her in respect. "Nice."

Hazel cleared her throat. "As I was saying, I'm going to get straight to the point of everything. We know who Semyon Markov is. He's loosely linked to a man named Alexei Kuznetsov." She paused for a moment and looked between the three of them. "And none of you seem surprised by that. You know who he is?"

All of them nodded.

She frowned at that, but continued, "We've also been watching Oleg Polzin. Or he's on our radar, at least. Suspected of a few crimes."

That was vague enough that she wasn't giving them any real details. Not that he was surprised. She and Leighton must really have a tight bond if she was here at all, listening to them. Or at this point, she was just talking. But she was here, and that mattered.

"Markov hasn't been on our radar. Not seriously anyway. We thought about trying to get to Kuznetsov through him, but from what we can tell, they aren't close. They have occasional business together, but... Anyway, now, what you guys are telling me is that he might be planning a bombing of a school? How reliable is the witness who overheard the conversation?"

"Reliable. She's soon going to be the sister-in-law of Markov's son," Brooks said, even though he knew that Leighton had already given the Fed the basic facts about Darcy. "She has a good relationship with her sister, likes her sister's fiancé, has never suspected anything strange going on with the family. And she is not prone to a wild imagination." *Plus I'm in love with her, so I'll do any damn thing it takes to protect her.*

"Okay, good. I'm going to want to talk to her."

"You can do it at my house, then." There was heavy security at his ranch, and it was so far out of the way that no one would see them meeting.

"Fine. Now you guys are going to answer some questions for me, like what the hell it is you do?" She shot a sharp look at Leighton.

"I already told you what we do. Consulting."

"And I don't buy it. I need to know more about what you're doing and whether or not I trust you."

At that, Leighton shoved up from the counter, a real spark of emotion rolling off him. Anger. One of the first emotions Brooks had seen from him in a long damn time. "Really? You're not sure you trust me?"

"I didn't mean it like that. I had one of my guys try to hack your system," she said, completely unapologetically. "And you have some serious encryption."

Gage stretched out in his seat, crossing one ankle over the other, obnoxiously casual. "Damn straight we do. And you guys tried to recruit me once upon a time."

"Why do you even need to bring us into this?" Leighton asked Hazel, his voice neutral. "You have a witness. And it will be easy enough to leave her out of it. All you have to do is say you received an anonymous tip."

She was silent for a long moment, and Brooks had a feeling that had been her intention all along. So why the hell was she here? "Where did you get the information about the specific schools?" she finally asked. "Because according to your story, the witness didn't overhear those details."

Ah, that was why. Well, Brooks certainly wasn't answering that question. He wasn't going to tell a Fed they'd broken into a cop's house and stolen the info.

"Good guess?" Gage murmured, trying to hide his grin and failing spectacularly.

"Bullshit. Did you guys break into Markov's house?"

"No," Leighton said immediately.

She narrowed her gaze at him. "You're telling the truth. But you didn't get that information legally." Not a question.

No one said a word. Even if Leighton trusted her, they weren't going to admit they'd broken into someone's house and stolen information. Finally Brooks said, "You're here, so the information must be good."

"Off the books, I had one of my guys run Polzin and Markov's faces through different programs."

"Let me guess," Gage said. "You found Polzin around a couple of the schools in the last few months. It's not obvious what he's doing, but to people like us, he's been doing recon."

The woman's eyes narrowed slightly, but she nodded. "As soon as I get the okay from my boss, we're going to check out the schools."

Brooks called bullshit. With the urgency of the situation he was fairly certain she'd already gotten the okay and had people either in place or ready to go. Or she wouldn't be here. "You want something from us."

She nodded at him. "Even if we find any explosive devices, unless we get lucky, nothing links us back to Markov or Polzin."

That wasn't exactly their problem, but no one said anything.

She continued. "I want to talk to your witness about potentially wearing—"

"Nope." Brooks knew exactly where the woman was going with this. "If you even mention that she wears a wire, we're done here."

Her jaw tightened slightly. "It doesn't have to be anything big, just a small recording device on her person while she's at the Markov residence. I've looked into her too. Her sister's wedding is Saturday, and she's going to be there for the next three days straight, basically. It wouldn't hurt to—"

"No," Brooks said. "We gave you a gift. Take it but leave her out of it. And if you try to go around us, you'll regret it." He didn't care if he was threatening a federal agent. If this woman tried to convince Darcy to do something like that, he would lose his mind.

Leighton nodded. "I'm with Brooks on this. We gave you solid information. What you do with it is up to you. You have a lot of resources, and I have no doubt that if they *are* planning something, you'll be able to stop it. But don't put the woman in danger. If you do, you and I..." He trailed off, and Brooks wasn't certain what the implied threat was.

The only thing he knew was his friend had his back. And he hadn't been sure Leighton would, not with the way he'd been looking at the woman covertly. Knowing that Leighton was on board completely with keeping Darcy out of this eased the band of tension around Brooks's chest.

"Fine. The woman stays out of it. I still want to talk to her, eventually. But for now, I have a shitload of work to do."

"You could say thank you instead of grumbling." Leighton actually smiled, sort of, for the first time in almost a year.

She nudged him with her hip. "Thank you. Seriously. And I will definitely keep your witness out of this. So far, I've got a small team ready to go. No matter what we find, I'll cite an anonymous tip started all of this. If we get what we need..." She rubbed her fingers against her temple and for the first time, Brooks could see she was exhausted. "Hopefully it'll be enough to get warrants."

"Well, you might not need one for Turner's place." Gage turned his laptop around. "The detective was killed last night in a gas station robbery gone wrong. The clerk was killed too. Place was trashed and cash registers emptied out."

Hazel cursed as she looked at Gage's screen. "Well isn't that just convenient."

It was possible it was simply a coincidence but Brooks didn't think so. If the detective had been murdered by Markov, or more likely Polzin on Markov's orders, they were likely cleaning up before the bombing. Which meant it was very likely that bombing would be in a couple days. *Shit.*

"I've got to run," she said.

"Where are you staying?" Leighton asked her.

"Bureau's putting us up in a place, not that I'm going to spend much time there," she muttered. "I'll text you later."

Leighton nodded once. "Call me if you need anything."

"I will. And I'll let you know...if we find anything."

Technically she shouldn't let them know anything. And the Feds could be sticklers about rules. This one maybe not so much. Brooks just raised an eyebrow at Leighton as the Fed left. "What's your history with her?"

Leighton simply shrugged. "She's solid. If they find a bomb, she'll let me know. And her word is good. Darcy won't be brought into anything."

That wasn't an answer, but Brooks let it go. Whatever his friend's history with the woman, it wasn't important right now. He turned to Gage. "Did you hear anything from the bugs in Turner's place?"

"No. But I think we should probably get those listening devices out of there now."

Brooks nodded in agreement. He'd worn gloves when he'd broken into the detective's home, but it was better to not leave any trace of themselves behind. "I can head there now."

"We'll go with you," Leighton said. "If no one is there yet, we'll be able to get in and out in less than five minutes."

There might be LEOs there already but Brooks doubted it. The detective hadn't been killed at his house. But they needed to move ASAP. "Let's roll," Brooks said. Now that the FBI had taken over everything, this job wasn't theirs anymore.

But that didn't mean he wasn't going to be protecting Darcy.

CHAPTER FIFTEEN

—I'm starting to question why I got out of bed this
morning.—

Darcy jumped when Emma silently stepped out from behind the door that led to the wine cellar and into the
kitchen, her reaction having more to do with her being on
edge than actually being surprised.

"Hey, Darc, hope I didn't scare you."

"No, I'm good." A lie, considering her racing heart. But it
had nothing to do with her sister and everything to do with
wondering and worrying about the meeting Brooks was at
right now. He might have left already, for all she knew. But
she hadn't heard from him and he'd promised to contact her.

Her sister set a pricey bottle of red wine on the counter.
She grinned at the bottle. "Peter's dad told us to take it."

Darcy let out a low whistle. "Part of your wedding gift?"

"I guess." Her sister shrugged and pulled out one of the
seats. "So, what's going on with you and Brooks? And don't
think I'm not annoyed that you've been avoiding my calls."

"I haven't been avoiding your calls. I've been texting you,
haven't I? I'm busy with wedding stuff, in case you forgot."

Her sister let out a disbelieving snort. "You think I don't
know you? You can ignore texts but you can't lie to my face.
So what's up with you guys?"

Darcy didn't want to lie to her sister so she decided to be
vague. "Things are complicated."

"That's not vague or anything." Her sister's eyes narrowed slightly. "And you've been weird the past couple days. What's going on?"

"Maybe I am being weird. Honestly, this whole thing with Brooks really is complicated. And I don't want you to think about it for one second. You're getting married in two days. Your rehearsal dinner is tomorrow. Those are the only things you need to be thinking about."

"That's what I have you for, so I don't have to worry about that stuff. Come on, you've forgiven him, I take it?"

"Yes." Even as she said the word, she knew it wasn't a lie. Because she *had* forgiven him. She was just all twisted up about the two of them.

"Peter's dad said something about Brooks. Apparently, he really likes the guy."

"Brooks is very likable."

"Yeah, but if he breaks your heart I'm seriously going to kick his ass."

She laughed at her little sister's tough talk. "You're very scary."

"I can be when I want to. And I'm not sure *I've* forgiven him for everything."

"Well, have you forgiven him enough to let him be my plus-one?"

Emma's eyes widened. "I can't believe you even asked that. Of course you can bring him. If it wasn't for you, we wouldn't even be having such an amazing wedding. I just...want to make sure that you're okay. It's not like you to be so tight-lipped about things." There was a touch of hurt in Emma's voice.

Darcy's heart twisted. She rounded the island and put her arm around her sister's shoulders. "When I have something to tell you, I promise I will. Honestly, I'm so confused about him right now. I don't even know what to say where he's concerned. We slept in the same bed last night but didn't do anything except talk." Falling asleep in his arms had felt so natural, and when she'd woken in the morning she hadn't felt weird about it either. Confused, yes. But that was about it. Because she didn't have any regrets. Just fear where he was concerned. She wasn't sure she could take getting her heart broken by him again. It would crush her.

Emma laid her head on Darcy's shoulder. "Do you still love him?" she asked quietly.

Oh yeah, she was *not* answering that question.

"I'll take your silence as a yes. What's holding you up about him?"

"Fear of getting hurt again." And there it was, the most honest she'd been to herself since Brooks barreled right back into her life.

"I get that. I never told you, but Peter and I broke up once."

Surprised, Darcy stepped to the side so she could look at her sister. "When was this?"

"In the beginning of our relationship. Way before we got engaged." Her sister tucked a strand of her dark hair behind her ear.

Darcy pulled out a seat next to her. "What happened?"

"Long story short, I did the same thing I always did with boyfriends before him. I wouldn't trust him—for no reason. I was creating conflict that wasn't there and he called me on it. I called him a jerk and he told me that when I finally decided to have a grown-up relationship to call him. Or something along those lines." Emma's lips curved up slightly. "I was stubborn and wouldn't call him. I figured he was just another loser I'd gotten rid of. But...he decided I was worth it and refused to let me go. He also called me on my bullshit and made it clear that he's not my father, and never will be. I knew that in my heart, but hearing him say it... I don't know, it was like a wakeup call."

"Wow." Her sister had definitely grown up a lot since she'd started dating Peter so her story didn't surprise Darcy. She just hoped that he wasn't like *his* father. Something she didn't want to think about right now. She was supposed to act normal and keep this wedding running smoothly.

"I know, right. I think about how different my life would be if he hadn't fought for me, come after me."

"Well I'm glad he did. You're a different person with him." It was as if her sister had let go of all of her anger toward their father in the last year. Or maybe not let it go so much as she'd stopped letting it control the way she reacted to the world.

"I don't know how you let things go with our sperm donor."

Darcy let out a sharp laugh with no humor. "I'm not sure that I let it go. I just refuse to let him take up space in my head. He's not worth it. Speaking of, he called me a few months ago." She hadn't told Emma because she hadn't wanted to upset her, but figured now was a good time to tell her. "I think he was fishing around for an invite to your wedding. And I'm pretty sure he was impressed by the man you're marrying." Peter was successful in his own right.

Emma shook her head. "Talk about ballsy."

"Right? What an idiot. Brooks told me that he got fired from his job a year ago." Darcy left out the reason why because it wasn't important. "And apparently he's been blackballed in the industry. Brooks might have had something to do with it."

"Okay, Brooks is completely and utterly forgiven," her sister said laughingly. "All right, I actually do need to get out of here. I still need to pack for our honeymoon, which I can't believe is so soon. I'm looking forward to it more than the wedding," she muttered before glancing around.

The place was milling with people, but thankfully no one had bothered them in the kitchen. Darcy pulled her into another hug. "You've been a champ with this whole circus of the wedding. I can say you're going to be the most beautiful bride ever."

"You have to say that."

"Yeah, but in your case, it's true." At that, tears pricked her eyes and she batted them away. "Damn it, I swore I wouldn't get emotional."

"Just get it all out now. There will be no crying on my actual wedding day."

"No promises." Because her baby sister was getting married. Brooks had told her that Peter looked aboveboard and didn't appear to have any type of ties to his father financially. And Darcy simply couldn't imagine that Peter was involved in any of this. If he was, she wasn't sure that she could forgive herself for not telling her sister about Mr. Markov.

But if she did tell her, and Emma mentioned it to Peter—and Peter was involved—things could get very bad for them. Especially since the FBI was now neck deep in this thing. No, deep down Darcy knew she was doing the right thing, but she still hated keeping this from her sister.

Whatever her own wants were, this wasn't about her. It was about innocent people who might be killed. She had to remember that.

* * *

"Everything will be wonderful tomorrow. I have faith in you." Darcy beamed at Mr. Singh. This would be one of their biggest jobs to date. All their food was quality and they never cut corners. They were pricier than some caterers in the area but worth it.

Mr. Singh nodded once. "He has a great setup in his kitchen. We'll be preparing everything ahead of time except the desserts. It will be better if they're done onsite."

Darcy nodded since they'd gone over this a few times. She was pretty sure that Mr. Singh was just nervous and triple-checking everything.

"And you already know all this." He laughed lightly. "I'm going to get out of here now. My crew has the setup under control. We'll be here three hours early tomorrow just so I can go over everything with the waitstaff one more time and do a dry run with the table layout. But my people are pros."

"Sounds good. And I'll be here when you are." Darcy planned on being here most of the day tomorrow. Well, first she had to go get a manicure and pedicure with her sister, which sounded fun, but part of her wished she could just skip it and prep more for the wedding. But in addition to being her sister's wedding planner, Darcy was also her maid of honor. Something she definitely couldn't forget. So she would be pulling double duty, trying to balance fun and work—and not freaking out about everything else going on.

She glanced at her cell phone and frowned when she saw the time. Seriously, why hadn't Brooks called her back? She knew he was fine. The man could take care of himself. But she still worried. It was impossible not to.

Sighing, she tucked her cell phone into the pocket of her black pants. Then she scanned the white-linen-covered tables. There were six in all, with eight covered chairs at each table. Just for the rehearsal dinner. Many more tables would be added once everyone had left the dinner. The giant room itself seemed to shimmer. A huge chandelier hung in the middle of the ballroom—there was no other word for the room—and Semyon had installed five more for the wedding. It created a sparkly, whimsical atmosphere.

The multiple sets of French doors opened out onto a huge lanai, where the actual ceremony would take place. Then people would be free to come inside, eat, mingle and dance. Emma had wanted to be married outside and hadn't been willing to compromise. So despite the cold weather, it would be an outdoor wedding. The warmers were already in place and would be ready to go long before the guests arrived.

Not that any of that mattered now. She was just stalling. She needed to tell Semyon she was leaving to go meet her sister. Emma wanted to try on her dress one more time. Darcy thought she really just needed some sister time, and that was fine with her. Almost the entire place had cleared out and there wasn't much for her to do at this point. Unless she wanted to give herself busywork.

After walking around the room and checking each door to make sure they were all locked, she stepped into one of the hallways. His place was huge, and not exactly a maze, but it would be easy to get turned around. And she had no desire to get lost here. She didn't even want to be here at all. In fact, she could just text him and tell him she was leaving. There was no need to hunt him down.

As she rounded the corner at the end of the hallway, she nearly ran right into Oleg. *Ugh.* Her immediate reaction to him was instinctive, and she knew she didn't hide it. That was the bad thing about wearing her emotions right out in the open. She tried to cover it up, and pasted on what she hoped was a smile. But she knew it didn't show in her eyes. Thankfully she didn't need to make small talk with the man. They had no business together. So she simply nodded politely and tried to sidestep him.

Instead of moving out of the way, however, he moved with her, blocking her way. And the first trickle of panic started to bloom inside her. That had been deliberately rude.

"Excuse me," she snapped. She'd learned that with him she couldn't be overly polite.

"You're looking lovely today." He had the barest hint of an accent. His pale blue eyes were frosty, and if it had been possible, they would have sliced right through her. For whatever reason, he didn't like her.

Well, the feeling was mutual. "Thank you. Now if you'll excuse me—" She tried to step around him again, but this time he moved lightning fast.

Before she realized what he intended, he had her pinned against the nearest wood-paneled wall, his hand wrapped around her throat. She grabbed onto his wrist with both hands as shock tore through her. He was *strong*.

"You stupid little bitch," he whispered. "You think you're too good for me?"

She couldn't answer even if she wanted to because of his tight grip. Gasping for air, she yanked at his wrist. Pain ricocheted through her when he grabbed her breast. Hard.

On instinct, she raised her knee, aiming for his groin, but he turned to the side, laughing at her.

"I've been watching you," he murmured as she continued to struggle.

Black spots appeared in her line of vision. Still clawing at his wrist with one hand, she slapped his face hard. She had to get him to release his grip. She couldn't breathe. He was going to kill her!

He reared back, his face mottled with rage. As he raised his fist back, she tried to shrink against the wall, but—

"Oleg!"

He squeezed her neck once before letting her go.

She crumpled to the floor, sucking in deep breaths as she crawled a few feet away. At the end of the hallway Mr. Markov stood there, his face flushed dark red. "Get out of my house." His words were savage, and Darcy was certain that if she hadn't been there, he would have killed Oleg.

Suddenly, Oleg pulled a gun from inside his jacket. Her heart skipped a beat as she stared at the gleaming weapon.

Mr. Markov didn't flinch at the sight of it, just stared him down. And two more men stepped out from an intersecting hallway, guns drawn.

She wished the ground would open up and swallow her. She wanted to be anywhere but here, but was afraid that if she moved, Oleg would focus that gun on her.

"Get out of here and don't come back." Markov's voice was calm but deadly.

Ice had completely frosted over her veins, her heart thundering in her chest. How was he so calm?

"You'll never make it out of here alive if you shoot me," Markov said. "So just go."

Oleg looked down at her, rage in his eyes. "I'll be seeing you," he whispered before racing down the hallway in the opposite direction.

She had a feeling that if she hadn't been there, Mr. Markov's men would have shot him on sight.

Mr. Markov shouted something in Russian to the two men with him and they took off. Before she could move from her position on the floor, he was crouched in front of her, concern in his expression. "Are you okay?"

She shook her head because she couldn't find her voice—and her throat hurt.

He helped her to her feet, steadying her elbow with one hand. "Do you need to go see a doctor?"

"No," she rasped out, trembling all over. "But we need to call the police."

"Don't worry about anything. Come, let's go to my office. You'll be safe there."

That was the last place she wanted to go, but she didn't plan to leave until she knew that Oleg was captured. Once inside his office, she collapsed in one of the plush leather chairs. Mr. Markov was quiet as he poured her a drink. Bourbon, she thought.

When he handed it to her, she took the glass tumbler automatically, her shaking hand making the amber liquid slosh.

"Drink," he said. "It will make you feel better."

"Why haven't you called the police?" she rasped out.

He was silent as he leaned against the front of his desk, crossing his arms over his chest. Looming there, he looked a little terrifying. She didn't think he was trying to, however. "If I call the police, they will come to my house, question you, and disrupt my son's wedding."

Darcy didn't point out that the wedding wasn't for two more days. "We can't just let him go. He assaulted me and threatened you."

"I won't be letting him go. I will involve the police on Sunday." Even though he looked sincere, she didn't buy a word of it.

She wondered how hard she should push. Because knowing what she did, she wasn't sure what he would do if she pushed too hard. She felt as if she were walking a tightrope right now. "I just don't understand why we can't call them now."

He sighed, sounding exhausted as he sat next to her. "Where I come from, we don't trust the authorities. I know it's different here. I just don't want to risk anything ruining Peter and Emma's wedding."

It was such bullshit, but she also knew that she'd gone as far as she could. She needed to appear to bend. "You need to tell Peter and Emma what happened, then. What if he goes after them? And why did he attack me?"

The tension in his shoulders seemed to lessen as he realized she wasn't arguing with him. He nodded once. "I will inform both Peter and your sister. And I will make sure they both have security with them—I'll insist they come stay here tonight."

Darcy could just imagine how that would go over with her sister but didn't respond. Instead she repeated, "I don't understand why he attacked me."

"I don't either. That is something we will let the police figure out."

"They're going to want to know why we waited so long to call them."

"Just let me worry about that." Then he actually petted her on the head, like she was a puppy. It was as if he was saying *Don't let your tiny woman brain worry about it.* Or maybe she was just projecting, but it sure felt that way. The fact that he assumed she would go along with this insanity—and the only reason she was, was because of what she knew about *him*— made her realize how stupid he must think she was.

"Maybe you should stay here tonight," he said.

"No, I'll stay at my boyfriend's." If she said anything different, it would look weird. And no way was she staying here.

He was silent for a long moment, as if weighing her words. Then he surprised her by saying, "Maybe you're right, and we should involve the police. But I will take you to the nearest police station instead of calling them."

She wondered if he'd changed his mind because of her mention of Brooks. He had to realize she would tell him, and a normal boyfriend would insist on calling the police. "Okay, thank you."

He nodded once and took the drink from her. "Let's go."

Unable to shake off the chill still running through her, she followed him. As soon as she made it to the police station, she was going to call Brooks. She wanted to call him right then, but didn't want to do it in front of Semyon. She didn't care if he hadn't called her back yet, he needed to know about this. And she wanted him with her.

Who was she kidding? She always wanted him with her.

CHAPTER SIXTEEN

—Absolutely no regrets.—

When Darcy stepped out into the lobby of the police station, she found Brooks, her sister, Peter and Mr. Markov—gah, Semyon—waiting.

There were other people sitting in the lime green chairs as well, but she only had eyes for Brooks. Her sister rushed at her first, however, eyes wide as she pulled Darcy into a hug.

"Oh my God! I'm so glad you're okay." Emma was petite, but very strong as she tightened her arms around Darcy.

"I really am." Her throat was a little sore, but she was otherwise unharmed. She'd made a report with the police and they were going to search for Polzin, but for some reason it didn't make her feel better. She wouldn't be able to rest until he was in jail. For what he'd done to her, or what he was potentially involved with. She wasn't going to think about that now though. Part of her wondered if Semyon's men had caught him and just killed him but there was no way to know. Squeezing her sister one last time, she stepped back and found herself facing a wall of rock-hard muscle as Brooks pulled her into his arms.

Unlike her sister, Brooks held her firmly but didn't squish her. He was a solid presence who wasn't going anywhere. For a long moment, she buried her face against his chest and simply inhaled his spicy, masculine scent. She didn't care if it looked weird either. She'd been keeping it together, she thought fairly well, but now she wanted to be in her own home, in her pajamas, with her favorite mug filled with hot cocoa, curled up with Brooks. She did *not* want to be at a police station on a Thursday night surrounded by strangers.

"I'm going to get you out of here in the next sixty seconds," he murmured against the top of her head. "Fair warning, I might be rude about it to the others. But you're leaving now."

It was really hard to argue with him when she was glad he was taking over. She was usually the woman in charge of things, and she liked it that way. She loved everything about her job and helping women on their big day. But right now, she didn't want to make any decisions. "Okay," she whispered, grateful for his strong presence.

When she stepped back, Brooks wrapped his arm around her shoulders and pulled her close.

"Do you think you should go to the hospital?" Her sister looked close to tears.

A few feet away, she heard Peter say to his father, "I told you that you should have let that bastard go a long time ago. I don't understand why you kept him on when he was clearly a creep. Darcy could have been seriously hurt!" he hissed.

"No," Darcy said, looking at her sister. She was glad that Peter cared so much, and she didn't think it was for show. It also made her think that he had no idea what his father was currently involved in. "He choked me—"

Darcy broke off when her sister let out a panicked little yelp. She'd thought that Emma knew what had happened.

"He choked you!" It was more a shout than a question.

"Yes," she murmured. "And let's take this outside." A few people had turned to stare at them and she hated being the center of attention on the best of days.

The sliding glass doors swished open, letting in an icy breeze that she felt straight to her bones. Despite wearing her thick jacket, she snuggled closer to Brooks. She had a feeling that her chilled body had nothing to do with the weather, or very little, anyway. She was still shocky and needed to get out of here. As far away from Semyon as possible.

"Darcy—"

Brooks cut her sister off, his voice gentle but firm. "We're leaving. I'm taking Darcy home right now. She's been through a lot and she needs rest. It's not up for discussion. She also won't be looking at her phone or working until tomorrow morning." There was the slightest hint of an edge to his words—as if he was daring anyone to argue with him.

Emma nodded immediately. "Of course, but I'll have my phone if you guys need *anything*. Or do you want me to stay with you?" she asked.

"Thank you, but no." Darcy loved her sister more than anything, but she wasn't up for conversation or anything really. And she knew that Brooks wouldn't push her. He would simply drive her home and take care of her. "I'll feel better knowing that you and Peter are at Mr.... Semyon's house. And I'll meet you tomorrow—"

"No, we're not going to do the manis and pedis." Now there was no give to Emma's words. "At least not at a salon. I know someone I can call. We'll set it up at Semyon's estate. I'll let Audrey know that there's been a change of plans," she said, referring to her other bridesmaid. "You deserve to be pampered so if you're up to it, it's happening." Darcy's instinct was to take over but Emma must have read her expression, because her sister simply shook her head. "I love and appreciate how much you're doing for our wedding, but I'm not helpless. I can take over from here. You need to go home and rest. Please."

Darcy pulled her sister into a big hug and then hugged Peter as well. Semyon, to give him credit, still seemed concerned, and was scanning the parking lot as if looking for danger. Which made her think that his men hadn't caught and killed Oleg. She seriously doubted that Oleg had come to the police station, but she would be happy to get out of here as soon as possible.

It didn't take long for Brooks to pull his truck around and bundle her up into the passenger seat. Before he'd even pulled out of the parking lot, he had the heater on full blast.

"What do you need from me?" he asked quietly.

"Honestly, nothing right now. Thank you so much for taking over." She laid her head back and closed her eyes.

"You never have to thank me for anything. But you're welcome. I want to hunt that bastard down and kill him." There was a dark edge to his tone. And she was pretty certain he wasn't joking.

"That's what the police are for."

Brooks snorted.

"Mr. Markov's guys ran after Oleg," she said. "They might have...taken care of him already."

"They haven't found him."

"How do you know?"

"Gage overheard a conversation Markov had on his cell phone in his vehicle with one of his guys—after you were already inside the police station. He disappeared from the grounds and Markov is pissed. He's increasing his security tenfold."

She swallowed hard. Great. Oleg really was still out there.

"Have you told your Fed friend what happened?"

"She's not my friend. But no, I haven't told anyone yet. As soon as I got your call, I came to the police station. So what happened?"

She wrapped her arms around herself but opened her eyes. There was no snow falling, but there was a blanket of white everywhere she looked as he drove down the quiet street. As she relayed what had happened in exact detail, Brooks gripped the steering wheel tightly, his knuckles turning white.

"Yep, I'm definitely going to kill him." The way he said it, it sounded more as if he was talking to himself than to her.

"Can the Feds use this against him?"

"Maybe. Right now, they're focusing on finding that bomb."

"Why didn't you call me back earlier today?" Ugh, did that sound like she was whining? Darcy inwardly winced at herself.

He shot her a sideways glance before focusing on the road. "I don't want to lie to you."

"Then don't lie."

"Okay, then I was retrieving some illegally planted listening devices in a now dead detective's house."

She blinked at his words. "What?"

"The detective you overheard talking, Turner, he's dead. Supposedly killed in a random gas station robbery. But I don't buy it."

"And you were... Oh, wow. That seems really dangerous." She knew he'd done a lot of very dangerous things when he'd been a Marine, but for some reason this hit home more. "What if you'd been caught or—"

"I wasn't. And if for some reason I was," he actually snorted at the thought before continuing, "I have a very good attorney."

"So...what exactly is happening with Semyon?"

"The Feds are looking into him. Apparently, he has a boss that they want a lot more. They're going to keep you out of everything. You're simply someone who left an anonymous tip. If that ever comes out at all. With Polzin and Markov clearly at odds, they might tear each other apart and bring

194 | KATIE REUS

themselves down. The anonymous tip might never come to light."

"What if...Semyon is never charged for the bombing? Or what if the Feds...don't find the bomb?"

Brooks's mouth pulled into a thin line. "We'll worry about that in the future. For now, I just want to get you home and in bed."

There was nothing sexual about the way he said "in bed" and for some reason she found that incredibly disappointing.

She closed her eyes and must have dozed because the next thing she knew, they were pulling into her driveway.

Darcy yawned as Brooks put his truck in Park. "I'm surprised you didn't insist on taking me back to your ranch."

"I'm not worried about Polzin. I can take care of him. And...I knew you would rather sleep in your own bed tonight."

His insight didn't exactly surprise her, but it did touch her. "You seem to know me pretty well."

"I do know you. Even if my past action says otherwise." He shot her a wry look. "I let the past dictate my reaction to something seven months ago. It was stupid."

"Stupid, yes. But not unforgivable." Despite how she'd felt before, she knew he'd made a mistake. But he was human. She was still scared of getting hurt by him, but he'd really stepped up recently. And the truth was she didn't think she could walk away from him. Not again.

He raised an eyebrow, but didn't comment. Instead he glanced around her little front yard. A light blanket of snow covered everything. "Where are your keys?"

She dug into her purse and handed them to him.

"Sit tight," he said. "I'm going to go in through the front door, turn off your alarm, and open the garage."

He had her code so she didn't need to give it to him. "Why can't I get out with you?"

"I doubt Polzin is waiting to attack you here, but I don't want you out in the open right now. My friend Gage is sitting across the street, keeping an eye on us."

Surprised, she turned around and, sure enough, there was a truck she didn't recognize across the street. The windows were tinted so she couldn't see inside, but if Brooks said it was his friend then it was. It made her feel even safer.

"I'll only be a few minutes. I'm going to do a sweep of your house as well." Then he was gone, leaving her alone in the quiet of his truck.

Most of the shock had worn off and she had time to think. She wasn't sure she wanted to think too much right now, however. What she wanted to do was give in to that little voice in her head telling her to make a go of things with Brooks.

A few minutes later, she nearly jumped out of her skin when he opened the driver's side door and slid inside. She hadn't even seen him approach the vehicle. Which probably had more to do with his stealth abilities than with her poor observational skills.

"Your house is clear."

A trickle of relief slid through her as he pulled into her garage. When the door shut behind them, she let out a little sigh. She was finally home. "Thank you for bringing me home. You were right, I really do want to sleep in my own bed tonight. And I would like you to join me." There was no mistaking what she was asking. She didn't want him to simply snuggle up with her. She wanted to feel him skin to skin, to feel him thrusting inside her over and over as they both came.

He didn't look directly at her, but his fingers gripped the steering wheel tightly. It was so quiet in the interior of the vehicle, his breathing overly harsh. Instead of responding as she'd expected, he got out of the driver's seat. Before she'd even unbuckled, he was at the passenger side helping her out. Not that she needed him to, but she still took his hand. Was he going to respond to what she'd said?

A bit of doubt crept in. She knew he wanted her. That much was clear in his every action the past few days. So why wasn't he jumping on this? She'd assumed this was exactly what he wanted.

He picked up her purse and as they stepped inside her laundry room, she slid off her jacket. She'd started to get too warm in the truck and was glad to take it off. He immediately took it from her and placed it on the hook by the door. Then, surprising her, he motioned for her to sit on the little bench. There was nothing sensual about the way he took off her boots. He moved with economical precision. And even if it felt a little silly letting him do this, she kind of liked it. Okay, more than kind of. Once he was done, they headed into her kitchen. Wordlessly, he headed for one of her cabinets and pulled out two cans of chicken noodle soup.

"I'm not that hungry," she said even as her stomach rumbled. Maybe it wasn't that she wasn't hungry, she simply didn't feel like eating.

"You need to eat something before you go to bed."

When he said bed, it made her think all sorts of things. Sexy, naked things. "Are you going to respond to what I said in your truck?"

He paused once before pulling two bowls down. "I'll sleep with you tonight, but we're not doing anything else. You just had a huge shock. I don't ever want to be something you regret." There wasn't much give in his voice.

"I'm not going to regret this." She had no doubt of it. "I need you."

He paused, his expression softening. But then he just made a sort of grunting sound and put one of the bowls in her microwave, then covered it with a paper towel. When he shut the door, he went to another cabinet, clearly having remembered where her stuff was. He pulled out a box of caffeine-free chamomile tea. Instead of making it in a pot on the stove, he placed one of the teabags in a mug and filled it with water. When the soup was done, she had no doubt he would simply put the tea in the microwave.

Since he wasn't going to talk more about what she'd said, she decided that she'd just get in bed with him naked later. That should make things easy enough between them. Because she seriously doubted he would argue with her then. Not when she wrapped her body around his.

She wanted more than an orgasm, because she could give herself one. No, she wanted that intimacy with him. Hell, right now she needed it.

CHAPTER SEVENTEEN

—You're my weakness.—

Feeling far too edgy, Brooks leaned back against the head-board as he waited for Darcy. He deserved a medal for telling her that they wouldn't be having sex tonight. She'd offered him everything he wanted but he couldn't do it. Not when she'd had such a rough night.

God, he couldn't even think about what she'd been through. What that psycho might have done if Markov hadn't been there. Brooks never thought he'd want to thank Markov for anything, but hell. He might have lost the woman he loved tonight. Right now he wanted to claim her more than anything, but he couldn't take advantage of her.

Darcy was okay because of Markov. Of course, if Markov hadn't had that bastard in his house in the first place, Darcy never would have been in danger. Brooks scrubbed a hand over his face. He kept trying to rein himself back in—and not go hunting Polzin down. Because if he left, Darcy would be alone. Or she'd be with one of his guys, but that still wasn't happening.

After what she'd just been through, he was going to be at her side.

When he heard the water from the bathroom shut off, he pushed up slightly against the headboard.

He wanted her more than his next breath.

But...he couldn't do that tonight.

Brooks sat up straight as Darcy stepped into the bedroom. Backlit by the open bathroom door, she was completely, utterly naked. He opened his mouth to say something, but nothing came out.

She gave him the cheekiest grin as she stepped into the room, confident in who she was. She was just as gorgeous as he remembered, all smooth skin and perfect curves. He didn't know where to look as he raked his gaze over her, greedy to drink in every inch. Her breasts were just a handful, her pink nipples tight and perky. He wanted to touch and tease her everywhere until she was panting from his caresses.

"Cat got your tongue?" She took another step toward him until she was at the foot of the bed.

He continued staring. They shouldn't do anything. She'd been assaulted earlier and she was in shock. Okay maybe she wasn't in shock anymore, but she'd been through a lot tonight. He hadn't been lying when he'd said he never wanted to be one of her regrets. That would carve him up inside—and might ruin any chance of a future they had. He wasn't sure that she'd completely forgiven him and if they slept together, it would carve him up if she regretted it in the morning. "Shock," he blurted. What the hell was he trying to say?

Her head tilted slightly to the side, and a cascade of her dark hair fell over her shoulder, highlighting one of her breasts. She crawled onto the bed, kneeling at the end of it as she watched him with a hungry gaze.

Fuck.

When she sat like that, *looking* at him like that, it was impossible not to be hard, not to want to throw out everything he'd decided earlier. "You were in shock earlier," he finally muttered, finding his damn voice. His cock was rock hard and his entire body ached with the need to touch her.

She let out a silvery laugh. "I'm not in shock *now.*"

He grabbed the covers and bunched them over his hard on, as if *that* would hide anything. God, he was acting like a ridiculous teenager. Scratch that—he never would have turned down a gorgeous, naked, willing woman as a teenager.

Her pale green eyes danced with laughter. "What's wrong with you?"

"I don't want to take advantage of you," he rasped out.

Her gaze darkened and she started crawling up the bed, her breasts full and so damn tempting. "I'm pretty sure that I'm the one taking advantage of you."

Okay, a man only had so much restraint. She was a grown-ass woman and if she told him she wanted this, they were doing this. But first... "No regrets," he rasped out. "Swear you won't regret this in the morning."

"I could never regret this."

Okay, that was going to have to be good enough for him. Moving lightning fast, he tossed the covers off and had her pinned flat on her back underneath him. She laughed in surprise as he stretched out on top of her, savoring every inch of her as she wrapped her legs around his waist.

God, he'd missed her. Now, having her like this, he wasn't sure where to start. Especially after that little preview last night, when he'd brought her to orgasm. That definitely hadn't been enough. He needed to taste all of her too.

"You're mine. Not letting you go," he murmured so she knew exactly where he stood—right before he crushed his mouth to hers.

His cock was rock hard and pressing against his boxers insistently as she moaned into his mouth and rolled her hips against his. It wouldn't take much to strip and be inside her but he wanted more than that. And she deserved more too.

Forcing himself to slow down, he gently sucked her bottom lip between his teeth.

She let out another little moan he felt straight to his cock and slid her hands down his back until she was cupping his ass. Then she made the most appreciative sound and squeezed.

"I've missed this ass," she murmured against his mouth, making him laugh.

"Oh yeah?" He'd never been one to need his ego stroked but...he loved that she was as into his body as he was into hers. And she'd never been shy about telling him. Okay, maybe she'd been reserved at first. But that was just one more thing he loved about her.

His Darcy could be serious, and when she let loose, let go with him—he knew it was just for him. That she trusted him enough to let her guard down.

And he swore that he was never going to lose her trust again. Life without her had been just existing.

"I've also missed this," she said, reaching between their bodies and stroking his hard length through his boxers.

He froze above her, all the muscles in his body going taut at the feel of her stroking him. And she wasn't even touching him skin to skin yet.

He groaned again before grasping her wrist. She gave him the most wicked grin.

"You're trying to push me over the edge," he murmured.

"It's what you get for trying to make decisions for me." She rolled her hips again. "And I don't think you'll be exactly sad if I do."

"I'm tasting you first." Then he'd come only when he was inside her. "Are you still on the pill?"

She nodded, her eyes heavy-lidded as she watched him. The desire he saw there nearly undid him. Reaching between their bodies, he cupped her mound and found her soaking. Oh yeah, it wouldn't take her long to climax.

And no matter how long it did, he was going to enjoy every second of getting her there.

She let out a strangled sound as he slid a finger inside her slickness.

"This for me?" He knew damn well it was for him. But the most primitive part of him wanted to hear her say it.

"Yes." The word came out harsh, unsteady.

Keeping his finger buried inside her, he dropped his head to one of her breasts. There was no rush right now. Even if all he wanted to do was bury himself inside her, lose himself in her and never stop. She was going to come against his mouth.

How the hell had he lived without her—and how had he ever imagined she'd betray him? That question would haunt him for a while, he had no doubt. But there was no room for that in his headspace now.

Slowly, he flicked his tongue over her already hard nipple, savoring the way she arched into his kisses and dug her fingers into his back.

"No foreplay," she rasped out.

Oh, she was getting foreplay. He lightly bit down onto her nipple in response. Teasing her had once been one of his favorite pastimes.

She arched into him and he continued his assault, moving to her other nipple, then back again, all while slowly stroking his finger in and out of her.

She made the sweetest little sounds of pleasure, her breathing as erratic as his heartbeat. By the time he made his way between her spread legs, he was desperate to taste her.

"Driving me crazy...on purpose." Her voice was unsteady as he dipped his head between her legs.

Hell yeah, he was. He was driving himself crazy too. But it was worth it. Her clit was swollen, the little bud peeking out from her folds, begging him to kiss it.

Oh so slowly, he flicked his tongue against her sensitive bundle of nerves and she nearly jolted off the bed. The woman was like dynamite and he wanted to be the one to set her off.

She slid her fingers through his hair and gripped his head. "No teasing."

"So much teasing," he murmured before flicking his tongue against her clit again. Over and over, he teased her as she writhed against his face.

He knew what it would take to get her off, to push her over that cliff, and while he wanted to drag it out longer, he wanted her to come more.

Last night had just been a reminder of how things had been between them. Tonight was different. When she'd said what he'd done was a mistake but not unforgivable, he knew she'd been sincere. That they had a chance again.

He wasn't letting it go. Wasn't letting *her* go.

Sliding two fingers inside her, he shuddered as her inner muscles tightened around him. His cock responded, shoving against his boxers, jealous of his damn fingers. He began stroking in a rhythm he knew would give her exactly what she needed.

"Oh, God."

"Oh, Brooks," he growled against her slick folds.

She gave a short laugh that quickly turned into a groan. "Brooks."

Over and over he thrust while teasing her clit, pushing her closer and closer until she arched off the bed, her back going bowstring tight as her orgasm slammed through her. He kept stroking, wanting to wring every possible ounce of pleasure out of her.

When she fell limp against the bed, gently sliding her fingers through his hair, he lifted his head. There was enough light streaming in from the bathroom that he could see every nuance of her expression.

Her eyes were heavy-lidded as she reached for him, the welcome of her open arms all he wanted. "Darcy," he murmured, moving until his body covered hers.

"Kiss me." A soft demand as she shoved at his boxers.

He quickly divested himself of them and then his mouth was on hers, giving her exactly what she wanted. What they both did. This woman owned him. Completely.

Reaching between her legs, though he knew she was slick he groaned against her mouth as he felt it. Hell, he still tasted it, knew she was tasting her own pleasure now. Sometimes she could be reserved but she didn't back away from anything in the bedroom. She'd given him her trust almost from the beginning. He'd had to work for it, but once they'd gotten there, she'd been all in.

"In me now."

Gladly. Poised at her entrance, he looked down at her for a long moment, splayed out, an offering for him to plunder. And treasure. Forever.

Thrusting once, he stopped only when he was buried fully inside her. She was tighter than he remembered, her inner walls clenching around him like a vise.

She raked her fingers over his chest, digging into his skin as he leaned down over her. Her muscles pulsed around him and his balls pulled up tight as he held back.

"I've missed you," she whispered, and the raw vulnerability in her expression and her voice ripped him open.

"I've missed you too." Slowly, he pulled back, hissing in a breath as her inner walls gripped him tight.

When she rolled her hips against his, arching into him, he lost all sense of thought and control. She met him stroke for stroke as he thrust inside her over and over. He lost track of time as their mouths and bodies tangled with each other.

And when he flipped her onto her knees, she pushed her ass back into him as she clutched at the sheets. This had always been one of her favorite positions.

He brought his palm down on her ass once before smoothing a hand over the sting. Then he was inside her again and time had no meaning as he thrust over and over. He wouldn't take long now and by the way her inner walls were pulsing around him, she wouldn't either.

It took all his restraint not to come right away but he wanted her to get off again. Needed it with a desperation he understood full well. She was his to take care of.

Reaching around her body, he cupped her mound, sliding his middle finger over her clit. She bucked against him, her inner walls clenching even harder and faster. Oh yeah, she was close.

Moments later she surged into orgasm again, crying out his name as her muscles stroked him harder and harder until he fell over that cliff too. Lightheaded with desire, he continued thrusting inside her, consumed by her as they both found release. Pleasure surged out to all his nerves in a wave of sensation until he was fully sated and barely breathing.

When he came down from his high, he collapsed on the bed, careful not to crush her. Instead he rolled to the side and tugged her into his arms.

She buried her face against his chest and inhaled deeply. When she pulled back she said, "Can't believe you tried to fight *that.*"

"I had reasons." He dropped a kiss on her lips, grateful that it was his right again. God, he'd missed her lips.

"Dumb reasons."

He laughed lightly at her haughty tone. "I was trying to do the right thing."

"Well, let me tell you, that was definitely the right thing." She threw a leg over his hip and wrapped her arm around him so they were chest to chest, skin to skin. "And I hope we do it again tonight."

"Are you too sore?" He gently traced his fingers over the light bruising on her throat. It was faint and might not develop into more.

"No... Maybe. We'll see," she finally murmured, her lips curving up in a sweet, satisfied smile.

He just held her tighter, resting his chin against the top of her forehead. An icy wind whipped outside against the window but they were safe and warm inside, exactly where he wanted to be. Tomorrow he was sure they'd have shit to deal with. But for now, he was going to savor this quiet moment with the woman he loved.

* * *

Gage tensed as he saw someone approaching the back of his truck... Wait, was that Nova in the rearview mirror? He glanced at his cell phone when it started blaring the song "Girl on Fire." "What the hell?" he muttered to himself, even as he realized that Nova must have changed the ring tone. That was what he got for giving her his code. "Hey, Nova," he said, glancing in the side mirror now. Yep, that was her.

That damn protectiveness swept through him as he realized the time. It was close to midnight. She wouldn't be here this late unless there was an emergency.

"Hey, jerk face. I'm about to knock on the passenger door of your truck. Don't shoot me." She ended the call.

A second later Nova, bundled up as if it was a snowpoca-lypse and holding two steaming to-go cups of something, knocked on the window. He quickly unlocked the doors and she slid inside. "What the hell are you doing here?" The question came out harsher than he'd intended.

"Well hello to you too, jerk face." She handed him one of the cups, then the other. "Hold mine," she said as she un-wrapped her scarf and pulled a sparkly cap with blue snow-flakes off her head. Her long, dark hair tumbled around her face and shoulders in waves he fantasized about wrapping around his fists as he tasted that sassy mouth.

"Why do you keep calling me jerk face? And seriously, why are you here?" Not that he was complaining. And it was pretty clear there wasn't an emergency or she would have said so al-ready.

"I think you can figure out *why* you're a jerk face." She lifted one of her dark eyebrows as she held out a hand. He gave her the cup. "And I'm here to keep you company. I heard you got stuck on security duty tonight."

"That's not part of your work description," he snapped, then felt like that jerk face that she kept calling him.

The hurt that flickered in her gaze stabbed him right in the chest.

"Sorry, I'm just tired and testy. I'm *glad* you're here." More than he would admit. But he was surprised to see her.

She let out a little sniff, but he knew he was forgiven when she smiled at him. "So have you seen anything exciting?"

"No. Just a couple neighbors bringing their dogs out to pee. So...what's up with the jerk face comments?"

"Seriously? You can't figure that out, Mr. Smarty-Pants?"

"Is it because I didn't want you going to the school for the faux interview?"

"Ding, ding, ding." She rolled her eyes. "What was that about anyway?"

He lifted a shoulder. "It didn't seem necessary." God, she smelled so good, like vanilla cookies. And in the interior of his truck, it seemed amplified, wrapping around him and making him crazy. "What is this?" he asked, lifting the cup.

"Taste it and find out."

He narrowed his gaze at her but did as she said. It was a latte, his favorite. "Thank you."

She shrugged and took a sip of her own drink. "So, you didn't actually answer my question. I know you guys didn't end up needing to go to the schools anyway because of the FBI, but why didn't you want me going? It wasn't dangerous."

"Just in case it *was* dangerous, I didn't want you involved." It was the truth, and he found that he didn't like the thought of lying to her.

"I don't know if I should be mad or not."

"Why would you be mad?"

"You wouldn't tell Skye not to go."

"I wouldn't tell her not to do anything." He valued his balls too much.

Nova laughed, the sound throaty and sensual. "Okay, fair enough. Bad example. Are you sure that wasn't some sexist thing with you not wanting me to go?"

"No. I mean yes, I'm sure it wasn't." Maybe it was, a little bit, but he felt too damn protective of her. And he didn't want her in any dangerous situation, end of discussion.

She let out a little *hmm* sound, but didn't push him any further.

"How many of my ring tones did you change?"

She grinned. "Guess you're going to have to find out."

Laughing, he took another sip of the drink and glanced across the street. Brooks had turned on the exterior lights and

Darcy had a security system. A good one too, courtesy of Brooks. He'd had the thing installed when they'd been together. And Gage was monitoring it when she was gone. He had an alert system set up to send his phone a message if any door or window in her house was opened while she wasn't there. Gage seriously doubted that Polzin would be stupid enough to come after her tonight, especially when Markov would be looking for him, but they were still taking all precautions.

"So have you heard any news from Leighton's Fed friend?"

"No. But they've got security set up at all the schools."

"Good. I got a call from Skye earlier. Sounds like she and Colt will be headed back tomorrow or Saturday."

Gage simply nodded. Skye had called him too. It turned out that their easy job wasn't as easy as they'd planned, but they were wrapping things up. He was glad. The office wasn't the same without the two of them.

"You think anything is going on with Leighton and his Fed friend?" Nova's question surprised him.

He turned to look at her. "Why?"

She simply shrugged. "Just curious."

"I'm not sure." Leighton had seemed at ease with the woman, but Gage hadn't been able to tell if there had been anything romantic between the two of them. Ever since getting out of the Marines, Leighton had been quiet, withdrawn. But when he'd been around Hazel, he'd come out of that self-induced shell, and Gage had seen a glimmer of the man he'd once been. But that didn't mean there was anything romantic between him and the special agent.

Nova simply made another *hmm* sound and Gage didn't push her. He didn't think she was interested in Leighton, and if she was, he sure as hell didn't want to know. He didn't need to analyze why he even cared.

Gage knew damn well why he did.

CHAPTER EIGHTEEN

—A sister is a little bit of childhood that can never be lost.—

"How was sleeping here last night?" Darcy asked her sister. It was the first time they'd had a chance to talk about anything non-rehearsal-dinner-related all day, and the dinner was finally winding down. At least she'd heard from her mechanic that her brakes showed signs of natural erosion. It made her feel a little better, but overall not so much. Especially since Brooks wasn't impressed by the news at all.

"Who cares about that? How are you doing? You've been like a busy little bee all night." Her sister made a buzzing sound.

Darcy laughed lightly and smoothed a hand down the taffeta of her navy blue dress. For some reason, the color seemed to make her green eyes a little darker. And she was vain enough to admit that she knew it looked good on her and had worn it for Brooks. "I'm fine. Promise."

"Have the police contacted you?"

She shook her head. "No, not that I really expected them to." They would only contact her if they'd found something. And in the last week she'd filed three reports. One for the mugging, one for the weird issue with her car—which appeared not to be sabotaged after all, *allegedly*—and one because of Polzin's assault. If she never had to see another cop again that would be fine with her. Semyon had told her not to worry, that Oleg would turn up, but according to Brooks—

and his team's eavesdropping—even Gage hadn't been able to find the man and Semyon truly didn't know where Oleg was. That scared her.

Her sister bit down on her bottom lip.

"None of that. You're getting married tomorrow. Then you're going on your honeymoon." And for that, Darcy was very grateful. If anything did happen with Peter's father, she wanted her sister and Peter out of town. And from what Brooks and the Feds seemed to think, Peter wasn't remotely involved in whatever his father was. Darcy prayed it was true.

"I'm allowed to worry about my big sister." Suddenly Emma's eyes filled with tears. "I really wish Mom was here."

"I do too. But if you cry, I'm going to cry too." Tears started to prick her eyes. "And then my makeup is going to get all messed up."

Emma started laughing, just like Darcy intended. "I don't know if I've properly thanked you—"

"Just stop right there. You don't have to thank me for anything."

"Except that I do. You've gone above and beyond what a wedding planner would do, let alone a big sister. And I don't just mean for this wedding. You're the best friend I ever could have imagined or hoped for, and I'm lucky enough to call you my family."

Oh, hell. Now Darcy did let a few tears fall. Not that she had a choice. Emotion swept through her at Emma's words and she swiped at her cheeks. "Well everything you said, right back at you. And get this all out now because there will be no more tears tomorrow."

Emma laughed again, and this time it was watery. "Uh oh," she murmured, looking past Darcy.

She turned to see both Peter and Brooks heading for them with worried expressions on their faces. For a moment, she thought something was wrong until Brooks reached them and said, "Are you okay?" with panic in his voice.

At the same time, Peter said to Emma, "What's wrong?"

Emma snorted. "Nothing."

"But you're crying." Brooks looked between the two of them, concern in every line of his serious expression.

Darcy stepped closer to him and wrapped her arm around his middle. She was so damn grateful he'd come tonight. She couldn't have kept him away anyway, not with the threat of Polzin, but it had been nice to have him at her side. Who was she kidding? It was nice to have him in her life again. Though nice was such a lame word. Especially after what they'd shared together last night. "These are just sister-related tears. Nothing to be alarmed about."

Peter didn't look convinced as he wrapped his arm around Emma's shoulders. "I'd like to say goodbye to a few people even though we'll see them tomorrow."

Emma nodded and looked at Darcy. "We're going to be staying here again tonight."

"I'll be back bright and early tomorrow morning. All the dresses are ready and—"

"You don't need to go over everything," Emma said, laughing. "I was just going to say that the offer to stay here is still open. Even though I know you won't take it," she said, looking at Brooks.

"I'll see you in the morning," Darcy said. There was no way in hell she would stay here. When her sister was out of earshot, she turned to Brooks. She felt safe with him here watching over her. "There are just a few things I need to take care of and then I'll be ready to go."

"No rush." He dropped a quick kiss on her mouth and stepped back. "I'll be in the kitchen if you need me."

It was a central enough location to meet. As he walked away, she scanned the room. The linens that had been used tonight would be removed from the tables and replaced with fresh ones in the morning. But they would be keeping most of the table settings and adding even more tables to accommodate how many people would be there.

She spotted Semyon talking to a man she didn't recognize from the rehearsal dinner. And she knew everyone who had been there, at least by face.

Standing near one of the open French doors, the man had on a long peacoat and his hands were in his pockets as he spoke quietly with Semyon. It was hard to read Semyon's expression. He didn't look angry, but his shoulders were tight, his body language tense.

She was curious who the man was, but had too much to deal with right now. As she turned away, she saw Brooks near one of the other doorways, his phone in his hand. He was looking at the screen, but for some reason she was under the impression he was taking a picture of Semyon. Or maybe it was the other man. She made a mental note to ask him about it later as Mr. Singh approached her, a smile on his face.

It was time to start wrapping things up tonight. Because as soon as she was done, she was headed back to her place with Brooks. That thought made her smile. No matter what else was going on, she was still reeling from what had happened between them last night.

They hadn't exactly spelled out what they were as of now, but it wasn't casual. She wasn't certain she wanted to put a label on them just yet. They still had a lot of catching up to do. Not to mention this whole mess with Semyon, Polzin and the FBI.

Her life had turned upside down in a matter of days, but no matter what, she was so glad that Brooks was back in it.

* * *

Semyon did his best to hide his frustration at Kuznetsov's appearance at his son's rehearsal dinner. "Do you really want to have this conversation here?" he asked quietly, aware of Darcy talking to the caterer and a few others still lingering nearby. The majority of the wedding party would be staying here for the night, with the exception of Darcy. But he understood that she preferred to be with her boyfriend.

"When I heard Oleg had gone missing, I thought I should check in with you directly." Kuznetsov was impossible to read, but Semyon knew that if the other man was aware of what he had planned, he would be dead. There would be no conversation like this.

"It's under control."

"Under control, like talking to the police?" His accent was thicker as he spat the last word.

Semyon motioned toward the open French door, preferring to take the rest of this conversation outside. Once they were out on the lanai, he switched to Russian. "I had no choice but to go to the police station. My soon-to-be daughter-in-law's sister has a wealthy, powerful boyfriend. She would have told him, had I insisted she *not* go to the police. It would have seemed strange."

His eyes narrowed slightly. "Who is her boyfriend?"

"Not in the same business as us. He's legitimate. Brooks Alexander."

Kuznetsov nodded slowly. "I vaguely recognize the name."

"Everything is under control, I promise. I will find Oleg and take care of him." As soon as Oleg was found, he would die.

"What happened with him?"

"He couldn't keep his head on straight." Semyon shrugged. "I think he has an obsession with the woman, the sister." He shrugged again, as if he had no concerns. "He will be found and dealt with."

"Bring him to me when you find him. By disrespecting you, he has disrespected me. I will make an example of him." For the first time since Kuznetsov had shown up tonight out of the blue, he gave a cold smile.

Semyon nodded even though he had no intention of doing such a thing. "Of course. I hope I will see you tomorrow at the wedding?" It was the only reason Kuznetsov was in town, and why Semyon had to use the man's proximity to his advantage. Somehow he kept his words steady and even, when all he wanted to do was gut the man right now and watch him bleed out all over the floor.

"I will be there. And I expect our problem to be taken care of soon. I have no time for loose ends." There was a not so subtle threat in his voice.

"Of course," he said again, keeping his expression as neutral as possible. Tomorrow one of his men would plant the explosive device in Kuznetsov's vehicle and, more importantly, make sure he died. Semyon himself would make sure Dimitri was covered in explosive residue. He would be at the wedding as part of Kuznetsov's security so making sure his hands and coat were covered in it would be simple. Someone had to take the fall for these crimes and Dimitri was simply unlucky.

Semyon tried not to think about all the people who would die at the carnival tomorrow. They were simply collateral damage. It was the only way to make sure Kuznetsov died, that his son Peter was safe. He needed to do this on his own turf, and things had aligned so perfectly he simply couldn't pass up this opportunity. Not after years of planning.

CHAPTER NINETEEN

—Mine to protect.—

Darcy slipped her thick coat on and buttoned it up as she headed to the front door of Semyon's mansion. It was thankfully time to go home. Brooks had texted her that he'd gone to get his vehicle. She was surprised he hadn't waited for her in the kitchen, but she knew he must have a reason. As she stepped outside, there were two men she didn't recognize.

Both were wearing dark suits and one was smoking a cigarette. Both had close-cropped haircuts, making them look like they might be military. Or former military, she guessed.

The one on the left subtly nudged the other one and they both looked her up and down, as if she was naked. The first said something to the other in a language she didn't understand. And the second laughed, giving her a lecherous grin. Normally she would have ignored something like that. But she was pretty certain that neither man worked for Semyon. He might be a bad person, but with the exception of Polzin, no one had ever made her feel uncomfortable. And tonight, she was at the end of her rope dealing with bullshit. She wouldn't smile and be polite.

Out of the corner of her eye, she saw Brooks's Tesla Roadster coming up the long driveway. Instead of driving his normal truck, he'd opted to drive what she considered his obscenely expensive "rich guy vehicle." She wasn't sure if seeing him gave her the courage or not, but she took a step toward them. "Do you need something?" she snapped, anger in each word.

They both straightened and the one who had spoken shook his head as he dropped his cigarette. Before she could respond, or before either of the men could, Brooks was out of the driver's side and moving toward her.

He shot the men a dismissive glance before placing his hand at the small of her back and helping her into the passenger seat. She didn't need the help, but she was definitely glad for his presence.

Surprising her, after he shut the door, he took a few steps toward them. She couldn't hear their conversation, but neither man appeared tough while talking to him. Less than a minute later, he was in the driver's seat and pulling away from the front of the house.

"What did you say to them?"

He shrugged.

"Really? You're not going to tell me?"

"Nope. Did they bother you?"

"Not really. Just two assholes. So why weren't you waiting in the kitchen? Is everything okay?"

"Yes and no. The Feds found a bomb at the elementary school." He let out a curse, shaking his head as he pulled out of the long driveway and onto the quiet street. "An elementary school."

Lead filled her insides as she sat back against the seat, suddenly cold again.

"It was set to go off tomorrow right in the middle of the carnival. It wasn't a remote type of thing, which is good. But still..." He shook his head.

"So what does this mean? Are they going to arrest Markov?"

"No. There's nothing tying it to him. And the Feds who were watching the school never saw anyone sneak in. They don't even have enough for a warrant to search his home. Not that I think he would be stupid enough to leave something at his home tying him to this."

"Jeez. That's scary." Even scarier that he could still be planning to do something else in the future. "What do you think he'll do when it doesn't go off?" she asked, even though there was no way Brooks could know. He seemed to understand her question was rhetorical and shrugged.

"I think the real question is, why is he doing it in the first place?"

"I…didn't think of that."

"The Feds have. And now that he's on their radar, they'll get him. Or if they don't, they'll make his life hell."

"All of this feels so unsatisfying." Obviously, she was glad there wouldn't be a bombing, but someone needed to be in jail. He nodded. When he didn't continue, she said, "Were you taking pictures of him earlier?"

"I was taking pictures of the man he was with."

"Feel like expanding on that?"

"No. But stay away from the man who was with him. He's not a good man." Each word came out tight and he gripped the steering wheel firmly.

She reached out and set a gentle hand on his leg. She wanted to ask who the guy was but Brooks didn't seem to want to talk about it. "Okay. I don't plan on spending much time over there anyway, not after tomorrow."

He set his hand over hers and squeezed. "There's something I need to tell you."

That lead felt even heavier in her belly. "What?"

"Leighton said his Fed friend talked about you potentially talking to Markov, or planting something in his house, trying to get him to say something to incriminate himself. Off the books. But if they could find something to use against him—"

"I could do that."

"*No*. I told them in no uncertain terms that it would never happen. I just wanted to let you know."

"I can talk to your Fed friend. Maybe—"

He glanced at her as he pulled up to a red light. "I'm not letting that happen. This isn't up for discussion." When she raised her eyebrows at his imperious tone, he continued. "I fucking love you, Darcy. I'm not letting you put yourself in danger. The Feds can do their job and put him in jail the right way. You went above and beyond by giving them information. You literally helped to stop the bombing because of what you passed on. You will not put yourself in any further danger. Period."

She had a lot to say about his dictatorial attitude, but the only words she'd really heard were "I fucking love you." How could he just drop that bomb in there with everything else? What was she supposed to say to that? She was open to more with him—*wanted* more with him. She wanted to be back to the way they were before everything got all messed up. But the last time she'd told him she loved him, made herself vulnerable, she'd gotten burned. And she still felt the remnants of it.

Silently, he looked over at her. Though he didn't say anything, it was clear he wanted her to respond to the bomb he'd just dropped.

But she wasn't touching that with a ten-foot pole. Not tonight. They'd literally just slept together for the first time in months last night. She wasn't even sure what their relationship was at this point. And he wanted to tell her that he loved her?

Was he trying to drive her insane? "Will you be going with me to the wedding tomorrow?"

"I can't believe you even asked that."

"Just wanted to make sure... I still can't tell my sister anything, can I?"

"No. Not now. The Feds can't risk Markov getting a whiff of anything off. Not while they're building a case against him."

And that was just something she would have to live with. Sighing, Darcy laid her head back against the leather seat and closed her eyes.

Everyone who would have been at that carnival was now safe. This would all be over with and behind her soon enough.

* * *

Brooks tightened his arm around Darcy's waist, pulling her back against his chest. She'd fallen asleep about ten minutes ago, but he was too restless. Even sex hadn't tired him out.

It was good news that the bomb had been found, but there were too many variables up in the air right now. And he really didn't like the fact that Kuznetsov had been at the rehearsal dinner last night. Well, he hadn't been at the dinner, but he'd shown up at the tail end when most people had left. The guy was supposed to be at the wedding, but him showing up at the dinner rubbed Brooks the wrong way so he'd passed that information on to Leighton's Fed friend, along with the images he'd snapped with his cell phone.

But there wasn't a whole hell of a lot they could do with it. Talking to someone wasn't a crime. Planting an explosive device was. Other than Darcy's word, they had *nothing* linking it back to Markov. Or Kuznetsov, for that matter.

And Polzin was still out there somewhere. Even Gage hadn't been able to track him down. The man had fallen completely off the grid, which meant he'd been prepared for the eventuality that he might have to run one day. His face hadn't shown up on any facial recognition software, and he wasn't using any of his credit cards. That wasn't too surprising. He would have known that Markov would be able to track him that way. There was the possibility that Markov had found and simply killed him in the last couple hours, but Brooks doubted it.

If it had been possible, Brooks would have broken into Polzin's place himself. But ever since he'd disappeared, the Feds had increased their surveillance of his house. There would be no sneaking in. Not that Brooks thought it really mattered. A man like that would have a backup plan. More than one.

While all of that weighed on his mind, the main thing bothering him was that Darcy hadn't responded at all when he'd told her that he still loved her. Of course, he'd more or less snapped it out in the middle of a conversation. He could have used a little more finesse.

But she didn't say *anything*.

He wasn't sure what to think about that. He didn't like it.

She'd still been intimate with him when they returned to her place, initiating things and dragging him into the shower with her. Not that she'd actually had to drag him; he'd gone willingly and had been planning to join her anyway. But he liked that she'd been the initiator.

Sighing, he closed his eyes and tried to force himself to sleep. It was difficult with her bare back and ass snug against his chest and cock. But he wouldn't change a thing.

At the sound of his phone buzzing across the nightstand, he gently rolled away from her and picked it up.

A text from Leighton. *Darcy's place is secure. Haven't seen any movement.*

Tonight, Leighton had volunteered to keep an eye on her place. This wasn't a long-term option, and if Polzin wasn't caught by the end of tomorrow night, he would insist Darcy move to the ranch, at least temporarily.

He wanted the opposite of temporary, but knew exactly how well that would go over with her. At least the wedding would be over tomorrow, and while she might still have other clients, he didn't care; she could work from his place.

Brooks texted back. *Thanks. Any news from your Fed friend?*

Nothing new. Still don't have enough for a warrant. But they'll be keeping an eye on him. Hazel said thank you for the pictures, BTW. They knew the two men were linked, but seeing K in M's house solidified it.

Go ahead and get out of here. Her place is locked down tight. And we'll be heading out in a few hours. There was no sense in Leighton sticking around. Brooks could take care of Polzin if the man was stupid enough to try to break into her place.

Nah. I'm good. I'll stick around a couple more hours. Hazel said I could tag along tomorrow at the carnival. They want to keep an eye on everything even though they already found the explosives.

Brooks raised his eyebrows. That was definitely against FBI protocol, bringing a civilian in. But he decided not to comment. Wasn't his business. *I'll be at the wedding with Darcy. You guys know where to find me if you need me.*

Before he'd put his phone down, he got another text.

This time from Gage. *Still no news on Polzin but I've been digging deeper into his past. Turns out he has a sealed juvie record. Issues with harassing girls, not understanding the word no. And one of those girls died in a car crash. Was deemed an accident. No way to know whether or not true.*

Before Brooks could text back, another stream of texts came through.

Started digging even deeper into his adult life. Things not on the normal radar. Found a few links between him and two women who have both died by car accidents. Both deemed accidental. The links weren't obvious and the cops never made the connection. Should I send the information to your detective friend Hernandez? Or the Feds?

Brooks thought for only a moment then texted back, *Both.* He was almost positive Hernandez wasn't involved in anything. It looked as if Turner had been the only dirty cop. And now he was murdered. A dead end to them, unfortunately.

If women who'd somehow angered Polzin had ended up dead via car accidents...it seemed clear that he'd been behind the tampering of Darcy's brakes. The mechanic had verified that they'd been worn down, though he hadn't been able to swear it hadn't been intentional. Still, Brooks had all the proof he needed.

Sighing, he set his phone back down, wrapped his arm around Darcy again and pulled her close. If he wanted to be fully functioning tomorrow, he needed at least a few hours of sleep.

Because he wasn't letting Polzin get to Darcy again. He'd kill the man first.

CHAPTER TWENTY

—Today will be one of those days where even my
coffee needs a coffee.—

Wearing a silly tank top with *Maid of Honor* and a skull and crossbones underneath the text—a gift from Emma—Darcy was officially ready for this wedding to be over. Her sister was supposed to be married in two hours and while everything was going according to plan, an underlying tension hummed through her, steady and annoying. Like bees living in her skull.

Looking down at her clipboard while simultaneously texting one of the vendors on her phone, she stepped into the kitchen to find Semyon on the phone. One of the caterers was laying out cranberry and brie bite appetizers.

He nodded briefly at her and continued talking in Russian. She frowned, wondering why he wasn't speaking in English. With everything going on, she decided to play detective and press record on her phone. She seriously doubted he would say anything of use, but just in case, decided to record his conversation. Brooks would probably be annoyed with her, especially after his "you're not getting involved" attitude last night. Not that she was particularly mad at him about it. She understood that he was protecting her. And she loved that about him.

God, she needed to tell him that she still loved him too. It was just that so much had happened, tensions were still high, and so much was up in the air right now. And okay, she was a big ole chicken. They'd barely gotten back together and yeah, she was scared about the future.

Shaking her head at herself, she flipped the page on her clipboard and did another run-through of items to be done in the next hour. Her sister's hair, nails, and everything possible was already done. Emma was the one person she didn't need to worry about. Darcy's hair and makeup were done too, and she would put her dress on in about an hour. But she had a few things to take care of first and didn't want to risk getting anything on the dress.

"Darcy, did you hear anything I said?" Semyon was now standing two feet in front of her and frowning.

Oh crap. She hadn't even realized he'd moved. "Ah, no, sorry."

"The priest is here. He just arrived. Is there anything you need from me?"

She shook her head. "No. I just have a few more things to check on, but we're all good."

"Good. Make sure you stay on the grounds." There was a touch of concern in his voice, and once again, she found herself conflicted about him.

Okay, maybe not conflicted. Not since the Feds had found that bomb. That was something only a monster could take part in. But it was still hard to reconcile who he truly was and who he appeared to be to the world. "I will. I won't be straying far from the house anyway." She knew why he was concerned. It had to do with Oleg Polzin, and she had no desire to run across him.

As he left the room, she stopped the recorder and turned to one of the catering staff. A short conversation later, she hurried out of the room and up the nearest set of stairs.

And nearly ran into Brooks—who was looking incredibly handsome in his custom-made Armani suit. Her mouth watered as she drank in the sight of him. For a moment, she forgot that she'd come up here looking for him, let alone was able to remember her first name.

He'd complained more than once in the past about wearing suits, but no matter his feeling on the subject, suits agreed with him. His broad shoulders strained against the fine material. Every inch of him was delicious, the suit merely his camouflage. Because underneath it, he was a trained warrior. One who would do anything to protect those he cared about.

She grabbed him by the lapels of his jacket and pulled him close. "I want to push you into the nearest room and have my wicked way with you."

It was clear she'd surprised him, but his expression quickly morphed into his charming, cowboy grin. "I'm obliged to let you do that," he murmured.

The low tone sent a rush of heat between her legs. She reached for the handle on the nearest door, clearly having completely lost her mind. "After this wedding, I swear, I'm going to strip—"

She paused as Audrey, her sister's other bridesmaid, stepped out of the room Emma was using as a dressing room. She smiled when she saw Darcy. "Hey, I'm going to go grab a couple glasses of champagne. Do you want one?"

She shook her head. "No, but I'll join you soon."

Audrey glanced between her and Brooks then winked at Darcy. "Take your time."

Darcy laughed as Audrey hurried down the hallway. Once she disappeared down the stairs, Darcy whispered, "It's probably nothing, but I overheard Semyon talking in Russian in the kitchen. So I recorded his side of the conversation. Just in case." She kept her voice low, so only Brooks could hear her, even though no one else was in the hallway.

Brooks glanced around then took her hand and opened one of the doors. She'd gotten a tour of the house before and was fairly familiar with the layout, so she knew it would be a guest room. They were greeted by a queen-sized bed and a lot of earth tones.

"I'm going to send the recording to Gage," he said, taking her phone. "He should be able to do something with it." In complete serious mode, his fingers flew across the screen as he sent the message off.

His jaw tightened as he looked down at the screen. His profile was enough to make her panties melt. Even the custom suit couldn't hide the raw masculinity and barely civilized edge lurking beneath.

When he looked up and met her gaze, her breath caught in her throat. Raw hunger sparked in the dark depths. "Keep looking at me like that and I'm going to fuck you right here." His words were a savage growl.

"Promise?" She took a step toward him. Right now, she didn't care that her hair and makeup were done. He could mess her up all he wanted.

They met each other halfway, and his big hand landed on her hip. His fingers flexed, holding her in place.

As if she had any desire to leave. It was completely irresponsible, but she didn't care. If he wanted to get naked right here, right now, she was pretty sure there was a lock on the door.

"Darcy—"

He broke off as his phone started ringing. Cursing once, he reached into his pocket and pulled his phone out and answered on the second ring. "Yeah..." A few tense moments, then, "I'm on my way."

In the span of a few seconds, his body language had changed drastically. All of his muscles were pulled taut and she could see...something in his expression. She wasn't sure how to describe it. He looked like a warrior. And it made her wonder if this was what he was like in battle mode.

"I have to go. Don't leave the grounds."

"Is it Polzin?"

"No. I wouldn't leave unless I had to. I might not be back for the wedding."

"That's fine." She knew without a doubt that he wouldn't leave unless it was an emergency, and right now she couldn't help but be worried about him. She'd never seen him like this before. "Can you tell me what's wrong?"

"No, but I'll call you as soon as I can." He crushed his mouth to hers for less than a second, but she felt it all the way to her toes.

"Be safe," she rasped out as he yanked the door open.

He nodded once and was gone in a blur of motion.

What the hell had just happened? She'd wanted to push, to ask for more details, but it had been clear that he needed to leave.

She just hoped he stayed safe.

* * *

Heart racing, Brooks tore down the driveway in his Tesla. As he cleared the gate, he slid his Bluetooth in.

Gage answered on the first ring. "I'm patching Leighton in right now."

The phone rang once then Leighton was on the line. "The Feds are on their way. But they're about twenty minutes out. I'm with Hazel. How close are you guys?"

Brooks took a sharp left at the end of the road. "Six minutes, give or take."

"Same," Gage snapped and a horn blared in the background.

Brooks slowed down as he reached a stop sign, then tore through it when he saw no one coming from any direction.

"You're sure about the translation?" Leighton asked.

Of course Gage was sure, Brooks thought.

"Nova is certain." Gage's words were clipped. "And I ran it through a translation program."

"What's the plan?" Brooks asked.

"I'm bringing fake FBI credentials," Gage said. "We should be able to get everybody out of the church. Then when the real Feds show up, they can find the bomb."

Yeah, if the thing didn't go off in the meantime. Brooks's heart kicked up a notch as he took another turn. Red light ahead. He swerved around an idling car, and pulled into the lane for oncoming traffic. At the four-way light, he raced into the intersection, ignoring the blast of multiple horns.

It was a risk for Gage to bring fake IDs, but Brooks also understood that it was the only way to get the church cleared out. According to what he'd said on Darcy's recording, apparently Semyon had a backup plan in place in case things went south with the first location. And he knew that the school bombing had been compromised, according to the overheard conversation. It sounded as if he believed Polzin had been the one to compromise it, so at least Semyon didn't know about the FBI involvement yet.

Unfortunately, he'd been confirming with someone about an explosive device at one of the other locations they'd found listed on Turner's computer. It was a private middle school that was also connected to a Catholic church. And there was a wedding there today. The *wedding* was the target. Not the school.

"The church will be packed," Gage said.

"Hazel wants you guys to wait until they get there," Leighton said. "She doesn't want you two to become casualties. They'll evacuate the church themselves and send in a—"

There was a distinct clicking sound. "I hung up on him," Gage said. "You want to wait for them?"

"Hell no."

"We might not come out of this. Wedding's in twenty minutes. And Markov didn't say when it was rigged to go off. For all we know, it could be remote detonation."

Brooks didn't respond. Instead he said, "Why didn't the Feds have someone watching all the locations?"

"No shit," Gage muttered.

Brooks had a feeling someone's head was going to roll for that oversight.

Less than three minutes later, Brooks screeched to a halt in front of a row of cars at the front of the small chapel entrance. As far as churches went, it was small. Right in the middle of the historic downtown district. Near expensive homes and established neighborhoods.

As he jumped out of his vehicle, Gage parked next to him right in the middle of the street. They were blocking anyone who might try to get by and he gave zero fucks about it.

Gage tossed him a navy blue jacket with FBI emblazoned on the back. Then he tossed him a black wallet with a fake ID and fake FBI credentials.

"This shit could get us put in jail," Brooks muttered.

"Whatever." Gage raced toward the double glass doors right next to Brooks.

Brooks yanked one of the doors open and came face-to-face with the bride and six bridesmaids, all in matching pale blue dresses.

"Ma'am, I need you all to exit quickly and move across the street. Move as far away from the building as possible," Brooks snapped out.

An older Hispanic woman next to the bride stepped forward, her expression haughty. "Young man—"

"Special Agent Blake," he shouted, using Hazel's last name. There's an explosive device in this building. Exit the building now. Now!" The woman gasped but he ignored her, moving through the narthex into the back of the church.

A priest was at the front with a man, clearly the groom, and the rest of the wedding party. And the church was indeed full. "Start with the back rows," Brooks said to Gage. "I'm going to talk to the priest and start getting everyone in the front out. There have to be more exits than the back." And without knowing where the device was, they simply needed everyone out of the building and as far away as possible.

Racing toward the front, Brooks pulled out his fake badge as he reached the priest, who was frowning as he moved down the steps of the altar toward him. "Father, we have a situation. And our time is limited. We've received a tip that there is an explosive device in this building." He spoke in quiet, even tones. "Backup is on the way. But we need to get everyone out of here now in a timely fashion and without panic. Can you get your parishioners to listen?" he asked.

A low murmur of panicked voices had already started and when Brooks turned around, he saw that those in the back were listening to Gage and moving out the back doors, but it was clear everyone was confused.

The man's eyes widened, but he nodded. "Of course." He pointed to the left and right of him. "We have two more exit doors here." Then without any further instructions, he stepped forward and spoke loudly, ordering the first six rows to get up and head to the left exit. Then he ordered the next six rows to move to the right exit.

All right, Father. "Are there any more people in here? Custodians or—"

The man paled. "The children. There are a few children upstairs in the nursery—"

"Where?"

"Second floor. Through there." He pointed behind him to an almost hidden door.

He'd barely finished before Brooks broke away from him. "Did you hear that?" he asked Gage, glad they'd kept their earpieces in.

"Yeah. I'm right behind you."

It didn't matter that Brooks and Gage hadn't served together—not directly. He knew without a doubt that Gage would have his back no matter what. The man was just as trained.

And they had to get those kids out of there.

Taking the stairs two at a time, his legs ate up the distance as he raced to the second floor. "Third door on the right," he said as he reached the open doorway where laughing little voices trailed out.

A woman in her early twenties was sitting on the floor with three kids playing a game. One set of twin girls. And another girl who might be their sister. All had to be under five years old. She looked startled when she saw him and shoved to her feet. "Wh—"

"I'm with the FBI. We need to get you out of here now. The church is being evacuated. I don't have time to explain. You're all in danger. Is there anyone else here?"

For a moment she was frozen, then nodded. "Ah, little Xavier is in the bathroom," she said, pointing to another doorway. As if on cue, Brooks heard the toilet flush.

"Go with my partner." Brooks motioned to Gage, who'd just hurried into the room, fake ID out. "Now. There's no time to waste."

Nodding, she scooped up one of the little girls. And Gage picked up the twins.

"I'm going to grab the other kid. We're right after you."

As they hurried out, Brooks pushed the bathroom door open. A small boy, who might be six, was standing on a stool and washing his hands at the sink. He frowned in the mirror when he saw Brooks and turned to face him. "Who are you?" he demanded.

"I'm the police," he said, because he figured the kid would understand that more than the FBI.

"Liar! My daddy is a cop."

Ah hell. There was no time to do this. Brooks picked the kid up in one swoop.

"Stranger danger!" the kid shouted as Brooks tossed him over his shoulder. Little fists pounded against his back and he almost felt bad for the kid.

"I'm taking you to your mommy, kid!"

"Liar! You don't even know my name! Stranger daaaannnnnnnger!" His shrieks pierced Brooks's eardrums as he hurried back down the stairs.

Instead of racing toward the back of the church, he hurried toward one of the nearest exits by the front, ignoring the continuing pounding of the kid's fists. As he burst out into the daylight, a rumble shook the ground.

No.

On a burst of speed, he sprinted down the little sidewalk toward the street. A crowd of people had gathered across it, all hovering with each other on a grassy patch. It wasn't far enough away. He waved at them with one hand. "Move back!"

People turned and started running. As he hit the pavement of the road, another rumble shook the ground before a piercing boom rent the air.

God, he hoped Gage and those kids were okay. His friend must have gone out another exit because Brooks didn't spot him.

Before the thought had fully formed, an explosion of concrete and stone burst out in every direction. A chunk of colorful glass flew past him as he dove toward the grass, tucking the kid under him as they hit. Using his arms to soften the blow, he tried to protect the kid from the force of their fall.

With his free hand, he covered the back of his head as debris fell around them. What felt like an eternity later, a deafening silence descended.

Shoving up, he looked down at the kid, whose eyes were wide. "You okay?"

The boy nodded, his eyes filled with tears. "I want my mommy," he whispered.

"I'll find her, I promise." Brooks just hoped that was a promise he could keep. Looking around, he saw that a few people had been injured, but mostly everyone looked okay. At least on his end.

Sirens sounded in the distance. *About damn time.* Standing, he lifted the kid with him and this time the boy curled up against him, tears in his eyes as he surveyed the destruction around them.

"Xavier!" A screaming, crying woman raced at them, her flowery black and peach dress ripped at the bottom, revealing a bleeding knee.

"Mommy!" The boy jumped from his arms. Okay, the kid was safe with his mom.

What kind of monster bombed a wedding? On the same day his own son was getting married? Brooks shook the thought off, would save his rage for later. He had to find Gage.

CHAPTER TWENTY-ONE

—Fuck this shit.—

Brooks stood by a huge oak tree across the street with Leighton and Gage. Leighton had taken the two FBI jackets and both their fake IDs and was planning to dispose of them very soon. So far they hadn't been questioned by the Feds—they'd had more important things to focus on—but Brooks knew that was coming.

"Doesn't seem to be any deaths," Leighton said quietly, relief on his face.

"Good... Here comes your friend." Brooks looked past Leighton to see Hazel moving toward them with a determined stride. In black pants and a thick jacket with FBI on the front and back, she looked grim.

As she reached them, however, her expression lightened ever so slightly. "Hey, guys. Hell of a thing you did. Thank you."

Brooks and Gage just nodded.

After a long pause, she glanced over her shoulder, then looked back at them. "So. According to Father Ramos, two men burst in with jackets and IDs and cleared everyone out."

Neither of them responded.

One of her eyebrows hiked up but she continued. "Maybe he's wrong, and two well-meaning citizens—not impersonating FBI agents—did this, but I'm pretty sure he's not. We can do this two ways..." She glanced over her shoulder again then back at them. "You can answer questions you probably don't want to answer, or you can get the hell out of here and we take all the credit for today. The two 'heroes' won't get any media attention either. We'll keep this locked down tight as a group effort. Unless you want to get your faces splashed across the—"

"Absolutely—"

"Not," Brooks finished for Gage.

Even Leighton let out a subtle sigh of relief after they answered. Brooks knew they wouldn't face any legal action. Not really. The Feds wouldn't do anything to two heroes even if they *had* impersonated agents—the Bureau would be crucified in the media for not stopping it themselves. But anyone related to Redemption Harbor Consulting did *not* want any media attention. This was a win-win for everyone.

Hazel nodded once. "Good answer. Here," she said, handing them a set of keys. "Your cars aren't going anywhere for a while."

Yeah, no shit. They were in the middle of everything, blocked in by an ambulance and other government vehicles.

She continued. "This is to my personal vehicle. Get the hell out of here."

"You gonna get in any trouble for this?" Leighton asked.

She snorted. "No. We thwarted a bombing at an elementary school and now there's absolutely no loss of life here. My boss is a dick who's got his *own* dick in a vise right now for something not related to this. He *needs* this win. He's not going to care how everyone made it out alive. I'll make it work. Trust me. And I'll make sure your vehicles are dropped off somewhere."

"I'll text you an address," Leighton said.

"What about Markov?" Brooks asked, not willing to leave just yet.

"We've got our techs out here combing over the explosion site. Once we're done, I'll let you know."

"He's into this up to his neck. You've got that recording."

"We do. But we're playing this by the books." She grinned. "Well, most of it. We want him *and* Kuznetsov." She lowered her voice even though they were across the street from everyone else and far enough away that no one could hear them.

"So?" Brooks asked. What the hell did that have to do with anything?

She lifted a shoulder. "We're going to bring him in. Just not right this instant. His son is getting married..." She glanced at her watch. "His son *is* married. He's not going anywhere right now. We'll bring him in tonight once the place has cleared out."

Brooks looked at Gage and Leighton. He didn't like it, but it was time to get out of there. "Fine. I'm heading over there now." He was a little scuffed up but he didn't care. He needed to see Darcy and he wouldn't be leaving her side. At least Peter and Emma would be leaving right after the wedding for their honeymoon and wouldn't be around for any of the follow-up bullshit. He knew it mattered to Darcy. She wanted her sister to be out of the media frenzy that would likely happen.

"Leighton knows where I'm parked." She turned to him, nodded once. "I've got my phone on me. Call if you need anything."

He nodded once before motioning to a side street. "Instead of trying to fight through the Feds and first responders, we can head that way." The Feds had been good about cordoning off the area and people were being let go as soon as they were cleared medically and had answered some brief questions. It was all very organized and efficient.

The street they headed down was small, with no sidewalks. Little cottages were interspersed with two-story homes that had to be at least five bedrooms. Everything was well-kept here—he was pretty sure his father owned a home or two in the historic district.

"Why the hell aren't they getting Markov now?" Gage asked, shaking his head.

"Hell," Brooks said suddenly as it hit him. "They want to bring him in *after* the wedding when Kuznetsov is gone. They don't want Kuznetsov to know. They're going to try to flip Markov on the bigger fish." At least that was his guess. He narrowed his gaze at Leighton, who hadn't responded but didn't look surprised. "Is that why?"

His friend shrugged. "Your guess is as good as mine. But...I wouldn't be surprised."

"Will she keep us out of this?"

"Yeah." No pause in his response. "From what I can tell, she hates her boss and will have no problem taking this win for her team."

"Good." The thought of being on the news as part of a res-cue—hell no. It could hurt everything they'd worked hard to create. Not only that, they definitely didn't want to get tangled up with the Feds. As it was, they were more on the periphery, which was exactly how they wanted it.

Plus, they'd given the FBI a huge win today without taking any of the credit. And anyone involved wouldn't forget that. It pissed him off that they might make a deal with Markov, especially considering what he'd tried to do, but they must really want Kuznetsov.

Right now, however, all he was concerned about was get-ting to Darcy. After what had just happened, he needed to hold her tight. He knew she was safe at the wedding with all those people, but that didn't ease the ache inside him. Nothing would, until she was in his arms.

* * *

"I'm not leaving you alone until you at least drink one glass of champagne," Audrey said.

Darcy laughed and took the extended glass from her sister's other bridesmaid. She really did adore the woman. "You're relentless."

"You've done so much for this wedding, and yes I know it's your job, but I've felt kind of useless. So my job is making sure you have a small buzz by the end of the night." She giggled, and Darcy was pretty sure Audrey already had one.

Darcy barked out a laugh, despite the ball of lead in her stomach. It had been hours and she hadn't heard from Brooks. Maybe that was a good thing. He'd told her that he might not make it back for the wedding and she was trying to be level-headed, but it was impossible not to worry about the man she loved. "You've been a great bridesmaid. Trust me, I've worked with enough and you've been wonderful for Emma. You show up when you're supposed to and don't complain about anything."

"Well she's easy to be wonderful for. Look at the two of them," Audrey murmured, staring across the dance floor at Peter and Emma, who were holding each other tight.

Darcy took a sip of her drink, pushing back the twinge of anxiety bubbling inside her. Even the Feds didn't think Peter was involved with his father, but it still bothered her, not being able to tell her sister anything. "I know."

"All right, I'll check in with you in a little bit and ply you with more to drink. Try not to work too hard." Then Audrey grabbed one of the nearest men standing by the dance floor and tugged him onto it with her.

Darcy nearly jumped at the feel of her phone buzzing in the pocket of her dress—and having the pocket specially sewn in had been ingenious, thank you very much. When she saw that it wasn't Brooks, but one of the catering staff, she pushed down the feeling of disappointment.

She frowned as she read the incoming text from one of the catering staff. *Something wrong with the front gate. Guard is having issue getting it opened. Help!*

Oh, hell. Of course something had to go wrong. She knew one of the catering vans had been leaving. The only thing she was really concerned about was if guests wanted to leave early and couldn't. This was not good. She would see if she could deal with this herself before involving Semyon. She simply couldn't be around him right now.

Winding her way through the tables where people were sitting and standing while many were dancing, she texted the person back. As she did, her phone buzzed, indicating an incoming call.

Brooks. She swiped her finger across the screen and answered immediately. She pressed a finger to one ear to drown out the noise. "Hey, are you okay?"

"Yes." He sounded tired, but if he was calling her, then he had to be okay. "I'm sorry for missing the ceremony."

She dropped her hand as she exited the ballroom. "Don't apologize. I know you would've been here if you could have." That much she knew about him. "Can you tell me what happened?"

"I will, but I want to do it in person. I'm headed there now."

In the foyer, she found one of Peter's coats in the coat closet and snagged it. Hers was upstairs and she wasn't going to waste time. It was black, puffy and came to her knees, looking ridiculous. But it was warm. "Good. I miss you," she said sincerely. Normally when she was in work mode all she focused on was that, work. But she'd been worried about

Brooks. And it felt good to tell him she'd missed him, to be open and honest.

"I miss you too." She went all melty inside at his words. "How was the ceremony?"

"Beautiful. The happy couple is now tearing it up on the dance floor and having a great time." And she loved seeing her sister so dang happy. They'd be cutting the cake in about half an hour and Darcy wasn't going to miss it.

"I'm glad...where are you?"

Her heels clicked against the stone driveway and she was sure he could hear the wind whipping against the phone. "Issue with the security gate. Coming outside to help the caterer."

Brooks was silent for a moment. "Can't someone else deal with it?"

"Ah...maybe. Why? It shouldn't take too long."

"I'll be there in a few minutes."

"Good. Hopefully we'll have the gate open by then. Otherwise you're going to be climbing it," she said jokingly.

"Who's with you?"

"No one. Oh, are you worried about Polzin?" She whispered the last word. And considering the gate wasn't even open, he wasn't getting inside unless he jumped it. And she doubted it, as Semyon had security all over the place.

"Yes," he said bluntly.

"I won't go outside the gates, how about that? I just want to check with the security guy and see what's going on." Then she would let one of the maintenance people deal with it. This was her sister's wedding, after all.

"Okay." His tone was muted.

"Is it really not okay?" She understood why he was worried, but the thought of Polzin showing up now was just insane. Unless there was something Brooks wasn't telling her?

He paused for a long moment. "It's just been a long day. Don't go outside the gates."

"Okay." As she reached the gate, she smiled because it was already open. "Well, I think the issue is solved, because—"

"What is it?"

Her feet were frozen to the spot as she stared past the open gate. Because of the huge brick wall she hadn't been able to see anything before, but the caterer was on the ground, hands secured behind her back, her expression terrified as she met Darcy's gaze. And one of the security men was lying next to her as well. It looked as if he was bleeding, but he was bound as well so he must be alive.

All her focus was on Polzin, however, who had a gun and was pointing it right at her. He was maybe twenty feet away. Oh God, where was Semyon's security? She'd seen men earlier but now she had tunnel vision, all her focus on the man with the gun.

"Get the fuck over here," he snapped. "And drop the phone!"

"He's here," she said into the phone. "He has a gun. I think he plans to put me in a white van with a sliding door." It wasn't the catering van, it was one she didn't recognize and didn't have a logo on the outside. He must have driven up in it. Maybe security assumed it was a catering van. She told Brooks everything she could think of because it would be up to him to stop this. The police certainly weren't going to be able to do anything.

Polzin started for her, his face red, and she dropped the phone. Every self-defense class she'd ever taken had warned to never get in a vehicle with anyone.

She tried to run, but it was impossible in her heels. Faster than she'd imagined, he was on her, grabbing her from behind. She let out a scream as he whipped her around to face him.

When she tried to fight back, he punched her in the stomach.

The shock of it made her double over and as she tried to suck in a breath, he wrenched her arms behind her back.

"Drop the weapon!" A man shouted from...somewhere.

Polzin pressed his gun to her temple. "Do anything stupid and she's dead," he shouted back to a man she couldn't even see. Then he was dragging her away.

She spotted a few guards moving out of the nearby trees, but no one seemed to have a good angle to take down Polzin—because she was in the way.

Oh, God! No, no, no.

She tried to scream again, but was in too much pain. She struggled against his hold even as he strapped ties on her wrists and yanked tight. Were the guards following? Pain cut through her wrists even as he shoved her through the van door. The interior was empty and hollowed out and her head slammed into one of the metal walls.

Pain ricocheted through her skull as she struggled to her knees. Without the use of her hands, it was almost impossible. Especially with her dress and jacket tangled around her.

By the time she'd pushed up, he was in the front seat. As the van jerked to life, she fell back, rolling and slamming face-first on the back of the door.

So much pain. She just hoped that Brooks got there in time.

CHAPTER TWENTY-TWO

—Keep calm and punch throats.—

"Faster!" Brooks shouted at Gage. He wished he was driving right now. Or maybe it was a good thing he wasn't because he wouldn't care who or what was in his way.

To give him credit, Gage didn't say a word. Just drove even faster as he neared the turnoff to Markov's street. As they made a sharp left turn, he gunned it again.

"That's the van!" he shouted, even though it was pretty obvious. But his adrenaline was racing.

The white van barreled toward them, toward the only exit from Markov's house. It was impossible to see the driver at this distance, but it had to be Polzin driving.

"What's the plan?" Gage asked, his voice tight.

Darcy was in the back, no doubt. She might get injured in a crash, but stopping this guy now was the only thing to do. They couldn't drag out a vehicle chase.

He pulled out his SIG. Shooting from a moving vehicle *at* a moving vehicle was difficult. But he was up to the task. Hell, he had the best training in the world for this.

Tuning everyone out, Brooks jumped up through the sunroof and aimed at the oncoming driver.

The wind ripped over him, but all of his focus was on the man behind the wheel. Twenty-five yards and counting.

More than anything, he wanted to aim straight for Polzin's head, but his center mass was a bigger target. And right now, there was no room for error. If he did miss, and the bullets flew past Polzin's head, they could strike Darcy.

The van suddenly jerked, swerving into their lane. Coming right toward them.

There was no time. Since any bullet that penetrated glass would automatically strike lower than aimed, he had to do this right. Staring down the sight, he aimed slightly higher than he wanted and pulled the trigger.

Glass fractured, spidering out, killing his visual of the driver. The van swerved sharply to the right, crashing into a brick mailbox with a sickening thud.

He had to get to Darcy!

"We'll get Polzin," Gage said, the tires of the SUV squealing as he jerked to a halt. "Get your girl."

SIG still in hand, Brooks was out of the passenger side and racing toward the back of the van. He trusted his guys to have his back no matter what. Still, as he yanked the door open, he had his weapon drawn.

It was unnecessary, as Gage was already at the driver's side, dragging Polzin through the door like a sack of garbage.

On her back, her jacket ripped and her forehead bleeding, Darcy rolled over and smiled at him. Actually smiled. "I knew you would come," she whispered.

Oh, hell. His entire body trembled as he put his weapon away and eased her up. Pulling out his pocket knife, he cut the zip ties on her wrists and lifted her up into his arms. He was never letting her go.

He didn't give a shit about Polzin now. The guy could bleed out for all he cared. "Are you okay?" He inwardly cursed as he asked it. Of course she wasn't.

"I hit my head a couple times, but I'm not seeing double. So that's gotta be good. Oh, he punched me and my stomach really hurts." Her voice was a little wobbly and he was worried she might have a concussion.

It took all of Brooks's self-control not to race over to where Polzin was and empty his magazine into the guy's head. Moving quickly, but not jostling her, he hurried to the SUV and gently set her inside. "Look at me," he said quietly, scanning her face and pupils.

She did and cupped his cheeks. "I love you. I should've told you earlier. I don't know why I was holding back. But I do. And I'm really scared of getting hurt again, but that's okay. Because you're worth it."

Oh God, maybe she really did have a concussion. He knew she had to be in pain but she seemed almost shocky. At least that was good but the adrenaline would wear off soon. Before he could respond, Leighton stepped up to them.

He glanced at Darcy, frowned, then focused on Brooks. "The guy isn't dead. He had on a vest. His ribs are probably broken, but he'll definitely make it."

Brooks reined in a snort. Polzin might have a temporary reprieve, but the man would be dead in a week. Brooks would see to it personally.

Leighton continued. "Called Hazel. We just gave the FBI another present. With Polzin kidnapping someone straight from this property, they've been able to expand their warrants to all of his known holdings and any they might stumble across in the course of this investigation. And," he looked over his shoulder, then back at Brooks, "they'll be arresting Markov soon."

He didn't want to talk about any of this right now, he just wanted to care for Darcy.

"Can they wait until after my sister's wedding?" Darcy asked, her voice trembling. "Or at least until after she's gone on her honeymoon? They're supposed to leave soon."

Brooks had a feeling that Emma wouldn't want to leave, even if Darcy insisted. He knew how close those two were. "Sweetheart, you don't worry about anything. Just sit tight. An ambulance is on the way," he said and gave his friend a sharp look. An ambulance better be on the way. And Leighton better stop talking about anything more in front of her.

"No, I'm fine," she insisted, shaking her head slightly. As she did, she winced. "Okay, bad move."

"Find a first aid kit," he said to his friend through gritted teeth. The only reason he wasn't shouting was because he didn't want to hurt Darcy's ears.

"You never responded," Darcy said, actually pouting as Leighton moved away. She stuck her bottom lip out and he thought she must have a concussion because he'd never seen this before.

"Responded to what?"

"I just told you I loved you."

"Honey, I love you too," he said quietly, gently cupping her cheeks. "I never stopped. And I'm never going to stop. You are it for me, darlin'," he murmured.

"I love it when you go all cowboy on me and call me darlin'," she said softly.

"Then I'll call you darlin' for the rest of our lives."

She closed her eyes and leaned back against the seat. "That better not be a proposal. Because I want a real one. With flowers. Maybe even fireworks."

He laughed even as he grasped her shoulders. "Open your eyes."

"I'm not going to fall asleep. I just hoped that if I closed my eyes, maybe I would wake up and this would all be a nightmare. Not the part with you, just the part with that psycho who tried to kidnap me."

Despite the situation, he laughed again. It was a miracle she was holding up so well, but all things considered he wasn't surprised. Part of her job was staying cool under pressure and clearly she was good at it.

He was never going to grow tired of this woman. Of that he had no doubt. He just hoped he could keep her as entertained for the rest of their lives as she would clearly keep him.

When he turned, Gage approached, a satisfied grin on his face. "Polzin is passed out."

"Passed out or knocked out?" Brooks had resisted going over to see the asshole on the other side of the crashed van because he hadn't trusted himself not to kill him.

Gage's grin grew. "Same difference. His face met the pavement. Repeatedly."

Before Brooks could respond, multiple sirens split the air. He was also aware of several of Markov's guards who'd converged on the area. He ignored them.

He didn't care what Darcy wanted, she was going to the hospital. He had a feeling she'd argue, but it was happening. He wanted her far away from this place. And he wanted to make sure she didn't have a concussion or other injuries.

His heart beat just a little faster than normal as he sat on the seat and pulled her into his lap. He needed to hold her.

Darcy curled right up against him, laying her head on his shoulder. "I'm not closing my eyes to sleep," she said. "Promise."

"What's your pain level?"

"Honestly...I feel okay. Which is probably the adrenaline talking."

She might be right. Brooks, who could actually lower his heartbeat out in the field, couldn't do a damn thing about the way his heart raced right now. Not when the woman he loved had come so close to being torn from his life.

He wasn't certain he'd ever get over what happened. Ever get over seeing that maniac tearing down the road and knowing she was trapped in the back.

Closing his own eyes, he laid his cheek against the top of her head. "It's going to be a short engagement."

"Still not a proposal." There was a bit of sass in her voice he loved.

"It's coming."

"Hmm," was all she said.

And it would be good. But he wasn't going to say any more. He'd just show her. Claim her—and lock her down so everyone knew she was his. He wasn't letting her go again.

* * *

Darcy shoved the surprisingly soft covers of the hospital bed off her, annoyed that she was even here. It felt ridiculous. Okay...it *wasn't* ridiculous. At all. She *had* been knocked around, she was incredibly sore now that the adrenaline had worn off, and she understood that they needed to check her over for internal bleeding and potentially a concussion, blah, blah, blah. But she hated that she'd missed the last part of her sister's wedding because of a maniacal asshole, and she was starting to get grumpy.

Mainly because Brooks had disappeared about ten minutes ago after receiving a text—and refused to tell her who it was from. She was fighting her annoyance at him and, okay, she was feeling overly emotional right now. He'd literally saved her life, and it wasn't as if he'd abandoned her, but man, she was feeling all the emotions.

When the door burst open and her sister ran in—still in her wedding dress—Darcy jolted upright in horror. "What are you doing here?"

Emma hurried around the bed, followed by Peter and Brooks. "What do you mean, why am I here? Where else would I be? Brooks said that you didn't have a concussion." She spun around and glared at him before turning a much softer expression on Darcy.

"I *don't*. I just thought you would be leaving on your honeymoon," Darcy said.

Both Peter and Emma looked at her as if she'd grown another head. "You really must have a concussion if you think I would leave you," her sister snapped. "Would you have left me?"

In that moment, Darcy felt like the biggest jerk on the planet. Of course her sister wouldn't have left, because no way would Darcy have ever left her after something like today. "I wasn't even thinking of it like that," she said. What she'd been more concerned about was her sister getting out of the country because she knew that Peter's father was going to be arrested in a few hours. "Blame it on getting kidnapped and tossed into the back of a van. I'm allowed to have a crazy moment."

Emma let out a strangled sound before pulling Darcy into her arms—gently. As her sister hugged her, she felt wetness on her neck as Emma cried. "When I think about what could have happened to you..." Sniffling, Emma pulled back and looked down at Darcy, concern in her gaze. "I'm just sorry that Brooks didn't kill him," she whispered loud enough for the *entire* room to hear.

Darcy's eyes widened. "That's bloodthirsty."

"That guy kidnapped you. He's lucky I didn't get ahold of him."

Peter, expression grim, came up and gave her a gentle kiss on the head. "I'm so sorry about all of this."

"You have nothing to be sorry for." She wondered how they were going to feel when they found out she'd known about his father's pending arrest.

"It happened at my father's house, of course we feel terrible. And that asshole worked for my father." Disgust was clear in Peter's voice. "He said he would be down here later, but he was dealing with the police and all the wedding stuff. The Feds were there too." He sounded a little confused by that.

Emma snorted. "Yeah, he wanted such a big affair, he gets to deal with all those people that we don't even know."

Darcy laughed at her sister's attitude. She felt terrible that they weren't going on their honeymoon yet, but knew better than to say so, at least right now. It would probably set her sister off.

"How was the cake?" she asked.

Her sister let out a startled laugh. "Oh my gosh, you're ridiculous. And I have no idea because we never cut it. But I'll make sure they save you some. Hell, you can have the whole damn cake. You deserve it."

Brooks chuckled behind them, his gaze steady on Darcy and full of the love she felt for him.

"By the way, these are some fancy digs. How did you swing getting a private room in *this* wing?"

Darcy's cheeks heated up, and she felt weird answering.

Thankfully Brooks saved her. "My dad donated a shitload of money to the hospital. He's here too, by the way," he added. "There are a lot of people here to see you."

She was surprised by that, but didn't ask who. She didn't plan on staying long enough to have a bunch of visitors. "Actually, he built the wing," Darcy added.

Emma's eyes widened. "Holy crap, I knew your dad was rich..." She trailed off, her cheeks flushing red as she looked away from Brooks. "I'm sorry, I have no filter right now."

Brooks just laughed and moved to the other side of the bed and took Darcy's hand. "It's okay. It's been a hell of a day. I'm sorry your wedding was ruined."

"Are you kidding? It didn't get ruined. I got to marry the man I love and now we have a crazy story to tell. It would have been ruined if anything had actually happened to my sister." She sniffled and teared up again then added, "Well, worse than what did happen. Oh my God, Darcy, I seriously can't believe what happened. I'm so glad you're okay. You look so much better than I imagined. I thought…" Swallowing hard, she shook her head.

Peter wrapped his arm around Emma's shoulders and pulled her close. "Is there anything we can get for you? How long are they keeping you?"

"I actually think I'm going to be discharged in the next hour, so you guys seriously don't need to stay."

Her sister snorted again and Darcy held up her hands. "Okay, okay, you can stay. But fair warning, I'm going back to my place and Brooks is taking over everything for the next couple days and being incredibly bossy about it," she said, smiling up at him. Because she was grateful that he was taking over.

"Good," Emma said. "I saw some of those little chocolate truffle things you like in the gift shop on the way up. Do you want some?"

Darcy nodded, smiling. "Yes, please."

"Okay, we'll be back up in a few minutes."

Once the door shut behind them, Darcy collapsed against the fluffy pillows. "Is there anything I need to know about right now?" She wanted to hear any details before her sister got back.

"I'm not sure how much I should tell you."

"I'm fine," she said, squeezing Brooks's hand once. "Just don't keep anything from me."

He looked so worried as he watched her.

She was achy and sore but at least she didn't need stitches. She'd only broken the skin on her forehead and her stomach barely even hurt anymore. She also didn't have internal bleeding, which was another win. She'd come out of this thing mostly unscathed, if a little terrified. And she had a feeling she was going to be reliving what had happened for a while. It was definitely the motivation she needed to start taking self-defense classes again. Not that she was certain she could have taken Polzin on anyway, but she needed to find something and be consistent about it. She never wanted to be a victim ever again.

Brooks glanced over at the door, which was still closed. "Markov will be arrested very soon. According to Leighton, the FBI is getting all their ducks in a row. And Polzin's already in custody. With what he attempted to do, they've expanded their warrant and found a couple more places owned by him. In one...he had pictures of you. He'd been keeping them on a tablet. It's clear he's been watching you for a while. All the pictures were long-range shots."

Her stomach sank. *Gross.* "Like, naked pictures?" Her voice trembled as she asked. Had he somehow spied on her in vulnerable positions?

Brooks shook his head. "No. Just pictures of you leaving home, heading to work, meeting with clients, stuff like that. They think that you getting back together with me is what set him off. They also figured out why so many of the guards weren't near the front gate. He knew the protocols there and used a cloned phone to text some of the guards as if he was one of them. He told them there was an issue in another area and it created the small window he needed."

She shuddered. "Do you think he'll try to cut a deal or something?"

"Probably. He'll try to flip on Markov. At least that's what Leighton's friend seems to think." His jaw tightened once.

Darcy narrowed her gaze. "Do you think they'll let him walk, or give him a reduced sentence?"

"Don't worry about that. He's not going anywhere. Listen, there's something I need to take care of tonight."

Darcy stared up at him. She wasn't sure how to respond. What could be so important that he had to leave her? Tonight of all nights? "Can you tell me what it is?" She tried to keep the tremble out of her voice and wasn't sure if she succeeded. She really didn't want to be alone tonight.

He was silent for a long moment then shook his head as he cupped her cheek. Oh so gently, he stroked his thumb against her skin. "No. I would if I could. Can you trust me?"

"Of course." She didn't even have to think about it.

He expelled a short breath. "Good. Savage and Olivia will be heading back to your place with you, and I'm sure Emma and Peter will be as well. What I've got to do shouldn't take too long. Listen, my dad wanted to come by and see you, but he said he understands if you have no desire to see him."

"Of course he can come up." She really wanted to know where Brooks was going, but there was something in his eyes that told her not to ask again. Right now, she was going to trust her instinct.

CHAPTER TWENTY-THREE

—Cowboys get shit done.—

Brooks stepped outside now that Peter and Emma were back in Darcy's hospital room. He knew she wouldn't be alone and he had something to take care of. Now.

As the door shut behind him, he came face-to-face with Savage, Olivia, Valencia, and Leighton.

Valencia was jumping up and down holding a clearly handmade pink and purple card covered in glittered hearts. "Can we see your girlfriend?" she asked, waving her card and sending glitter flying everywhere.

Brooks smiled and, using ASL, signed back that yes she could go inside. He was still learning ASL and was rewarded with a huge smile. Sometimes Valencia signed and sometimes she spoke aloud. Savage had once told him that it just depended on her mood. She liked to go back and forth.

Olivia smiled indulgently at her daughter and gave Brooks a quick kiss on the cheek. "We'll watch out for your girl," she said. "I'm glad you're okay too."

Brooks turned to Savage and was pulled into a tight hug. "I'm glad you're okay, brother." Savage's voice was thick with emotion, taking him off guard. "Though I can't believe you guys did that without calling me," he muttered as he stood back.

"We had literal minutes to get to the church."

"I know, I just feel like I'm the only one left out of all the action."

Brooks snorted. "Well I'm sure Olivia is fine that you got left out."

Grinning, Savage shrugged. "True enough."

"They're going to be moving in on Markov soon," Leighton said quietly.

"Any news on Polzin?" At the moment, dealing with that asshole was all he cared about. If possible, he was taking care of the problem tonight.

"Yes. She shouldn't have told me but Hazel said he's trying to cut a deal. He's given them some info on Markov and says he has more on Kuznetsov. He's also saying that Markov was ultimately targeting Kuznetsov. It sounds like a clusterfuck of info. They're going to transfer him from the hospital tonight to protective holding. Look...he might end up going into WITSEC if he gives them enough. You need to be ready for that possibility."

Yeah, that wasn't happening. Brooks would make sure of it. Polzin wasn't walking. If he went into WITSEC there was no way Brooks would be able to find him—and there was no guarantee he'd leave Darcy alone. He could come after her later. Not a risk Brooks was willing to take. It was no surprise Polzin had been taken to a hospital, what with his broken ribs. And his broken face. At least he wasn't at this one. And Brooks knew exactly where he would be transferred from. "What time?"

Leighton watched him carefully. "She didn't say."

"Can you find out?" If not, he would find out on his own. His father had enough contacts everywhere, including the hospital Polzin was at.

Leighton's gaze narrowed. "Are you planning what I think you are?"

Brooks didn't respond. This couldn't be a surprise to his friend. Because if there was even remotely a chance that the

Feds would cut a deal with that bastard, he wasn't letting it happen. Darcy was his to protect. And protect her he would. Through any means necessary.

"You need backup?" Savage asked, clearly knowing what he intended to do.

"No. I need you to keep an eye on Darcy." Savage was his best friend. Someone he trusted more than anyone, but the man had a new family. He wasn't bringing him in on this.

Brooks glanced at his watch. If the Feds were going to make a transfer it could be at any moment. And he had some shit to get together first. Not to mention he needed to talk to Gage about erasing any CCTV footage in the area.

"I'll see what I can find out." Leighton didn't look happy about it but he also wasn't arguing. *Good.*

"I need to go." All of his gear was at the office so at least he didn't have to drive back to the ranch.

"You sure about this?" Savage asked quietly.

Brooks didn't bother responding. Of course he was sure. And Savage would do the same thing for Olivia and Valencia.

CHAPTER TWENTY-FOUR

—One shot. One kill. —

Brooks looked through the scope of his rifle, only partially contemplating the morality of what he was about to do. He didn't do something like this lightly. And he didn't plan to do it again.

The only time he'd ever killed had been during wartime. And he hadn't taken any joy in it. That had been about the job—about keeping his friends and others safe. Period.

This... He was doing this to keep Darcy safe. And to keep a monster off the streets. He knew he didn't have the right to be a judge, jury or executioner. But he was still doing this. Because once Polzin went into protective custody, he'd never be able to get near him again.

Though it was night, there was more than enough light for him. He stayed in the shadows of the window of the apartment he was using. Unlike in the movies, snipers didn't use rooftops. Not if they could help it. Thanks to Gage's genius he'd found an unused apartment as his final firing position.

There had been five different places he could have chosen, but in the end he'd gone with this apartment because of the angle, the concealment it provided him, and the exfil. One of the most important things a sniper had to consider—the escape.

He flicked a glance at a nearby flag from a neighboring building. Wind was barely existent tonight.

He returned his gaze to the scope. The hospital exit Polzin was supposed to be escorted from was lit up like a Christmas tree. It was like they were trying to make this easy for him.

A black SUV with tinted windows pulled up under the overhang. His breathing was as steady as his heart rate as he watched. This was the first time a kill had ever been personal.

This time it truly mattered. Once he did this, there was no going back for him. He'd made this decision and if there were any consequences, he would face them.

But for now, he shut those thoughts down.

Two FBI agents got out of the vehicle, almost as if they'd synchronized it. One stood by one of the back doors while the other moved to the exit door.

A moment later a shackled Polzin shuffled out wearing light blue scrubs. Both his wrists and ankles were restrained, making his movements slow.

Brooks quickly calculated the distance and wind, and on his natural respiratory pause, he pulled the trigger.

Polzin dropped while the agents quickly moved into action. Brooks didn't bother watching what they did. He didn't care. He'd done what he'd come to do.

It was possible they'd set up a grid and do a search for the shooter, but they'd be disappointed. Gage had hacked into every system in the area—because yeah he was that fucking good—so they wouldn't be caught on camera. But that didn't mean he could stick around.

Slipping on gloves, he stood and shut the window. Then he folded up his stock and, moving with a practiced efficiency, stored his rifle in the carrying case.

There were people in this building, so he'd have to be careful as he left. But he'd planned his escape. Because of the acoustics, it would be almost impossible to pinpoint his location. The Feds would do it later using all the technology at their disposal, of course, but there wouldn't be a trace of him left here by the time they figured out the location. And he had no connection to the building either.

Easing open the door, he peered out into the hallway. All clear.

No way was he using the elevator. Though carrying the rifle was bulky, he made it down the stairs in record time.

As he stepped out into an alleyway, his heart rate kicked up just the slightest bit when he didn't spot Gage. But a moment later two headlights flipped on, showing Brooks where his friend was waiting. Just as quickly they turned off. Their signal.

He glanced around again, just to make sure, but he didn't see anyone. Pulling his ball cap down low, he waited as Gage started the engine and pulled up next to him.

It was time to go home. Time to go to Darcy.

CHAPTER TWENTY-FIVE

—Life is full of surprises.—

"Is that the doorbell?" Darcy asked, snuggling closer to Brooks under the covers.

It felt surreal that barely half a day had passed since the insanity of yesterday.

"Yes," he murmured, kissing her. It wasn't obscenely early, but early enough that neither of them wanted to be bothered. He'd kicked everyone out practically the moment he'd gotten back to her house last night. When he'd shown up with enough food to stock her place for a week, Emma had given him a big hug and thanked him for taking care of her sister. He couldn't actually take credit for shopping for the food since his father had paid someone take care of that with no questions asked. But he'd needed a reason to be away from her that made sense. "Stay here, I'll grab it." Picking up his discarded jeans and sweater, he quickly got dressed before hurrying down the stairs.

He knew Darcy would be right behind him, but he hoped she took her time. She'd been through a lot and he really hoped this wasn't her sister coming by. Markov had been arrested by now, and he didn't want Darcy to have to deal with anything else.

After looking through the peephole, he stiffened. Not a friendly visit. Or maybe it was, but he kind of doubted it. He disarmed the security system and pulled open the front door.

Special Agent Blake didn't seem surprised to see him standing there. She nodded once, her expression polite. "Is Miss Cooper here?"

"Yes." He stayed where he was, and shoved his hands in his pockets. There was a chance she'd pull him in for questioning for Polzin's murder, but he knew for a fact the Feds had no proof of what he'd done. In addition to all the precautions he'd taken, there were no witnesses and the gunshot residue on Brooks was easily explainable from what had happened after Darcy had been kidnapped. "What kind of visit is this? I don't want her upset right now. She's been through a lot and because of her, you guys stopped a massacre."

"Technically, you stopped it." A pause. "It's a friendly visit. I promise. I just wanted to give her an update in person."

"Brooks, please let the woman in, it's freezing out." Darcy's sweet voice trailed from behind him. He turned to find her moving slowly across the foyer. She might be technically fine, but she was banged up and sore and that wasn't fine, in his opinion. He didn't want her doing anything.

He stepped back so Hazel could enter. "Would you like any coffee?" There, he still had some manners.

"No thanks, this won't take long. How are you feeling, Miss Cooper?" Hazel asked, her voice gentle.

Darcy smiled. "Please call me Darcy. And like I got run over by a truck. But I'm incredibly grateful to be alive. I know this could have ended up a lot worse."

"Is there somewhere we can sit?"

"Of course. This way," she said, indicating the living room right off the foyer.

Brooks helped Darcy onto one of the couches and wrapped his arm around her shoulders when she leaned into him.

The federal agent sat across from them. She hadn't even bothered to take her coat off so he figured she was telling the truth and this really wouldn't take long. Not to mention he'd noticed that it was just her, no partner waiting out in her vehicle. So at least she wasn't here to arrest him. Not that he was worried if she did.

"I'm going to get right down to it. I just stopped by as a courtesy. I wanted to let you know that Polzin was killed last night. During his prison transport."

Darcy sat up and let out a little gasp even as Brooks feigned surprise. "Was anyone else hurt? Were the police hurt?" she asked.

"No. He was shot once. In the head. He died within moments of the bullet impact." She flicked a quick glance at Brooks, but her expression revealed nothing. Just as quickly she looked back at Darcy. "I'm also going to tell you something else, and if you say anything, I'll deny it. Markov was killed last night as well."

This surprised Brooks. *Holy hell.* Someone had decided to clean house fast. And he knew exactly who'd done it. Had to be Kuznetsov.

Darcy put a hand over her mouth. "Do my sister and Peter know?"

Hazel nodded. "Someone is on their way over there right now."

"I don't even know what to say. I want to ask if you know who did it, who killed them, but you probably can't tell me anything, can you?" Darcy asked.

"Officially I can't comment on an ongoing investigation, but you stepped up when most people wouldn't have. You put your life on the line and saved hundreds of lives. So while I can't directly comment about the investigation, I can tell you that we are almost certain you are not in danger anymore. You were never listed as the source who tipped us off. Your name hasn't been in any memos or official files. And whoever killed Markov and Polzin... Well, I can't imagine why anyone would want to come after you."

Next to him, Darcy shuddered and laid her head on his shoulder. "I'm glad this nightmare is over, but I feel so bad for Peter."

Standing, Hazel simply nodded. "He'll likely deal with some media scrutiny but he's not dirty, and as of now, I can say that we have no plans to arrest him. We're still continuing our investigation so that could change, but I don't think it's going to. Thank you again. I might be in touch again as we continue investigating the murders of Markov and Polzin."

Darcy frowned at that but simply nodded.

Brooks stood and when Darcy started to move, both he and Hazel motioned for her to sit down.

"I'll walk you to the door," Brooks said quietly.

As he stepped outside with Hazel, she paused on the front stoop as she slid her sunglasses on. It wasn't early enough to need them but he figured this was part of her FBI armor. "Whoever killed Polzin was a really good shot."

He kept his expression neutral. "Okay."

She tilted her head slightly to the side, as if trying to figure him out. "I might bring you in for questioning later."

"Go ahead. You can go through my lawyer. And I can already tell you what his argument would be if you're stupid enough to suspect me. If I wanted him dead, I would have killed him when he was in the van." If she had proof or a witness, he'd already be in handcuffs.

She gave him a half-smile and nodded. "That would be the smart defense." She paused for a moment then held out a hand. Surprised, he took it as she said, "Thank you again for what you did at the church. There are a lot of families that are still whole right now because of you."

Brooks locked the door behind her and took a moment to himself before heading back to the living room. "Do you want to go back to bed, or do you want coffee?" he asked Darcy.

"What I'd really like is some hot cocoa and my laptop. I need to call my sister. Then check on some clients and—"

He shook his head, having been ready for her to say this. He hadn't expected it so soon. "No. Absolutely not. I mean, yes to the hot cocoa. But no to work. Not today. You're taking the day off." And a few more after.

Frowning, she crossed her arms over her chest. "My hands and brain are fine. I'm just a little sore."

"Fine, then humor me."

Instead of arguing she gave him a curious look. Then she said, "Will you be okay with the FBI?"

He scooted closer to her on the couch, trying not to jostle her too much. "What do you mean?"

"I'm just saying that if you need an alibi, I'm it. I'll lie my face off to the FBI for you."

Her meaning sank in, shocking him.

Holy shit. Leaning forward, he brushed his lips over hers and forced himself not to deepen it too much when all he wanted to do was consume her right now. He'd been debating whether he would tell her what he'd done—and he'd been leaning toward a ninety-nine percent hell no. He'd been worried it would change her opinion of him.

But it turned out she'd figured it out on her own. "I didn't kill Markov," he said quietly.

"I didn't think you did. You seemed surprised when Special Agent Blake said he'd been murdered."

But he hadn't been surprised by the mention of Polzin's murder even if he had put on the appropriate expression of surprise.

It was a relief that she knew. He didn't want to hide anything from her. "So, you know what kind of man I am. Is this the kind of man you want to be married to?" he asked quietly. "I'm not sorry for what I did and I'd do it again." He wanted that much clear. Because he didn't want secrets between them.

"First, I know what kind of man you are. You're a good, kind man who protects those he loves. And second, you keep talking about marriage, Brooks. But I still don't see a ring on this finger." She lifted her left hand and wiggled her fingers.

Leaning forward again he kissed her, careful not to jostle her too much. She was definitely going to get a proposal, the kind she deserved. She'd just surprised the hell out of him, had been willing to lie to the Feds for him. This woman owned him. After kissing her he said, "I'm going to get that hot cocoa now."

"Marshmallows, please." Then she gave him a cheeky grin. "If you're going to make me be an invalid today, I might take advantage and let you wait on me hand and foot. And...other places too."

He lifted an eyebrow. "Oh yeah?"

Her grin went pure wicked. "Oh yeah."

Laughing under his breath, he headed to the kitchen. Even if she wanted to get him into bed, that wasn't happening. Not now, maybe not for another day or two. Not when she was still so sore and bruised. But he definitely didn't mind waiting on her hand and foot in the meantime.

* * *

Brooks looked around the conference room table at his friends—at the cofounders of Redemption Harbor Consulting. Though he'd hated to do it, he'd had to leave Darcy for a little while this afternoon—but not before inviting Olivia and Valencia over to keep her company.

Before he got back to her, everyone at this table had some serious decisions to make about how they were going to go forward regarding the murder of Markov—meaning, how they were going to handle Kuznetsov.

Skye polished off the rest of her taquito and wiped her hands on the napkin Colt handed her. "It had to have been Kuznetsov. It's the only thing that makes sense. He must have been worried that Markov would cut a deal. Or who knows, but my bet is on him being the one behind the murder. We're already sure he was behind the death of Olivia's ex-husband during the Miami job—same MO and everything."

Everyone around the table nodded.

"Have you talked to Darcy's sister and Peter Markov?" Colt asked.

Colt and Skye had just gotten back in town and they hadn't even debriefed everyone on the Oregon job. They'd come straight to the office for this meeting.

Brooks shook his head. "No. As soon as we're done here, I'm picking Darcy up and we're going over to see the two of them. They're both distraught." Something he understood, considering all of this had come as a shock, and right after their wedding. Literally one day after saying "I do," they were dealing with Peter's father being arrested and then murdered.

Skye's expression was grim. "Kuznetsov might come after Peter."

Brooks nodded. "I know. Which is why I wanted to talk to you guys in person. I'm going to set up a meeting with him." Technically, he was going to ambush the guy into having a conversation with him.

When no one spoke up to say it was a bad idea, he continued. "I want to use those blackmail pictures from the Miami job."

The room went impossibly quiet, as he'd known it would. He couldn't just take those pictures without asking the team. The flash drive—a treasure of information—they'd stolen in Miami was basically their "get out of jail free card" if they ever needed it. And Brooks wanted to use part of what they'd taken, which opened them up to scrutiny from Kuznetsov.

Finally, Savage spoke. "What are you thinking?" Savage and Olivia had been the ones to extract a whole lot of blackmail material on a lot of very important people. Including pictures—and video—of Kuznetsov's married-to-a-woman son engaging in extracurricular activities with a very married and publicly straight male senator. Nothing illegal, but they knew for a fact that Kuznetsov didn't want it getting out to the public.

"I just want to give him some pictures and tell him to leave Peter and Emma—and anyone related to them—alone. I'll make it clear that if he goes after them, I'll destroy him." It was a risk, and he would use more finesse than that, but he had to talk to the man. Because Darcy was related to Emma. And sometimes people like Kuznetsov took out anyone they wanted, as a message. So anyone related to the Markov family would be in danger. That included Darcy.

Not acceptable.

"I don't like it, but I think you need to do it," Skye finally said. "How are you going to approach him? As an employee of Redemption Harbor Consulting?"

"No. I'm going to come to him like a rich asshole businessman. I'm going to talk the same language as him."

"He's already left town," Gage said.

"I know. I want to leave tonight on the jet and confront him tomorrow." Kuznetsov would feel better on his home turf, would think he had the advantage. Brooks didn't care. Once he'd said what he had to say, the ball would be in Kuznetsov's court. And if he decided to come after Peter or Emma—or Darcy—Brooks would keep his word and destroy him. He was aware that Kuznetsov might just try to put a bullet in him, but he'd be beyond stupid if he did. And Brooks didn't think the man was stupid. It was one of the only reasons Brooks wasn't putting a bullet in the man's head outright. He didn't want to risk doing that, however. Not now. They didn't know enough about his organization yet and what type of potential enemies they might make.

"Well, we planned to go after him anyway. We can just move the timeline up." Skye shrugged slightly.

Brooks shook his head. "I don't want to go after him. Not yet. I just want him to back off." Technically he did want to take the guy down. Kuznetsov was a piece of shit running humans and drugs up and down the East Coast. But for now, he needed Darcy safe. And they didn't have enough intel on Kuznetsov to declare war on him.

Skye watched him for a long moment. Then she said, "I need to make a call. I know one of his associates and I *might* have something that can help you. Something more than the blackmail."

Brooks nodded. He hadn't known Skye that long, but he trusted her with his life. Pushing up from the chair, he said, "I'm going to head out now. I've got my phone on me." It was time to get back to Darcy.

"You need backup," Colt said.

"I can do this—"

"I'm not asking." His friend, who'd gone all lone wolf on the crew a year ago, looked dead serious. "At least one of us is going."

Damn it, the man was right. "All right. I'll let you decide who." Because he trusted any one of them to have his back.

They nodded and started conversing among themselves. He'd grab what he needed later from Gage before flying out tonight.

As he headed down the hallway, Savage ducked out after him.

"You going to tell the others it was you who killed Polzin?" his best friend asked.

Brooks lifted a shoulder. "I kind of figured they already knew." It wasn't a secret and Gage had helped him make a clean getaway.

The corners of Savage's mouth kicked up. "Yeah. Skye pretty much called you out before you got here."

"They pissed about it?"

He snorted. "Skye was just mad you didn't ask for her backup."

Feeling awkward, he rubbed the back of his neck. "Darcy said..." Brooks cleared his throat. "She said that if I needed an alibi, she'd give me one. I'd never planned to tell her what I did, but she knew." It still floored him.

Savage squeezed his shoulder once. "Marry that woman as soon as possible."

He planned to.

CHAPTER TWENTY-SIX

—It's the unexpected that changes our lives.—

Darcy took solace in Brooks's presence next to her on Emma and Peter's couch. They'd been living together for the last six months and she could see her sister's touches everywhere. Throw pillows and blankets on the couches, the place smelled like warm vanilla cookies, and there were pictures of the two of them everywhere.

"I just don't understand everything that's happened." Peter looked so lost, and nothing like the confident man she'd come to know. Next to him, Emma held his hand tightly in her own.

"We might be able to shed a little light on some things for you," Brooks said. "But it's going to be very hard to hear."

Darcy looked at her sister and gave her a small and what she hoped was reassuring smile. "I don't even know how to say this so I'm just going to get it all out." She went through everything, starting from when she'd overheard that conversation in Semyon's office between the detective and Oleg, to the involvement of the Feds and then the bombing on their wedding day. She hadn't even found out about the bombing until later, after Brooks had come back from...well, what he'd done to Oleg. As she wrapped up, both Emma and Peter had gone very still. And Peter looked sick.

"The FBI agents we talked to didn't say anything about that," Peter finally said, his voice hoarse. "Just that he'd been arrested for multiple crimes, that there were explosives at his estate, and that he had been murdered during a prison transport—and that they were investigating who killed him."

"Do you know who killed him?" Emma asked, looking between the two of them.

Darcy shook her head even as Brooks said, "No. Your father had a lot of enemies. It's very clear he kept that part of his life a secret from you. From the world."

"I'm sorry I couldn't tell you earlier about what I overheard," Darcy said, focusing on her sister. "At the time, I didn't know if Peter was involved in his father's business." She shot Peter an apologetic look and he gave her nothing. He just stared almost blankly. "I couldn't risk kids getting hurt—or *anyone* getting hurt."

"Of course you couldn't tell me," Emma said, tears filling her eyes. She quickly swiped them away. "You were in an impossible situation. I'm so sorry that you've been holding all of this in. But I'm glad Brooks was able to help you and that the FBI stopped that bombing. I...I just can't imagine why he would have been involved in something like that. It seems so pointless and heartless."

Peter rubbed a hand over his face. "I had no idea he had this double life." Standing abruptly, he strode from the room.

"He's not handling this well," Emma said quietly, stress lines bracketing her mouth.

"We'll leave you guys alone," Darcy said. "Unless you want us to stay?"

Her sister shook her head. "No. I think he needs more time to adjust to this new reality. If you find out any details... Will you tell us? If you can?" she asked, looking at Brooks.

"If we hear anything and we're able to, we'll let you know anything we find out."

Darcy hugged her sister and was grateful that Emma didn't squeeze too hard because she was still sore. "Call me if you need anything," Darcy whispered, fighting her own tears. She hated leaving Emma right now but understood that the two of them needed time alone. What should have been the happiest time in Emma's life was being shadowed by a dark cloud.

"Right back at you," Emma said.

Once they were outside, Darcy sucked in an icy breath. The temperature seemed to have dropped ten degrees since they'd gone inside, or maybe she was simply chilled. "I expected her to be angry at me."

"No, your sister loves you. And she's very pragmatic. I'm not surprised by her reaction. They're going to be in for a rough road, at least in the beginning. It's going to be hard for Peter to deal with the reality of his father."

"I know. Plus with all the media scrutiny they'll be facing." Darcy simply shook her head. "I almost wish they would leave on their honeymoon just to get out of town."

As they settled into Brooks's truck, he said, "Speaking of getting out of town. I have to take a short trip."

"Where?"

"I can't tell you."

"Nope. I understand what you did before. But if you're doing something related to any of this, I'm going with you. I'm not saying I need to be in the thick of things, but we are a team. And this isn't up for discussion."

He watched her for a long moment. "You're incredible, you know that?"

"I do."

That earned her a laugh, which was the point. "I need to talk to someone. Someone who might still be a threat to Peter—and in turn, you and Emma."

"I thought you said Peter wasn't involved with anything."

Brooks started the truck. "He's not. But the man who might have killed his father won't care. If he chooses to, he might want to make an example."

"Why?"

"At this point, we don't actually know if he wants to or if he will. The only thing we do know is that another man was killed in the same way during a prison transport about seven months back. And the man who killed him had a connection to—"

"Okay, I'm going to need an actual name. All these pronouns are giving me a headache."

Brooks barked out a short laugh. "The man we suspect of being behind Markov's murder is named Alexei Kuznetsov."

She vaguely recognized the name, but wasn't sure where from. From the wedding maybe? "Why do you think he killed him?"

"We don't know for certain, but he probably considered him a liability. Once Markov and Polzin were arrested, they might have been willing to give information on Kuznetsov—if they had it, and I think they did—to the authorities in order to get less jail time or be put into witness protection. This is all conjecture, but a man like Kuznetsov wouldn't wait for them to make a deal. He would just eliminate the problem."

She fought off a shiver. "And you know for a fact he's done it before?"

"Yes."

"And you plan to just what, talk to him?" *What. The. Hell.*

"It's not as simple as that. But yes, I'm going to talk to him and make him see things my way."

Fear filtered through Darcy, but Brooks looked so damn confident. So she said as much. "How are you so certain he won't just do the same thing to you?" She tried to keep her voice steady, but failed.

"Because I have information on him that he won't want to be made public. If anything happens to me, it will be." A dark smile curved his lips as he glanced at her. "I'll tell you everything on the way there."

"So I'm going with you?"

"Not to the meeting, but you're right, we are a team. And there's more I need to tell you about what I do for a living."

Good. That was all she needed to know, that he saw her as his partner. If they were going to give this a second chance—and she desperately wanted to—she was going to be all in. But only if he opened up completely to her. "When do we leave?"

"In the morning. On my jet." He gave her another wicked grin, this one very different from the one before.

Her eyes widened. Back when they'd first started dating he'd offered to take her on it more than once, but it had seemed so extravagant that she'd always declined. Plus they'd both been working so hard and she hadn't been able to take away much time from her job. Now... Well, she was going with him wherever he went. She could work from her laptop if necessary. If there was ever a time she was going to take a break from work, it was now. Getting kidnapped and almost killed had changed her perspective on things. "Does this jet have a bed?"

"It does. But we won't be sleeping." The sensual note in his voice sent very different kinds of shivers running through her.

Whatever they were facing tomorrow, they'd face it as a team.

CHAPTER TWENTY-SEVEN

—If you see the lion's teeth, do not think he's
smiling.—

Keeping his expression neutral, Brooks strode through the lobby of the newly purchased New Orleans hotel owned by Kuznetsov. He'd called the man's personal cell phone—and he'd only gotten the phone number courtesy of Gage—half an hour ago and told him they needed to talk. At first the man had tried to dismiss him until Brooks had casually brought up Kuznetsov's married son. That had gotten the man's attention.

Instead of dressing in his normal cowboy gear, he'd worn a casual Armani suit—custom fit. When walking into a den of wolves, he had to look the part. Good thing he was a fucking lion.

Coming in here alone was definitely a risk. But it was one he was willing to take. Both Gage and Leighton were nearby and while they wouldn't be able to do a damn thing if Kuznetsov tried to kill him, they'd be able to get Darcy out of town—and come after Kuznetsov later.

A lot of light streamed in from the skylights and everything gleamed. The marble floors, the overhead chandeliers and the huge sculpture of a half-clothed woman balancing an intricate headdress.

When he reached the entryway of the seafood restaurant that wouldn't open for a few hours yet, a man in a suit stopped him. He recognized the guy from the other night. One of the assholes who'd leered at Darcy.

"Hold out your arms," the man said.

Brooks did and was quickly scanned with a wand. Then he was patted down quickly and efficiently. When the man pulled out a sealed manila envelope from Brooks's jacket and started to open it, Brooks shook his head. "Unless you want your boss to put a bullet in your head, I wouldn't open that."

The man paused, then to his surprise, froze. That was when Brooks saw the small earpiece in his ear. Someone, likely Kuznetsov himself, had just told him to stop. "This way."

Brooks followed after him through the empty restaurant and was led to a back corner booth where Kuznetsov sat alone, a glass of what might be vodka in front of him, and a tablet. He appraised Brooks as he approached then nodded at him to sit down. Brooks took him in up close. Sharp bone structure, pale, wolf-like eyes, and blond hair cut in a buzz. His suit was expensive but not flashy. Same with the watch Kuznetsov wore.

Brooks slid into the circular booth, so that he was opposite the other man. He was aware of at least four others in the restaurant watching them, but wasn't sure if they were close enough to hear. As soon as he sat, Kuznetsov dismissed the other man with a flick of his wrist.

"Why are you here?" Kuznetsov demanded softly.

"We need to talk."

Kuznetsov watched him for a long moment. "We're not in the same business, you and I. Yet you flew all this way to interrupt my breakfast. What could we possibly have to talk about?"

"A man loosely linked to the woman I love was recently murdered. I don't know why he was killed and I don't care.

What I *do* know is that it's possible his killer might want to make an example of the dead man's family."

"Don't speak in riddles."

Fine, if that was how he wanted it. "Semyon Markov was killed. I want to make sure that his son, his son's new wife, and her sister will be safe from any 'examples' Markov's killer might try to make."

Kuznetsov looked annoyed. "I barely knew Semyon."

Yeah, Brooks wasn't going to play that game. "Good. Then we shouldn't have a problem." He nodded once at the envelope the thug had left in the middle of the table. "But just in case…"

Frowning, Kuznetsov opened the envelope and pulled out the pictures.

"I have video too." Brooks kept his voice icy.

The other man's jaw tightened, but other than that his expression remained neutral. "You think to blackmail me?" he asked quietly.

"No. I never want to talk to or see you again after today. I just want to make sure that we're on the same page." That the woman he loved was protected.

After a moment of silence, Kuznetsov spoke again. "I looked into you. You're the boyfriend of Markov's sister-in-law."

Yeah, no shit. He'd just said that.

"You must care for her a lot to come here with this. How did you even get this?"

Brooks was silent.

Kuznetsov tapped his finger on the table as he watched Brooks. "Making enemies with me isn't smart."

"The way I see it, we don't have to be enemies. I want nothing from you other than to leave Markov and the Cooper sisters alone. Forever. This will never go public as long as you stay away from them," he said, nodding at the envelope. "But if any of them so much as stub their fucking toe because of you, I will come after you."

The other man's head tilted to the side slightly, as if trying to figure Brooks out. "You are walking a very dangerous line right now."

"I know. I also know about Liliana." Brooks continued, giving the name of her private school in the UK as well as the names of two of her teachers. It wasn't in his nature to threaten children, or threaten people in general, but right now they had to speak the same language. The man in front of him had to understand that he would cross every line—or he had to make the man *believe* he would. There was no way Brooks would actually kill a kid, but he needed this man afraid. And not much would scare a man like this one. But threatening the daughter that Kuznetsov had been very careful to keep secret from the world? Yeah, that would do it.

It was as if all the air was sucked out of the room as Kuznetsov's gaze went nuclear. Out of the corner of his eye, Brooks saw one of Kuznetsov's men step forward. But Kuznetsov let out a harsh-sounding order in Russian and the man froze. All his concentration was on Brooks.

Brooks stood and adjusted his jacket. "You leave the three of them alone and I leave your family alone. It's as simple as that. And if you think to cross me, I'm not working alone. If I die, or if anyone in my family is harmed, you and your *entire* family will be erased." He let the truth bleed into his gaze as he stared down at Kuznetsov.

The man's jaw tightened again as he stared back, fury and rage clear in his pale eyes. Finally he spoke, and his words surprised Brooks. "I didn't kill Polzin." There was a question in Kuznetsov's gaze now.

Brooks gave a dark smile. "I know."

When he strode from the restaurant, no one attempted to stop him as he made his way back through the lobby—though he half expected a bullet in the back of his head. Now it was just a waiting game to see how Kuznetsov would deal with this.

Either Kuznetsov left Peter, Emma, Darcy—and now Brooks and anyone else he loved—alone...

Or there would be war.

CHAPTER TWENTY-EIGHT

—Be with someone who makes you, and your
orgasms, their first priority.—

When there was a knock on the door of the penthouse suite, Brooks rose from the couch. In a hotel on the other side of town from Kuznetsov, he wouldn't rest easy until he had an idea how things would play out with him and the criminal. Now it seemed Brooks might get his answer.

He'd received a text from Leighton that someone in Kuznetsov's crew had arrived downstairs five minutes ago and handed a note to the concierge. Even so, Brooks pulled out his weapon. "Stay here," he said quietly to Darcy. He'd left Kuznetsov a couple hours ago and, according to Gage, the man had been busy since then.

He'd tried to do a deeper search on Brooks, Brooks's father, and Kuznetsov had checked in with his daughter's school to ensure that his daughter was safe. The man had gone to a lot of trouble to ensure that the world didn't know she existed. But apparently Skye worked magic. He wasn't even certain where she'd gotten that information about Kuznetsov having a daughter, but she'd certainly come through. The threat to his daughter was what had gotten through to him. He'd been angry about the blackmail to his son, but the knowledge of his daughter had snagged his attention.

Brooks had seen the raw reaction in the man's eyes and hadn't been certain that Kuznetsov wouldn't lunge across the table. He'd been ready for an attack and surprised when it hadn't come. But that was a good sign.

After checking through the peephole, he opened the door to find a bellman. The man handed him a white envelope and walked away.

He shut the door and tucked his SIG in its holster and opened up the envelope. Inside was a simple photograph of a white flag. On the back, a handwritten note read: *We are not enemies. Your family is safe as long as mine is safe.*

He allowed himself a trickle of relief. That would have to do for now. One day he and the crew planned to take down Kuznetsov's operation, but it wouldn't be today.

"Is everything okay? Darcy asked, standing from the couch where she'd been sitting in the living area.

He shoved the envelope and picture in his pants pocket. "I think it is." He would still keep an eye on Kuznetsov, but for now he took a deep breath and wrapped his arms around her. They were safe. They were free.

She stepped into his embrace willingly, wrapping her arms around his waist as she laid her cheek against his chest. "Do you want to head home?" she asked quietly.

"We can. Or we can take advantage of this hotel room." He let his voice drop an octave, his meaning clear.

She looked up at him, eyebrows raised. "You talk a good game, but you wouldn't even do anything on the plane." And she sounded dangerously close to pouting, which made him internally smile. This woman owned him.

Laughing, he said, "Leighton and Gage were with us."

She grinned cheekily. "Fair enough."

He'd been worried about hurting her since she was still healing. But his Darcy was clearly strong. And... "Is it selfish that I don't want to wait until we get back home?"

"You don't have a selfish bone in your body," she murmured.

"If you're hurting or if you feel any discomfort, we stop. You have to let me know. Promise." He couldn't stomach the thought of hurting her in any way.

"I promise," she said, smiling as she lifted up on her tiptoes to kiss him.

He claimed her mouth with his, teasing slowly and sensually. Her taste—a mix of coffee, something fruity, and something that was all her—drove him wild. His body trembled with the need to claim her, but he was going to take things slow, to ensure she experienced only pleasure.

When she reached for the buckle of his belt, he stilled her with his hands. But she pulled back to look up at him.

"I'm touching you everywhere I want. I'm in charge now." Her voice trembled slightly, more a question than a statement, and he couldn't fight his grin.

"Yes, ma'am." Lifting her in his arms, he brushed his lips over hers as he carried her to the bedroom.

Gage had hacked into the security system of the hotel—the hotel Brooks's father owned—so if anyone tried to infiltrate the room, Brooks would know long before they tried.

He was free to explore Darcy's body, to kiss her everywhere he wanted. In the bedroom he gently set her down on the thick gold duvet.

"I'm not made of glass," she murmured, reaching for his pants again.

He let her push them down even as he stripped off his jacket and shirt. When he was naked she ran her fingers up his stomach and the simple action made him pull back. If she started touching him, he wouldn't be able to think straight.

"You. Naked."

She laughed at his rasped-out words but lifted her arms as he reached for the hem of her sweater.

It didn't take long for him to have her completely naked and stretched out on the bed in front of him. Her dark hair spilled out around her face and her breasts rose and fell rapidly as she watched him.

It was still afternoon and light spilled in from the big windows, bathing every inch of her in its warmth.

He was able to see her bruising clearly and forced himself to take a deep breath as he climbed onto the bed and up her delectable body. He had to trust her that if she said she wanted this, she was okay. Gently, he kissed above the bruise on her stomach, then made his way to her breasts.

He kept his hands on the bed, using just his mouth to brush over her smooth, soft skin.

She made a little mewling sound as he pulled one nipple between his teeth and flicked his tongue over it. Her fingers speared through his hair, clutching onto his head as she arched into him.

Reaching between her legs, he cupped her mound and slid a finger through her delicate folds. She was wet, but he wanted her soaking. Slowly moving his finger in and out of her, he continued teasing her breasts, so slowly he knew it would drive her crazy.

She squirmed beneath him, gasping and moaning out his name. "You're driving me crazy," she finally rasped out.

He lifted up, looked down at her. "I've barely started."

"I know." There was a desperation in her voice and her sweet expression that normally would have made him drag this out even longer but...he wanted to see her come. Wanted to taste it on his tongue.

More than anything, he knew she needed this. Keeping his gaze pinned to hers, he slid another finger inside her.

She arched up, sucking in a breath. "No more teasing."

Oh, he wasn't teasing. Not now. Hell, for how he felt, he wanted to fuck and fuck until he erased the image of her tumbling out of that van. Though he wanted more than just sex. With Darcy it had always been more.

The memory of carrying her from that van had been seared into his brain and he'd been so damn careful about touching her since then, so careful not to hurt her. The last couple days he'd wanted to claim her, mark her as his in the most primal way. But all the muscles in his body were pulled taut, as if he was walking a tightrope of control.

"Can you be on top?" He sounded as if he'd swallowed gravel.

Surprise flickered across her expression—because he usually liked to be on top or take her from behind—only to be replaced by a smile.

As he flipped onto his back, his cock dragged against her abdomen and he sucked in a breath. He was hard as stone and she was testing all of his control.

"Are you okay?" he asked as she settled her legs on either side of him, slowly rubbing her slick folds over his erection. He groaned.

Laughing lightly, she shook her head at him. "I should be asking you that." Reaching between their bodies, she grasped his cock and stroked once. "I like having you underneath me," she whispered.

She could have him any way she wanted. He tried to tell her that, to get the words out, but his throat seized as she stroked him again. He could not come. Not now. Not in her hands. He made a sort of growling sound and she must have understood because she let go and positioned herself on top of him.

She looked like a goddess poised above him, her dark hair fanning around her breasts, her breathing as erratic as his as she looked down at him. Though his instinct was to take over, he wanted her to set the pace, wanted her to be in control.

Right now was all about her pleasure.

When she slid fully down on him, he groaned and grabbed onto her hips, holding her in place as he savored the sensation of being buried inside her.

Her green eyes were heavy-lidded as she watched him, the pink tips of her nipples hard and aroused.

"Touch your breasts," he ordered even as he reached between their bodies and began teasing her clit.

Just soft little strokes that would drive her crazy. The second he started teasing her, he felt her inner muscles contract around him. There was no better feeling in the world.

That familiar tingling sensation at his spine started as his balls pulled up even tighter but he gritted his teeth. Hell no. Darcy was going to come and he wanted to be inside her for a hell of a lot longer. He could drown in her and die happy.

As she cupped her breasts, she started oh so slowly grinding against him. Not really moving up and down, just barely rolling her hips against his in the most erotic way.

The entire time she watched him, he couldn't look away. Didn't want to. Something had shifted into place between them. He hadn't been joking about proposing later, even if she thought he had been.

Nope. Darcy was his. For always.

Soon he'd have a ring on her finger. And hopefully one day they'd create a family of their own. For now, he just wanted her. Only her.

He wasn't sure how long they stayed like that, watching each other while he was buried deep inside her. Time didn't exist now. Nothing did except her.

When he increased the tempo, teasing her clit a little faster and with more pressure, her eyes closed and she fell forward on him, her fingers digging into his shoulders as she began riding him.

Oh, hell. He watched the soft sway of her breasts as she moved up and down, and nearly lost it. His control snapped and though he tried to hold back, his hips rolled up to meet hers stroke for stroke.

He knew the moment before she climaxed—her inner walls pulsed around him as she threw her head back, moaning out his name.

Grasping the back of her neck, he crushed his mouth to hers as her climax shuddered through her. It pulsed through her in waves, consuming her—and him.

God, this was heaven.

She bit his bottom lip and rasped out, "Come in me." The softly spoken words set something off inside him.

And that was it. He was hers to command. Grasping her hips, he thrust inside her over and over until he found his release in long, hard waves of pleasure. He never wanted this to end.

Eventually she sprawled on top of him, her breathing as uneven as his. Their bodies were slick with sweat and sticky from their release and he had no desire to move. Ever.

He stroked a hand up and down her back, wanting to stay that way forever.

"I could stay like this forever," she murmured, as if reading his mind.

"Me too." He tightened his grip on her, holding her close. She was his. For always.

* * *

Stretched out on the king-size bed, Brooks grabbed his buzzing cell phone. Darcy was still in the shower and he was impatiently waiting for her to return so he could wrap her up in his arms—then bury his face between her legs.

"Hey," he said, answering on the second ring.

"Heard things went well," Skye said.

"I think so. How'd you get that information, anyway?" He hadn't asked her before but he was damn curious. Because even Gage hadn't found out that Kuznetsov had a daughter.

"David Ramirez." Two simple words. But nothing about that particular man was simple.

"*He* told you?" Damn. Skye had infiltrated the man's compound, rescued Mary Grace and killed some of Ramirez's best men. But...she and Colt had also let the man know that his brother had killed their father and had planned to kill David.

"He owed me."

"That's..." Hell, he didn't know what to think. A year ago Brooks never could have imagined that he'd be cashing in favors from known drug lords. It was a whole new world right now. When he'd been in the Marine Corps, things had been black and white. Right and wrong.

"Don't overthink it too much. Listen, I called for a reason... Olivia is insisting I wear a bridesmaid's dress for her wedding."

"Ah...okay. Why are you telling me?"

"I wanted to see if you could talk to Darcy. Maybe she can convince Olivia that it's a stupid idea. That—"

He stifled a laugh. "This is ridiculous, even for you. It's a dress. Suck it up and wear it."

Skye started cursing at him as Darcy stepped out of the bathroom, steam billowing behind her—completely naked.

He hung up on Skye.

CHAPTER TWENTY-NINE

—Happiness often sneaks in a door you didn't think
was open.—

"Are you sure you don't want me to go with you?" Darcy asked, her tone anxious. "Seriously, just turn around and pick me up."

Brooks laughed lightly. "I think you're more nervous than me. And I'm sure. I think this is something I need to do alone the first time. If she's nice...then I want to introduce her to you and everyone."

"I'm crazy nervous but I'm also excited for you." They'd returned home early this morning, and once he'd gotten her settled back in her house, he'd had one more confession.

Well, not really a confession, but news. He was ninety-five percent certain that the woman who'd been following him was his half-sister. He'd had Gage dig into her a little bit more, and it fit. His father had lived in Jupiter for a while, and right after the woman had been born, her mother had up and moved. No one was listed as her father on the birth certificate, however. And though he might have issues with his dad, he didn't think his dad knew.

Which left a lot of unanswered questions. And he planned to get them. Now that things were mostly back to normal, he wanted to talk to Hadley.

According to her school schedule, she should be getting out of class soon. He did feel kind of like a dick for ambushing her, but she'd followed him at least twice that he knew of. It was clear she wanted to reach out, but was maybe too afraid. He just hoped she wasn't going to hit him up for money. He could afford it, and he would give her whatever she asked for if they were related, but he didn't want a relationship like that.

It didn't take long to find where she was parked—Gage might have had something to do with tracking her car—so he parked in the same lot and leaned against the driver's side door of her little red car.

Have you met her yet? a text from Darcy read.

He shook his head at her enthusiasm as he responded. *I'm still in the parking lot. She hasn't come out of class yet.* Which Darcy very well knew. She was simply impatient.

OMG, this is so cool! I really hope she's nice! I swear I'll stop bothering you, but you better call me as soon as you can. Her text was followed with a bunch of smiley face and cat emojis.

God, he'd missed her. He'd missed their phone conversations, the cute little texts she sent him during the day, all of their naked time, just being around her. He hadn't realized how empty his life had been without her until he'd lost her.

Never again.

When he looked up from his phone, Hadley was approaching him, almost timidly. She wore jeans, brown boots and a thick jacket that had nothing to do with fashion and everything to do with keeping her warm. With her hair back in a ponytail and her backpack on, she looked younger than twenty-two. She gave a small smile as she reached him and said, "Hi."

"Hi...I'm Brooks Alexander."

"I know who you are. I'm Hadley." She clutched onto the straps of her backpack and watched him, not exactly warily, but she was nervous and vulnerable in that moment.

"You were following me the other day," he said bluntly.

Her cheeks flushed red and she nodded. "I didn't know how to approach you. I don't even know what to say now. This is nothing like I imagined."

"Was it the first time you followed me?"

She shook her head.

"Why have you been following me?" He had a feeling he knew the answer, but he wanted to hear what she had to say.

"I...think I might be your half-sister," she said in a rush. "I mean, I don't know for sure. My mom said Douglas Alexander was my dad, but...I don't know." It was clear she was getting flustered and nervous. And this wasn't the place for a conversation like this.

"You want to grab coffee somewhere close? We can talk?"

"Oh my God, yeah! I mean..." She cleared her throat. "That would be great." Her smile was blinding, and in that moment, his ninety-five percent went up to ninety-nine point nine that they were related. She had the same damn dimple he did, and while he thought it looked stupid on him, it looked adorable on her.

She also had the same dark hair and dark eyes, which might mean nothing but...he could see the family resemblance. And it was like a sucker punch.

He had a sister.

CHAPTER THIRTY

—Always act like you're wearing an invisible
crown.—

Two weeks later

"I can't believe you convinced Skye to wear a dress. She's not even whining about it," Nova whispered. "And if you say I used the words whine and Skye in the same sentence, I'll deny it until the day I die."

Darcy looked up from the screen of her cell phone and smiled at Nova, the beautiful woman getting fitted for her bridesmaid's dress. Olivia was with her daughter Valencia looking at tiaras because the six-year-old was determined that both she and her mother wear one on Olivia's wedding day. Darcy was pretty sure the kid was going to win this argument.

"I just showed her who was boss." Darcy grinned as the other woman's eyes widened.

And even as she said it, Mary Grace and Martina—two women she'd gotten to know a lot in the last couple weeks—strode over, their eyes wide as well.

"Are you serious? Because Skye is crazier than a bag of cats," Mary Grace said. "I should know," she muttered.

Darcy wasn't sure about the last part, but she nodded. "I told her if she didn't wear a dress she wouldn't be in the wedding—and it would seriously disappoint Valencia. Then I sent Valencia in to talk to her. This isn't my first wedding," she said, grinning. Though Skye was the first bridesmaid Darcy had met who carried a gun around. It was holstered, and Skye had assured her that she had a license for it, but it had still surprised Darcy a little when she'd seen it.

"Taken down by a six-year-old." Mary Grace seemed to think that was hilarious as she reached for another glass of champagne on the nearby table.

The women were here at Darcy's shop for their final fitting since Savage and Olivia were getting married in about a month. The dress designer had blocked out a few hours and the women were having a great time. The wedding was going to be small, just family and friends, and perfect. Of that Darcy had no doubt.

As if she knew she was being talked about, Skye came out of the dressing room wearing the lavender, one-shoulder, floor-length gown with lace and chiffon—looking stunning. Her auburn hair was pulled back into a tight braid and her expression was sulky. Approaching the stand, she stepped up on it and held out her arms as if going to her execution. "All right, let's finish this," she said to the seamstress.

Hannah, the seamstress on loan from Faith, gave Darcy a covert look and rolled her eyes. Darcy had to hide a laugh at the woman's antics.

"At least I can hide my weapons in this thing," Skye muttered, twisting on the stand so that the dress flared out.

"Stand still or I'll poke you," Hannah said, her voice light and cheery.

Which just made Darcy grin. Hannah always had a smile for everyone.

"I think we're going to do the tiaras," Olivia said, coming to stand next to Darcy.

She turned all her attention on the bride-to-be. "Good. And it's not like you have to wear them for all the pictures."

"I'm going to be wearing mine to sleep tonight and every day until the wedding," Valencia said matter-of-factly.

Her mother simply looked at her and ran a gentle hand over the top of her head.

"When are you and Uncle Brooks getting married?" the little girl asked, her jet-black ponytail swinging as she hugged her tiara to her chest and rocked back and forth.

Darcy choked on air as she struggled to find an answer. "Ah…"

"Honey, why don't you go grab a cookie? Miss Darcy just set some out. Chocolate chip, your favorite."

Apparently, *cookie* was all Valencia needed to hear because she was gone in a flash, her dark hair flying out behind her.

"Sorry about that," Olivia murmured. "At that age they don't have a filter."

"It's okay," Darcy said, laughing. "So how are you feeling? Are you ready for the big day?"

"Honestly, house hunting is proving to be more difficult than planning this wedding. But that's thanks to you since you're doing everything." Olivia laughed lightly. "I feel like I should be more stressed, but I'm not really worried about anything. I just want to be married to Savage."

That was a good answer.

"How's your sister?" Olivia asked before Darcy could respond.

"Surprisingly good. Or maybe not good, but they're dealing with everything." And from what Darcy could tell, they were facing things as a team. Namely the media scrutiny, which thankfully in the last couple days had seemed to taper off. There was a new scandal in New York, which had taken the heat off. Not that Emma and Peter had been involved in anything, but the media were like vultures, trying to find a story that wasn't there.

Darcy had learned the truth about why Semyon had planted those bombs—or rather his men had on his orders. One of his security guys, who was now in jail, had helped with planting the one at the school. And the Feds had proof in the form of his DNA, so he'd been willing to talk. Apparently, years ago Alexei Kuznetsov had killed Semyon's wife and son—Peter's older brother. Darcy knew he'd had one, but only because Emma had once mentioned it. Semyon hadn't had proof, not that he would have gone to the cops anyway. Instead he'd been patiently waiting to kill Kuznetsov. He'd even framed a fall guy, Dimitri, to take all the blame, so that Semyon would never be suspected—and then kill Kuznetsov in his own vehicle. Make it look like Kuznetsov's man had an agenda, including killing someone at the wedding who'd wronged him. Semyon simply hadn't cared who'd died in the process. There'd also been a loose link to Dimitri at the elementary school, in addition to the wedding. A woman he'd once dated worked there. Semyon had been planning this for *years*, looking for the perfect person to take the blame for killing Kuznetsov.

That way, he would have been free of scrutiny from others in Kuznetsov's organization and able to walk away and live his life. Unfortunately for the FBI, the guard had nothing on Kuznetsov the Feds could actually use, but at least they had a why for what Semyon had done. That reason would never be released to the public or media, however. And Dimitri? He was now missing—probably dead simply because Kuznetsov didn't want him to talk to the Feds—and unable to be questioned by the FBI. Darcy only knew because Leighton had told Brooks—and he'd told her. She was glad he didn't keep secrets from her.

"Good. I've texted her a few times, but I didn't want to bother her," Olivia said.

"Thank you. She definitely needs friends right now." And Emma had lost a few in the last couple weeks. Obviously they hadn't been real friends, but Darcy knew that knowledge wouldn't make it any easier on her sister.

At the sound of the little bell over the front door of the shop jingling, she turned to see Brooks and Savage entering.

For a moment, all her focus was on Brooks. How could it not be? The man was incredible, all broad shoulders and raw masculinity. Plus, that sexy little dimple when he smiled made her panties melt. And he had on his Stetson today. Which just made her mouth water. He was definitely rocking the sexy cowboy look.

She was vaguely aware of Savage saying hello before moving on to his bride-to-be. Darcy might have responded, she couldn't be sure. Smiling up at the man she loved more than anything, she said, "I thought you had to work today."

"I let the foreman take over."

Technically he had more than one job, she'd discovered. He still ran the ranch—if peripherally—and had cofounded Redemption Harbor Consulting. She'd also learned that their mission statement and what they actually did were two different things. Basically they helped people who couldn't afford it and, in some cases, couldn't go to the police for help because their situation was tricky. But for the next couple weeks, Brooks was sticking close to home. He didn't think Kuznetsov was a threat to any of them, and according to Gage, the man didn't seem to be showing an interest in any of them, but Brooks had been protective and possessive.

Not that she was complaining. "Good. You're wearing the Stetson later tonight," she whispered. "And nothing else."

The grin he gave her made her insides melt. "Sounds like a plan. And speaking of later tonight, do you want to stay at my place?"

They'd been staying at her little house the last couple weeks since it was closer to town and she'd been dealing with various work things. But it wasn't fair to him to always stay at her place, so she nodded. "Of course. I just need to pack a bag."

"Do you think you can take off tomorrow?" he murmured, setting one big hand on her hip.

Warmth ribboned through her. She wanted to lean into him, but if she did, she was pretty sure she wasn't going to stop at a brief kiss. "I'd already planned it."

His eyes seemed to darken as he watched her and the heat there was unmistakable. "Good."

She wasn't sure how it was possible but there was a wealth of emotions in that one word and she felt them all the way to her core. Tonight couldn't come soon enough.

CHAPTER THIRTY-ONE

—I will always choose you.—

Darcy eyed the ladder leading to the top of Brooks's barn. Well, one of them, because there were a few barns on the property. "I'm going to be honest and tell you that if you plan on getting lucky...I'm not sure I'm adventurous enough to do it in a bunch of hay." She shuddered at the thought of little bugs that might be hiding in it.

He barked out a laugh she felt all the way to her toes. God, she'd missed that laugh. And his smile. "I just want to show you something."

"Is that like...a euphemism?"

He laughed again. "Come on, or I can't give you your surprise."

She eyed him once more before climbing upward. As she reached the top, a bunch of lights flipped on. She let out a little gasp and climbed onto the hayloft floor. There was no hay up here, just a bunch of twinkle lights, throw blankets and pillows right by the huge open windows. And what looked like... "Is that a picnic?" she asked, turning to him as he joined her on the platform.

He simply grinned and wrapped his arm around her shoulders as he led her to the blankets.

"I can't believe you did all this." It was incredible.

"I might have had a little help getting it set up. Hadley was here earlier."

Aww, his sister. Darcy absolutely adored Hadley, and was glad that she and Brooks were becoming friends.

As Darcy sat on one of the pillows, she let out another gasp. It was such a clear night with a near full moon that she could see for miles out the windows. Rolling hills, quiet live-stock sleeping, and a huge pond glistening under the moon-light. "This is incredible."

"I'm glad you like it. Champagne or hot cocoa?" he asked, sitting across from her.

She eyed the open picnic basket and loosened her scarf slightly. "How about champagne?" It had been a long day and this was the best surprise ever. As he pulled out two glasses, she couldn't help but stare at him. "This is incredibly sweet, thank you."

He looked at her then, a seriousness in his eyes. "I love you, Darcy."

She would never get tired of hearing that. "I love you too."

After opening the bottle, and pouring their glasses, he handed her one and took his own. "We've got chocolate and cheese, your favorites, but first..." He motioned outward to the wide open night sky in front of them.

She wasn't sure what he wanted her to look at—until the fireworks started.

Actual fireworks. Because he'd remembered what she'd teasingly said to him weeks ago.

The sky lit up with a kaleidoscope of reds, greens, yel-lows... Her eyes widened at the shapes they created. Flowers, starbursts, and even— "Is that a horse?" she practically squealed, not caring that she sounded like a teenage girl. It was incredible.

His grip around her tightened and she leaned into him, laying her head on his shoulder. Champagne forgotten, she set it down and wrapped her other arm around him. This was the sweetest gift ever.

As a burst of red hearts filled the sky, followed with *I love you*, Brooks turned her toward him. And that was when she saw the little jewelry box.

She stared, not quite comprehending as he shifted and knelt in front of her.

He opened the box, his hand only slightly trembling. "Marry me, Darcy?"

"Yes!" She wasn't sure why it came out as a shout but she couldn't control her happiness. "Yes, yes, yes!" Since she was too flustered to take her gloves off, he helped her and slid the diamond ring on her left-hand ring finger.

She barely glanced at it as she cupped his face with her hands. He crushed his mouth to hers in a clear, dominant claiming that thrilled her to her toes.

When he finally lifted his head, his smile was adorable. "I was so nervous," he murmured.

She couldn't imagine why, but she brushed her lips over his again. Did he seriously think she might have said no? "This was amazing."

"You're amazing. And I'm never letting you go."

"Right back at you, cowboy."

He grinned, revealing that little dimple and once again she melted. Well, melted even more. "There's no hay up here," he murmured, reaching for the buttons on her coat.

She laughed at the gleam in his eyes and reached for the buttons on his jeans. No, there wasn't. And she didn't care how cold it was... With Brooks at her side for the rest of her life, she'd never be cold again.

—The End—

Thank you for reading Dangerous Witness, the third book in my all new Redemption Harbor series. If you don't want to miss any future releases, please feel free to join my newsletter. Find the signup link on my website:

http://www.katiereus.com

ACKNOWLEDGMENTS

First, I'm grateful to Manda Collins and Angela Quarles for our caffeine-fueled plotting day. To Kari Walker, I'm very grateful for all your insight into this book and series. Kelli Collins, thank you for such thorough developmental edits. Julia Ganis, thank you for copy editing. Jaycee, once again I'm in love with your design work, thank you. To my wonderful readers, thank you guys for embracing this new series! For my family, I'm grateful you deal with my deadlines. And as always, I'm grateful to God.

COMPLETE BOOKLIST

Red Stone Security Series
No One to Trust
Danger Next Door
Fatal Deception
Miami, Mistletoe & Murder
His to Protect
Breaking Her Rules
Protecting His Witness
Sinful Seduction
Under His Protection
Deadly Fallout
Sworn to Protect
Secret Obsession
Love Thy Enemy
Dangerous Protector
Lethal Game

Deadly Ops Series
Targeted
Bound to Danger
Chasing Danger (novella)
Shattered Duty
Edge of Danger
A Covert Affair

Redemption Harbor Series
Resurrection
Savage Rising
Dangerous Witness

ABOUT THE AUTHOR

Katie Reus is the *New York Times* and *USA Today* bestselling author of the Red Stone Security series, the Darkness series and the Deadly Ops series. She fell in love with romance at a young age thanks to books she pilfered from her mom's stash. Years later she loves reading romance almost as much as she loves writing it.

However, she didn't always know she wanted to be a writer. After changing majors many times, she finally graduated summa cum laude with a degree in psychology. Not long after that she discovered a new love. Writing. She now spends her days writing dark paranormal romance and sexy romantic suspense.

For more information on Katie please visit her website: www.katiereus.com. Also find her on twitter @katiereus or visit her on facebook at:
www.facebook.com/katiereusauthor.

Made in the USA
Lexington, KY
29 January 2018